MORE PRAISE FOR BLOODTHIRSTY

"That rare second novel that is as impressive as the first…Karp writes compelling fiction without resorting to stomach-churning, *CSI*-style theatrics…Suffice it to say that the largest mystery in this series is never really answered: Where has Marshall Karp been all these years?"
—Louisville *Courier-Journal*

"*Bloodthirsty* is a TKO of a book—wry, poignant, exquisitely written, and funny as hell. Karp should be considered a national treasure."
—Cornelia Read, Edgar®-nominated author of *The Crazy School*

"With its har-har banter and well-paced, undemanding plot, Karp's Tinseltown kiss-off reads like a solid Hollywood buddy-cop thriller."
—*Entertainment Weekly*

"Karp keeps the jokes moving as fast as the action…As with Janet Evanovich's mysteries, we are swept up in the humor, the quirky characters, and the frenetic pace."
—*Library Journal*

"[*Bloodthirsty*] just cemented my admiration for Karp's humor and inventiveness. I'll be right there waiting for the next in the series."
—*Deadly Pleasures Mystery Magazine*

"A hottie of a read, a fast-paced (and very funny) story of blood and bullets set in the bloodthirsty town of Hollywood."
—Ann LaFarge, "Constant Reader"

PRAISE FOR THE RABBIT FACTORY

A *Deadly Pleasures Mystery Magazine*
"Best First Mystery/Crime Novel of 2006"

"...the comedy never overshadows this smart, many-layered
thriller...Lomax, Biggs, and the FBI have their work cut out for them in a
clever plot that will keep readers guessing to the very end."
—*Publishers Weekly* (starred review)

"...irrepressible and often poignant...Like the best of Donald Westlake and
Carl Hiaasen, *The Rabbit Factory* is deftly plotted and deliciously askew."
—*Booklist* (starred review)

"Totally original, a sheer roller coaster ride, packed with waves of
humor and a dynamic duo in Lomax and Biggs.
Karp shows a master's touch in his debut."
—David Baldacci, *New York Times* bestselling author of *The Whole Truth*

"...brings to mind Robert B. Parker, Janet Evanovich, Dean Koontz,
Stuart Woods and a lot of other fast-paced authors."
—Janet Maslin, *New York Times*

"Razor-sharp wit and intricate plotlines aside, *The Rabbit Factory*
is powered by the author's amazingly strong and insightful
characterization. The detective duo of Lomax and Biggs make this
novel an absolute delight to read...Prediction: Instant cult classic."
—Barnes & Noble *Ransom Notes*

"4-stars...An hilariously sharp debut thriller."
—*Daily Mirror* (UK)

"It's refreshing to have so many likeable characters in a crime novel.
Lomax and Biggs in particular are an engaging pair, with a nice line
in witty repartee...Karp's genial style and humorous
anti-establishment digs make an entertaining read."
—*Sunday Telegraph* (UK)

BLOODTHIRSTY

a Lomax & Biggs Mystery

MARSHALL KARP

MACADAM CAGE

MacAdam/Cage Publishing
155 Sansome Street, Suite 550
San Francisco, California 94104
www.MacAdamCage.com

Karp, Marshall.
  Bloodthirsty : a Lomax and Biggs mystery / Marshall Karp.
    p. cm.
  ISBN 978-1-59692-209-9 (alk. paper)
  1. Police—California—Los Angeles—Fiction. 2. Gangs—Fiction.
3. Los Angeles (Calif.)—Fiction. I. Title.
PS3561.A684B58 2007
813'.54—dc22
                              2006103276

Paperback edition: April 2008
ISBN 978-1-59692-288-4

Manufactured in the United States of America.

10 9 8 7 6 5 4 3 2 1

Book and jacket design by Dorothy Carico Smith.

For my blood:
Mom, Dad, Jody, Harold, Pearl, Icky,
Dennis, Matthew, Cori, Adam, Sarah, and Zach

*It's a bloodthirsty town, Hollywood is. No matter how popular you are, there's always someone who'd be happier if you were dead. And in some cases, you can be so despised, that **everyone** would be happier if you were dead.*

CHAPTER ONE

Roger and Aggie held hands as they watched the kid bleed out. He was on his back, head flopped to the left. The gurgling in his windpipe had stopped, and now there was just a silent stream, as if Roger had left the tap open.

"Practice makes perfect," Aggie said.

Roger accepted the compliment by giving her hand a gentle squeeze. He was definitely not the type to slit somebody's throat without doing some serious prep work. So he had practiced. On pigs. He tracked down a copy of *Comparative Anatomy and Physiology of the Pig* at the Texas A&M library. After that it was just a matter of working on his technique.

"Did you know that swine have the same basic characteristics as people?" he had said to Aggie. "That's why they use 'em in biomedical research. You could live for years with a pig heart in you."

"I think Ermaline Hofsteader's already got one in her," Aggie said. "You see how that girl eats?"

Roger slaughtered four hogs in all. By the third one he got the hang of it, but he did one more for insurance.

"You sure you can't switch over to cows or chickens?" Aggie said one night at dinner. "I'm getting pretty damn sick of pork."

Four pigs, one Mexican, Roger thought, looking down at the kid. The only difference was that the kid's blood wasn't bright red like the pigs'. In the murky light under the freeway it looked more like Hershey's syrup.

The pool of chocolate soup got wider, caught a crack in the concrete, and one satellite stream oozed its way toward Roger's left foot.

"Careful it don't get on your boots," Aggie said.

Roger backed up a few steps. "The boots are fine," he said. "More'n I can say for my..." His lips started to form the F-word, but he caught himself. He had given up profanity for Lent. The results had been spotty at best, so on Easter Sunday he made a silent vow to try and hold off cursing another fifty days till Pentecost. "More'n I can say for my dang shirt."

He looked down at his right sleeve, sopping with the kid's juices. "Darn kid spurted. Got blood all over my good Roper."

"Told you ten times not to wear that shirt," she said.

"I must not have heard you," he said. "And it was more like a hundred and ten times."

"Don't worry. I can get it out. I'll take it to a laundromat tonight."

"Good idea," he said. "And make sure you buy a big box of that new Tide with DNA Remover."

"I can get out the blood."

"Blood's not DNA. Trust me, this muchacho's genetic code is in this shirt till I burn it. Besides, a lot of these laundromats in Los Angeles have security cameras, and I don't want to star in no movie about you and me washing blood out of no shirt."

"It wouldn't be you and me in the movie," she said, "because when in the past twenty-seven years did you ever help one time with the washing?"

"Same amount of times you ever split one stick of firewood."

Aggie looked down at the body. Eighty feet over her head she could hear the hum of tires rolling along concrete. She inhaled a noseful of freeway fumes and caught a whiff of garlic. The kid's last meal, probably.

Roger knelt down beside the body and tightened his grip on the knife. It was a seven-inch Ka-bar, the same Marine Corps fighting knife he had carried with him since Nam. "Let me get this over with," he said.

"Don't," Aggie said, grabbing his arm. The shirt was wet and sticky, but she didn't let go. "Leave him be."

"Ag," he said, "we decided."

It had made sense when they were planning it. Make the murder look like a rival gang did it. Mutilate the kid's face beyond cosmetic repair, so that even his own mother couldn't look at him. Street revenge.

"It ain't necessary," she said. "The cops won't investigate a dead gangbanger. How old is he? Fourteen? Fifteen? You gave some poor woman a dead son. At least give her one she can bury in an open coffin."

"I don't know why I bother planning, if you're gonna change everything last minute." Roger felt the F-word welling up in his throat. "Fine," it came out.

She released the grip on his arm and rubbed her hands together to dry off the blood. "Thank you. You saying he got his DNA in your shirt?"

Roger stood up and slipped the Ka-bar back into its leather

sheath. "Yep. Never get it out."

"Then fair is fair. We should leave him a little DNA of our own."

She puckered her lips and sucked them in and out, gathering up a generous gob. She let it fly. The frothy mix of saliva and bile hit the kid's vacant left eye and trickled down his brown cheek toward an ear.

A few minutes later, they were in the Chevy pickup creeping along the freeway with the rest of the rush-hour traffic. He could feel her eyes on him. Reading him. "You upset?" she finally said.

"About what?"

"About the high cost of chintz in China. You just cut a boy's throat. You upset about killing someone?"

Roger forced a little laugh. "No big deal. I've killed people before."

"But that was always in the line of duty."

Roger wiped one watery eye with a wrinkled blue bandana. "Yeah. Well, that's what this was, Aggie. Killing this little fucker was the line of duty."

CHAPTER TWO

If you're looking to get rich, being a cop is not the way to go. Especially the honest variety.

Last year I made ninety-three grand working homicide for LAPD. My partner, Terry Biggs, who is one pay grade lower, managed to make eighty-eight with overtime. Not bad money. Except that my plumber cleared one-fifty. And he didn't get shot at. Of course, I don't have to snake toilets. Life is full of trade-offs.

Then one day the phone rings and some guy offers me and Terry fifty thousand dollars to option our last big homicide case for a movie. I hang up. It's a con job. Ever since we cracked the Familyland murders and got our minute and a half of fame, every cop we know has been busting our balls.

The guy calls back. He swears he's Halsey Bates, the director. "Sure, you are," I say, as I Google him. "Where'd you go to college?"

"Penn," he says.

"Wrong," I say and hang up.

Next day Halsey Bates shows up at the station house, in the

flesh. "You might have solved a big murder case, Detective Lomax," he says, "but you don't have a clue where I went to school." He holds up his college diploma. *"Universitas Pennsylvaniensis.* Penn."

"Hollywood Online says Penn State," I tell him.

"They also say Clay Aiken's dating a supermodel. Let's talk."

Two weeks later, Halsey hands us each a check for twenty-five big ones. "And that's just your first taste," he says. "This movie catches fire, and you boys will be building yourselves swimming pools."

"I already have a swimming pool," Terry told him.

"This one would be for your money."

"What if I just drained the pool I have?" Terry said. "How long would it take you to refill it with cash?"

"Depends on how long it takes me to find someone with sixty million bucks to bankroll us."

"I got three daughters. The twins are starting college in September."

"It took ten years to find the money to make *Forrest Gump*," Halsey said. "How were you planning on paying for college if I didn't option your story?"

"Mike and I were going to stick up the Wal-Mart over on Crenshaw. My other choice was to sell a kidney, but Mike refuses to part with one."

"Well, if you're in a hurry, we could sell our souls to the devil," Halsey said. "I have his home number."

The devil, in this case, was Barry Gerber, a legendary industry prick. Over the years he made dozens of films, zillions of dollars, and zero friends.

"I hear he's a real Hollywood asshole," Terry said.

"That's redundant," Halsey said. He gave us both a big toothy smile and ran his hand through his thick, straight, dirty-blond hair. The hair is the only thing straight about him.

I've met a lot of schmucks in the movie business. Halsey Bates isn't one of them. He's a decent guy, with an ugly past.

Seven years ago he was directing a movie and met Kirk Jacoby, a struggling young actor who had the three basic ingredients guaranteed to make him a star. He was talented, great looking, and bisexual. Kirk would sleep with anyone if he thought it could help him get ahead in the business.

They spent the day shooting at an LA country club, first on the tennis court, then the locker room, and finally the showers. Halsey was so hot for Kirk he wrapped early, and they drove to Halsey's house, which was well stocked with booze, dope, and condoms.

Jacoby had one agenda. He wanted a bigger part. Halsey offered him a few more scenes, but Kirk wasn't stupid. He knew they'd wind up on the cutting room floor, so he said goodnight and staggered toward his car. He was not only too drunk to drive; he was too drunk to walk. He cut across the lawn and fell into the koi pond. Halsey offered to put him up for the night, but Jacoby insisted on leaving. *Absolut* logic prevailed, and they decided that Halsey should be the designated driver. Jacoby flopped into the director's Saab convertible and immediately fell asleep in the passenger seat.

He never woke up. They weren't the only drunks on the road that night. Heading east on Beverly Boulevard they were T-boned by a young couple in a pickup running a light at Highland. Jacoby, unbelted, was thrown 120 feet and killed instantly. The driver of the pickup had his chest crushed and his girlfriend's head was severed when she went through the windshield.

Even with the best lawyers money could buy, Halsey spent the next four and a half years in prison. But it was time well spent. From his jail cell he used his clout, his talent, and his ingenuity to raise enough money to open a drug and alcohol rehabilitation center in downtown LA.

By the time he got out he had added a rescue mission and a battered-women's shelter, and his charity, One Brick At A Time, had become as popular among the rich and famous as Japanese hybrids. Hollywood is nothing if not forgiving.

The day he got out was a media gangbang of O.J. proportions. TV crews from around the world were camped outside the gates. The first one to welcome him back was Barry Gerber. He announced that he was hiring Halsey to direct his first post-prison film. He then whipped out a contract and a pen, offered up his back, and the cameras rolled while Halsey signed on the dotted line. It was a great stunt, and the media gobbled it up.

"What's the movie about?" half the reporters yelled at once.

Gerber just smiled. "I can't say."

It was an old Hollywood ruse. Tell them what you're trying to pimp, and you're lucky if they print a word of it. Don't tell them, and they'll invoke the First Amendment.

"Come on, Barry," a woman from *People* demanded. "Give us something."

Gerber held his hands up and shook his head. The man was a master at getting millions of dollars' worth of publicity without spending a dime.

The press refused to take no for an answer.

Finally, Gerber acquiesced. "Alright, just a taste. It's about a good-looking, charming, successful man who makes a terrible mistake," he said, putting his arm around the good-looking, charming, successful man, who had spent four and half years paying for his own terrible mistake.

"What kind of mistake?" came the inevitable response.

Gerber grinned. "He kills his boyfriend."

CHAPTER THREE

It took the better part of a month for Halsey to set up a meeting between us and Barry Gerber. Living legends have busy schedules, so I figured we'd be lucky to get five minutes with him in his office. But that wasn't Barry's style.

"He wants you at the premiere of our new movie," Halsey said. "Sunday night. The Pantages Theatre. Red carpet, black tie."

"Do you really think we should pitch him the Familyland idea when he's surrounded by a theater full of people?" Terry said. "Why doesn't he just meet us in St. Peter's Square and bless us from the balcony?"

"It's the perfect time," Halsey said. "He loves making deals when he's feeling triumphant and expansive. I once saw him green-light a feature at a Lakers game. They had just won in double overtime."

"Can I bring my wife?" Terry said. "She hates when I go to these Hollywood premieres on my own."

"Bring your entire posse," Halsey said. "We'll make a night of it."

Our posse consisted of Terry's wife Marilyn, my girlfriend Diana, my father Big Jim Lomax, and his wife Angel. Jim has a fleet of cars, trucks, and production vehicles that he rents out to film crews. He decided that the best way for us to show up at the premiere was in a thirty-foot stretch Hummer.

Jim is about the size of a Hummer himself, loud as a Harley, and prone to bear hugs. He was sitting across from me in the limo, Angel's tiny brown hand resting on his picnic ham of a thigh. She's twenty years younger, two hundred pounds lighter, and at least three times as stubborn. When my mother died six years ago, Angel did what anti-depressants, shrinks, and weekly visits from our parish priest couldn't. She made him smile. I grinned at the happy couple and gave Jim the official Lomax Wink of Approval.

He caught it, directed his gaze toward the lovely Diana Trantanella sitting at my side, creased one eyelid, and tossed back a paternal wink of his own.

"So, what's this movie about?" Marilyn asked Halsey. Marilyn is Terry's fourth and, I'll bet every nickel of my movie-option money, final wife. She's one of those plus-sized women, so it's ironic that she wound up changing her last name to Biggs. But she's Biggs and Beautiful, with delicate pale skin, fiery red hair, and a quick wit that lets her go wisecrack for wisecrack with her wannabe-comedian husband.

"It's called *I.C.U.,*" Halsey said. "It's a thriller, so all I'm going to tell you is that Damian Hedge plays a neurosurgeon who murders someone he's having an affair with."

"I love Damian Hedge," Marilyn said. "Do you think you can direct him to have an affair with me?"

"Marilyn, my pet, you are far too good for Damian Hedge."

"I'm far too good for Terry, but I still sleep with him."

"Excuse me, folks." It was Dennis, our driver. "I don't think Damian will be at the premiere. We have the contract with his studio, and I've been driving him around for the past three or four weeks, but he canceled the limo."

"Maybe he heard Marilyn was stalking him," Terry said.

"It's more likely that he hates Barry Gerber's guts, and he's standing him up just to screw him over," Halsey said.

"Oh God, Halsey," Marilyn said. "Do you know why Gerber fired him? I would kill to find out."

The Barry Gerber–Damian Hedge feud had been one of the hotter topics in La-La Land. It started out as gossip, but the threats of lawsuits and countersuits got it kicked up to the business pages. Frankly, I didn't give a damn.

Halsey had filled six glasses with champagne, and his own with Perrier. "I have no desire to discuss why the most obnoxious man in this town isn't talking to the rudest one," he said, passing out the glasses. "But I do have a toast to a much more promising business relationship."

Big Jim tapped on the divider. "Dennis, slow down. You got designated drinkers back here, and I don't want them spilling this stuff on the upholstery."

The stretch eased to a smooth glide, and Halsey raised his glass. "To Mike and Terry, my new partners in crime. If the gods are smiling tonight, you'll meet the man who will put up the money to make the movie that will make you rich."

Terry raised his glass. "Halsey," he said, "if you're right, and this movie sells, you will have single-handedly destroyed the very principle on which I have based my entire adult life."

Halsey turned on the Big Toothy Grin. "And what would that

be, Detective Biggs?"

"I've been working under the ridiculous assumption that crime doesn't pay."

CHAPTER FOUR

We were in a caravan of limos on Hollywood Boulevard inching our way to the Pantages Theatre.

"Explain something to me," Terry said. "They can orchestrate a twelve-minute car chase through the streets of LA, but they can't figure out how to drop people off at a movie theater without creating a major traffic jam."

"It's all part of the game," Halsey said. "People drag their asses getting out of their limos so they get more camera time. They know everybody else is behind them, and they're thinking, let those losers wait."

"But you're the director," Angel said. "You shouldn't have to wait."

"Everybody sits in traffic," Halsey said. "Streisand, Scorsese, everybody. Just play the game. They won't start without us."

It took us ten minutes to go three blocks. When we got to the front of the line, two hunks of beef in tuxedos opened the doors and helped unload the precious cargo onto the red carpet. A third gave Dennis instructions on where to park and how to pick up his passengers at the end of the night.

Big Jim exited the Hummer first, then helped Angel out.

The mob behind the velvet rope sized them up. One woman actually said, "Who are they?" Half a dozen fans quickly fielded the totally uncool question. "Nobody. They're nobody."

Of course, celebrity stalkers know that Nobodies never arrive alone, so the crowd strained to see which Somebody would finally emerge from the limo. Terry, Marilyn, Diana, and I followed, and I could see that the crowd was getting impatient. I stepped away from the car door, so Halsey could have his moment.

But Big Jim stepped in front of it, threw his arms up in the air, and yelled, "You are the greatest fans in the world."

The man is a six-foot-four, 300-pound people magnet. People started cheering. A few of us Nobodies waved, and the cameras started snapping.

"Ladies and gentlemen," the Trucker Ringmaster bellowed, "the man you've all been waiting for, the director of *I.C.U.*, Mr. Halsey Bates."

Halsey stepped out and the crowd let out a roar. *So you got drunk and killed someone. You make great movies. All is forgiven.*

I could see Terry lapping it all up. I slammed the car door, and Dennis started to drive off when we heard the siren. One of the beefy parkers slapped the side of the Hummer and yelled, "Hold it up; let him pass." He pulled out a walkie-talkie and said, "I thought LAPD was redirecting all traffic to Sunset."

I couldn't hear the comeback, because the siren got louder and the flashing lights of an ambulance came into view. Then a reporter on the red carpet started yelling at her cameraman, "Freddie, shoot it, shoot it."

She shoved me and Diana out of the way so Freddie could get a better shot of the ambulance as it passed.

But it didn't pass.

It came to a screeching stop right in front of the Pantages. The front doors opened and two big-titted blondes in skimpy nurses' outfits jumped out, ran around to the back, and flung open the rear doors.

Out stepped Damian Hedge. The fans started yowling, reporters started shoving, and the LA cops who thought they could coast through the evening began shoving back.

Damian was wearing a white tux and had a stethoscope around his neck. One of the blonde nurses bent forward so he could listen to her colossal chest. Apparently the stethoscope didn't work. He tapped it, hit it against his palm, and finally shrugged and tossed it into the crowd. Then he buried his ear into her cleavage and pronounced her extremely healthy. The crowd ate it up.

Halsey shook his head. "Big stupid douchebag ham."

"And he didn't have to wait in traffic," Terry added.

By now the crowd was chanting, "Day-mi-an, Day-mi-an," and the big stupid douchebag ham walked past us into a sea of cameras and microphones.

"Let's not wait for sloppy seconds," Halsey said. We headed inside.

CHAPTER FIVE

The Pantages Theatre is a piece of Hollywood history. Even without a movie, it's worth the price of admission. It's art deco heaven, with ornate ceilings, massive chandeliers, and thousands of thick, plush, red velvet seats.

The ushers were all wearing green hospital scrubs with a red I.C.U. logo on the back. One escorted Big Jim and the women to the mezzanine level. Halsey, Terry and I were walked down the aisle to a section marked Reserved.

We barely sat down when a man with a Bluetooth headset in his ear appeared and knelt down beside Halsey's aisle seat. He was about thirty-five, but it was a weary thirty-five, and the lines around his eyes told me he had either spent too much time in the sun or in the line of fire.

I could make out the Waspy good looks that must have served him well at Yale or Dartmouth, but his cheeks were doughy, his jaw was sagging, and his sweat glands were working overtime. The theater was cool, but his face was glistening and his tuxedo shirt had wilted. He looked like a *GQ* cover boy gone to seed.

"Hey, Tyler," Halsey said. "Fellas, this is Tyler Baker-Broome, the man who runs Barry's life. T.B., I'd like you to meet—"

T.B. didn't want to meet anybody. "We have a problem," he said.

"I know. I saw Damian make his grand entrance. I'll bet Barry is livid. Where is he? I want him to meet Mike and Terry."

"He's not here," Baker-Broome said. "That's the problem."

"Where is he?"

"I don't know where he is," Baker-Broome said, lowering his voice into a nasty whisper. "I only know where he isn't."

"Did he walk out because of Damian?"

"He didn't walk out because of anything. He never showed up. I spoke to him this morning. He was fine. I called him again at noon. No answer, so I left a message. I called him again at one. Since then I've been calling every ten minutes. I tried the office, the house, his cell, everything. He was supposed to be in the theater an hour ago. He's never missed an opening in his life."

"Did you call the cops?"

"Are you out of your mind? You know Barry. He's probably got his nose in some blow, and his dick in some underage coke whore. You want me to call the cops?"

"Excuse me," Terry said. "None of my business, but he hasn't been missing long enough for the cops to get involved."

Baker-Broome had ignored us so far. Now he gave Terry a condescending sneer. "You're right. It's none of your business, Mister..."

"Biggs," Terry said, getting up from his seat. "Detective Terry Biggs. Los Angeles Police Department."

Terry Biggs is not a pretty man. In fact, he'd be the first to agree that he's ugly as a mud fence. His face is pitted and has an unfortunate bone structure that makes him look like a cross between Mick Jagger and a weasel. At six-foot-three, he doesn't have to work hard to look menacing. He loomed over Baker-Broome, who was still squatting, all of two-foot-nothing.

Baker-Broome clenched his face like he had just missed the final Jeopardy question. He stood up and nodded toward me. "You a cop too?"

"Detective Mike Lomax," I said. "You have the right to remain silent."

"A little late for that," he said, holding out his hands to be cuffed.

"Relax, Tyler," Halsey said. "They're cool. I'm sure they don't give a shit that Barry is out somewhere getting his brains fried or his knob polished."

"Actually, we do," Terry said. "I only rented this tuxedo so I could meet him and pitch him a movie."

"I make most of Barry's appointments and all of his apologies," Baker-Broome said. "Sorry he stood you up. As soon as I talk to him, I'll get you on his calendar." He handed each of us a business card.

"Tyler's been with Barry for years," Halsey said.

"Sixteen and a half," Tyler said.

"His job description says he's supposed to be making deals or movies, but he spends most of his time cleaning up after Barry. We call him Tyler Baker-Broome-and-Shovel."

"So this is not the first time he's gone missing," I said.

Tyler laughed. "Hardly. He's pulled his disappearing act before. He's got a few perverse habits that get in the way of his judgment. But he never did anything like this. I can't believe he hasn't showed up for your opening, Halsey. Once again, I apologize. And speaking of deals and movies, I hope we're still on for lunch Thursday."

"Chiseled in stone," Halsey said.

The audience burst into applause. The four of us turned and looked up to see what triggered it. It wasn't Barry. It was Damian Hedge.

"Elvis has entered the building," Halsey said.

"Let's give Barry five more minutes," Baker-Broome said. "If he doesn't show, could you get up there and welcome people?"

Halsey agreed and T.B. went off to make more frantic phone calls.

"Sorry you had to hear all the deviant details about the man I picked to fund our movie," Halsey said. "I hope it won't keep you from taking his sixty mil."

"You said we'd be doing business with the devil," I said.

"Underage coke whore?" Terry said. "One would think Barry Gerber's taste would run to high-class hookers and movie starlets."

"He's done them too," Halsey said, "but his first choice is always street trash. Usually young, so that even when they consent, it's statutory rape. Barry's biggest problem is that he hates himself."

Halsey waited ten minutes, then stepped to the front of the theater and took the microphone. "I just got a call from Barry," he lied. "He's running late."

"You know Barry," a voice yelled out. It was Damian Hedge. "He's always getting *a little behind.*"

The crowd laughed. Apparently Barry's love of young ass was legend.

"Now, Damian," Halsey said. "Everyone is late from time to time. When we were working on this film, there were a number of mornings that you missed your call time. Rumor has it you were *all tied up.*"

Advantage, Halsey. One of the tabloids had just done a cover story on Damian's penchant for an erotic form of Japanese rope bondage called Shibari. This time the crowd responded with hoots and yells.

Halsey held the mic close to his face so his voice filled the hall, drowning out any possibility of a retort from Hedge. "Ladies and gentlemen, forgive me for being prejudiced, but I think *I.C.U.* is a terrific film. I know you're going to embrace it, and I'm sure Barry will join us at the party later this evening."

With that, the house lights went down. Halsey Bates got the last laugh. And he was right about the movie. It was damn good.

But he was wrong about Barry. The bastard never showed up. There's no people like show people.

CHAPTER SIX

When my wife Joanie died a year and a half ago, I never thought I'd feel joy or love or anything but pain again. And then I met Diana Trantanella.

"Met" is a poor choice of terms. I was sandbagged by my meddling father. Big Jim invited me to dinner one night and there she was. I was totally pissed. What kind of an overbearing, interfering, fat jerk of a father blindsides his forty-two-year-old widowed son with a surprise dinner date? And only six months after Joanie died.

I was as uncooperative, unfriendly, and unsocial as I could be. Actually, I acted like a complete asshole. Jim wanted to kill me. Diana was more forgiving. At the end of the evening I walked her to her car and apologized. She smiled and gave me a gentle peck on the cheek. Apology accepted. Pain understood. Diana's husband had died two years before. She knew we had both just been manipulated by a Machiavellian teamster, and she forgave my bad behavior.

You don't let a woman like that go. Especially when she looks like Diana.

Ever since my hormones were old enough to form opinions of their own, when I hear the Beach Boys sing "California Girls," I picture a sun-streaked blonde with blue eyes, golden skin, and a knockout smile, running in slo-mo through the surf. Diana is the early-forties version of my fantasy girl, and if they ever met her, I bet Brian Wilson and Mike Love would update their lyrics in a heartbeat.

Diana and I are now living together. Sort of.

I still rent the little house in West Hollywood where I lived with Joanie. A month after Diana and I started dating, she moved some of her things in. But not all of her things. She keeps the rest in an apartment on Wilshire, where she had lived with her late husband.

When I realized she wasn't going to move in with me full time, I brought some of my stuff over to her apartment. So for the better part of a year it's been your place or mine. There is no ours.

Big Jim, who is never short on solutions, especially when they're for somebody else's problems, offered up his unwanted fatherly wisdom on our living arrangements. "Stop holding on to the past, and buy a house together."

When I informed him that we were happy the way we were, he informed me that we were not. He may be right, but I'll be damned if I let him know.

Halsey's movie ended at 9:30. Diana and I left the party at 11, blew off the limo, and took a cab to her place.

The sun came up about 6:20. Little Mike was up shortly after that. Diana loves to make love in the morning. Personally, I'm not fussy about the time. Just the woman. We were in that half-asleep, totally naked, post-coital spoon position, her belly pressed to my back, her fingers stroking my chest.

"I think we got this backwards," I said. "Roll over."

We twisted a hundred and eighty degrees, until I had arranged myself comfortably behind her and could cup a breast in each hand.

Diana has fantastic breasts. Tits that tit men fantasize about. Full, firm, and oh, so real. The kind that God provides, not the ones approved by the FDA.

We lay there in silence, breathing in perfect sync.

"What are you thinking about?" she said.

"Nothing." I shifted my body ever so slightly because Little Mike had actually started thinking about an encore.

"You're thinking about Paul McCartney, aren't you?"

"No," I said, "and if you bring it up again, you're going to give me a serious case of erectile dysfunction."

"Paul McCartney" is code for the state of our relationship. He was married almost thirty years when his wife died. Four years later he remarried and had a child. Four years after that, his second marriage ended in an ugly divorce.

The sociologists pounced all over it. Their bottom line is that men are quick to remarry, but that the new wife has a tough time measuring up to the memory of the sainted dead original.

Sir Paul's divorce made all the papers. The first mistake I made was to read about it. The second mistake was to share it with Diana.

"They call it the Rebecca syndrome," she said. "Widowers who were happily married have expectations that the replacement wives can't live up to. But we're fine. I'm not a replacement wife."

True. But I had thought about it. According to what I had

read, the average widower waits two and a half years before remarrying. My brain started heading in that direction by the third date.

"So marry her" was Terry's solution. "If it works, it works. It took me three miserable marriages before I found Marilyn."

"It's not the same thing," I told him. "Marilyn didn't have a gold standard to live up to. All she had to do was not shoot you with your own gun, and you'd have called it a roaring success."

"You know what your problem is? You overthink everything."

He's right. Thinking is bad for me. Getting laid is good. I stopped thinking, kissed Diana's shoulder and pulled my body as tight to hers as I could. Penis trumps Brain every time. Both Mikes were ready for Round Two when my cell phone rang.

"Somebody needs a cop," Diana said.

"It's Terry. Let it ring."

"Whatever happened to Protect and Serve?" she said, unspooning. She reached over to the night table and handed me the phone.

I flipped it open. "Have I told you lately that your timing sucks?"

"And good morning to you too, Detective Lomax. I'm sorry to interruptus your coitus, but there's a body in a trash can up in the Hollywood Hills, and you're invited to the opening. If you tell us where you are, we'll send a limo."

"I'm at Diana's and I don't have my car, so yeah, come and get me."

"My pleasure. But first, ask me what this guy died of."

With Terry anytime is comedy time. "I give up, Terry. What killed the poor fellow?"

"He got a Viagra stuck in his throat. Died of a stiff neck."

"I'm hitting the shower. Pick me up in twenty minutes."

Diana grabbed the phone. "Make it thirty minutes. I'm hitting the shower with him."

CHAPTER SEVEN

Diana's apartment building has a semi-circular driveway, and Terry's five-year-old silver Lexus ES 250 was already parked at the far end when I got downstairs.

"Morning," I said, getting in. "How late did you party last night?"

"Some time around midnight Marilyn realized she wasn't going to live out her fantasies with Damian Hedge, so she decided to settle for me."

"At least you got laid," I said.

"One would think." He turned left out of the driveway onto Wilshire. "But on the ride home she brought up a sore subject."

"Your lackluster past performance in the sack?"

"My dick is fine. It's my bank account that's all shriveled up. Rebecca and Sarah will be in college any minute now, and Emily is only two years behind them. I think Marilyn was expecting Barry Gerber to show up last night and start writing tuition checks. So after four glasses of champagne, Marilyn decides to rehash the shortcomings of the Biggs family budget."

"Definitely not conducive to romance."

"Thank you, Dr. Ruth. You want to solve the world's over-population problem? Mandatory husband and wife financial discussions. It's the ultimate form of sex prevention."

"Fortunately, Diana and I file separate returns, so we had fantastic sex."

"Swell. I'll make a note of it on the official Lomax and Biggs scorecard."

"Oh, well, if you're keeping score, as of 7 a.m., it's Lomax 2, Biggs, nothing."

Terry looked at his watch. "And as of 7:35, we're both getting fucked. Do you believe this crapola?"

"I'm not sure which particular crapola you're complaining about this morning."

"A body in a trash can? That's the case we catch? And before that, we get a junkie in an alley, a Jane Doe under a pier, a night clerk at a flophouse, a pimp. Do you see a pattern here?"

"Dead people."

"Boring dead people. Ever since we signed the movie deal with Halsey, Division is sending us out on the lowest of the low profile cases."

"Obviously, somebody is determined to teach you some humility," I said. "And as your partner, I'm forced to suffer the consequences. But look on the bright side. We work out of Hollywood. We're bound to catch a superstar sooner or later."

The good news is, it was sooner. The bad news is, it was the guy who was supposed to write Terry's tuition checks. The body in the trash can turned out to be Barry Gerber.

CHAPTER EIGHT

Hollywood Hills is one of the more prosperous neighborhoods Terry and I cover. But we don't get to spend much time there. People who live in the Hills have better things to do with their lives than kill each other.

It's also the easiest part of our turf to get lost in. Most of our jurisdiction is laid out in neat little grids. Wide streets. Straight lines. La Brea is parallel to Fairfax. Hollywood intersects with Vine. But there's no such pattern to the Hills. The narrow, winding roads have as much logic as a bowl of linguini. It's so confusing that LAPD issues us area maps with turn-by-turn directions.

"We're going to the 2400 block of El Contento Drive," Terry said. "Get out the cheat sheet."

"Don't need it," I said. "When I was ten, Frankie was born. Mom was busy, so I spent most of my summer vacation driving around with Big Jim. That's the year they shot *Chinatown*. Every Tuesday after they wrapped we would drive Jack Nicholson to an all-night poker game at a buddy's house on El Contento. We'd pick him up the next morning."

"Nicholson? It was probably an all-night fuckfest. How contento did he look in the morning?"

"Actually, he was always pretty chipper. I just figured he was a good poker player."

I navigated Terry through the quiet streets. "Zero traffic headed south," he said as we turned onto Ivarene. The roads were wide enough for two cars, but nothing passed us coming down. No Moms in Volvos driving the kids to school. No Dads in Beemers heading for the office. It was just pure suburban serenity. Until we turned onto El Contento.

It was a total logjam. Six squad cars were parked at six different angles. There were two County Coroner vehicles, a gaggle of media vans, and, from the Sanitation Department, a supervisor's car and a green top-loader garbage truck.

"Looks a little discontento," Terry said, adding our car to the tail end of the chaos. "Like New Year's Eve in Tijuana, only without the gunfire."

Cop car lights were strobing, police radios were crackling with static, and clueless reporters were sticking microphones in the faces of equally clueless gawkers, one of whom ducked under the crime scene tape, pissing off one of the uniforms, who yelled, "Hey, shit-for-brains, this is the last time I'm gonna tell you nice. Get your dumb ass behind the tape."

We headed for the cluster of people who were at the eye of the storm, wielding cameras, calipers, cotton swabs, and other weapons of modern forensics.

There in the middle of it all was Jessica Keating. She was partially hidden behind a black garbage can, but I could see the blonde curls and hear the flat, nasal Chicago twang butchering all words that contained the letter *A*.

Jess is the best crime scene investigator in LA County. If you're going to spend your day trying to figure out how dead people got dead, you need what Terry calls the Forensics Trifecta. Brains, heart, and a twisted sense of humor.

We waited quietly behind her while she held a pair of tweezers up to the sunlight and squinted at it. Whatever she had plucked from the garbage can or the dead guy was imperceptible from where I was standing. She dropped the invisible clue into an evidence pouch and marked it. "Good morning, Detective Lomax. Good morning, Detective Biggs," she said.

"Nice police work," Terry said. "You didn't even turn around."

"Terry, if you keep wearing that Eau de Road Kill, even a blind man could pick you out of a lineup." She sealed the pouch and stood up tall. Very tall. I'm six-one, and we were eyeball to eyeball. She was a little rounder than the last time I saw her. She was five months pregnant, and you didn't need to be a detective to figure it out.

"I love what you've done with your boobs," Terry said. "And that motherly glow. Any day now, some bureaucrat will pick up on it and tell you no more field work."

"Well, I'm glad I caught this one. Looks like we got ourselves another headline homicide."

"That's Hollywood for you," Terry said. "Throwing out the rich and famous with the trash. Who you got?"

"You ever hear of Barry Gerber, the movie producer?"

"Oh, shit," Terry said.

"You a fan?"

"Mike and I were supposed to meet him last night, but he never showed."

"That's because he was already dead. Would you like to meet him now?"

Terry and I put on rubber gloves and knelt beside the garbage can, which was lying on its side. Gerber's head and bare shoulders were visible, but the rest of him was still wedged inside the plastic coffin.

"Can you get him out of there?" I asked.

"Not without a crowbar and a gallon of KY. This boy is in full-blown rigor. I put the TOD somewhere between 4 p.m. and 7 p.m. yesterday. They can cut him out of the can at the morgue, but he'll need another twenty-four hours to limber up."

"Damn," Terry said. "This sucks."

"My professional opinion is that it sucks for him too," Jessica said. "So, was he going to produce the movie on the Lamaar Familyland case?"

"We never got that far," I said. "Last night was supposed to be our first meeting."

"Does this mean you guys have a conflict of interest handling this case?"

I shook my head. "No, it just means Terry and I have to find some other rich guy to make our movie."

"*Our* movie," Jessica said. "Don't forget I was CSI on that case. My husband thinks Nicole Kidman should play me, but I'm leaning toward Uma."

"Uma doesn't do supporting roles," Terry said, studying the dead man's face. "Are you sure this is Gerber? A lot of these Hollywood fat cats have the same look."

"This one's also got a wallet with a driver's license and six credit cards that say Barry Gerber. The killer left it in a plastic bag inside the can."

"Any cash?" I said.

"A little over two thousand bucks."

"Not enough to make a movie," I said, standing up, "but it does rule out robbery."

Terry stood up too. "This totally blows," he said.

"Sorry for your loss, Detective," Jessica said. "I'll do everything I can in my supporting role to help you find your benefactor's killer."

"For starters, you could tell us how Mr. Gerber met his demise."

She shrugged. "Honey, I can't see most of this guy's torso. The best I can give you right now is loss of blood."

Loss of blood is often the official cause of death. But it's a catchall that covers a lot of possibilities. The critical question is what made the hole from which the blood got lost.

"So he bled out," I said, "but you don't know if it's from a bullet, a machete, or a hat pin."

"He's got to have a hole in him somewhere," she said. "But I can't find it without destroying the evidence. Once the turkey carvers at the morgue get him on the table, they'll find the wound and give you the weapon. But I'll go out on a limb now and rule out hat pin."

I took a flashlight and crouched down again, shining the light into the can so I could get a better look. I got back up, fast. Barry stunk.

"No blood on the can or the body," I said.

"Not as far as I can see," Jessica said. "They must have cleaned him up before they tossed him out."

"Alright," I said. "Let's canvass. Who's the first responder?"

Jessica pointed to the beefy cop who had cursed out the civilian for sneaking under the yellow tape. "Sauer," she said, puckering her mouth like she just sucked a lemon. "Good luck."

Ed Sauer. More than two hundred uniforms work out of the Hollywood station with us, and if they gave an Asshole of the Month Award, Sauer would keep winning it till they retired his badge number. He's a forty-something beat cop whose foot slips every time he tries to climb a rung on the ladder.

"Good morning, detectives," he said. He didn't like us. He didn't like anyone who made grade.

"I hear they're giving a remedial course in Courteous Crowd Control at the Academy," Terry said. "It's never too late."

"That guy who tried to cross the tape?" Sauer said. "He wanted to touch the body. He said touching famous dead people is his hobby. Like an autograph hound who chases movie stars, only he waits till they're dead. The sick bastard. If he wants to file a civilian complaint, let him. It won't be my first."

"What went down here?" I said.

"Garbageman, the black guy over there, found the body."

"Did you question him?"

"Yeah, for what it's worth. Let's face it. None of them are too bright."

I didn't want to know if Sauer meant garbagemen or black guys. "What did he say?"

"Basically nothing. He's picking up garbage, finds a body. End of story."

"Who lives here?"

"A couple of Arabs. But it looks like they took off."

There are more than a hundred thousand Muslim Americans living in LA. Sauer made these two sound like a terrorist cell. "Anything else?" I said.

"Hey, what do I know? I'm not a detective. I'm just here to

charm the crowd. That's what us beat cops do."

"Well, why don't you use some of that charm and help us find a murder weapon," Terry said. "Get a few more uniforms and rifle through all the garbage cans in a six-block radius."

"You want me doing garbage cans?"

"Yeah," Terry said. "That's what you beat cops do."

CHAPTER NINE

The garbageman Sauer had labeled as not too bright turned out to be the smartest, best-looking sanitation worker I'd ever met. Otis Hairston was a light-skinned African American with dark intelligent eyes, a jaw that a team of plastic surgeons couldn't improve on, and a ready-for-my-close-up-Mr.-Spielberg smile.

"Jesus," Terry said. "If Barry Gerber had discovered that guy instead of the other way around, he'd be starring in our movie."

I reminded Terry that we didn't have a movie. And now we didn't have Barry Gerber.

"Just as well," he said. "Gives us more time to solve this damn murder."

Hairston handed me his city ID before I even asked for it. "I discovered the body," he said. "This is my supervisor, Javier Ortiz. I radioed him right after I called 911."

Ortiz was short, chunky, and not happy that a dead movie mogul had screwed up garbage collection in his little corner of California.

Los Angeles County is anal retentive about garbage. They issue every residence three types of plastic receptacles. Black for household garbage, blue for recycling, and green for grass clippings. On pickup day, cans have to be set out at the curb and lined up perfectly so the trucks can drive up alongside them. Without ever leaving his vehicle, the driver lowers a pair of pincers, which lifts the can and dumps it into the belly of the truck. Hairston had been collecting the nastiest of the three. The putrid stuff in the black cans.

"How long before we get this cleared up?" Ortiz asked. "I got two more trucks coming for recycling and yard waste."

"Tell them to take the rest of the day off," I said. "We have to canvass the neighborhood to see if any weapons were trashed."

"What about the stuff I already picked up?" Hairston said. He smiled as if he already knew the answer, but he didn't want to be the one to break the bad news to his boss.

"Your truck will be impounded," I said, "and some lucky cops will get to wade through it looking for evidence."

"Can I help?" Hairston said. "I took the LAPD exam last month. I'm almost a cop."

"Thanks, but no," Terry said. "Almost a cop doesn't count."

"You shoulda took the exam sooner," Ortiz said. "Then instead of driving a garbage truck, you could be one of the cops crawling around inside."

Terry pulled out his notebook and a pen. "Otis," he said, "tell us how you found the body."

"This is my regular run. I know the homes, I know the people, I know the cans. This house belongs to Dr. and Mrs. Hammoud. They've got the standard three cans, a black, a blue, and a green. First thing I notice is they have a second black can.

And it's backwards. Instead of the wheels of the can being up against the curb, they're the other way around. So when the pincers grab it and dump it, the garbage could wind up on the street instead of in the hopper."

"He's supposed to pass 'em by," Ortiz said. "If they put their garbage out wrong, we let it sit there. That's the only way people are going to learn."

"It's a dumb rule," Hairston said. "I wasn't gonna stick them with a full can, so I get out of the truck and go to turn the can around. Besides, I'm suspicious. Where did the second black can come from? I go to move it, but it weighs a ton. I open the lid. There's a dead guy inside, so I call the cops."

"Did you see anything out of the ordinary from the time you started collecting this morning?" I asked.

"No. Totally normal day. But you realize I don't actually look at the garbage. The truck does all the work. It lifts the can, flips it, dumps it, and puts it back. If that can wasn't backwards, I might have pitched that guy right into the belly of this beast and been on my way. For all I know, I could have already tossed in a dozen more dead passengers."

"Did you ever see the victim before?"

"On TV," Hairston said. "He's a movie producer. But he doesn't live around here. And the can isn't from around here either. It was stolen from an apartment building in Westwood."

"How do you know that?" I asked.

"It was probably a question on the cop exam," Ortiz said.

Hairston ignored him. "Every can in the county is coded. While I was waiting for you guys, I called our dispatcher and gave him the barcode number on the can that had the body. It was issued to a sixteen-unit building on Weyburn. I got the address and the super's phone number for you." He handed me a piece of paper with the information neatly printed on it. "I bet when you talk to him, he'll know when the can was stolen."

"Otis," Terry said, "if you tell us who murdered this dude, you'll be wearing a badge and a uniform by tomorrow."

Hairston flashed a smile that would make Denzel's career counselors nervous. "At least you guys listened to me. That first cop, Sauer, he pulls his patrol car in front of the garbage cans. I tell him he should move it, because maybe whoever dropped off the body left tire marks or footprints. He tells me he's the one who gives the orders, and I should keep my mouth shut and pick up the garbage."

"Officer Sauer is a critical part of LA's finest," Terry said. "His job is to contaminate evidence and piss off witnesses. You pass that exam, and he'll be your brother in blue."

"How does the department manage to turn out idiots like him and heroes like you?" Hairston said.

"He was an idiot before the department got him," Terry said, "and who told you we were heroes?"

"Come on, man. You cracked the Lamaar murders. You sold your story to the movies. You're celebrity cops."

Celebrity cops. I could see Terry's body language change as the magical words danced around in his brain. He cocked his head and smiled. He went from bored cop to bemused superstar. His pen rested on a blank page in his notebook. I was sure he was going to ask the garbageman, "Who do I make this one out to?" Instead he said, "What makes you think we're celebrity cops?"

"I read all about you guys in the trades."

Terry was enjoying this. "Garbagemen have trades?"

Hairston laughed. He was enjoying it too. Ortiz, on the other hand, looked like he was personally constipated by the tons of waste that were backing up on his watch.

"My wife is an actress," Hairston said. "She's on a soap, *General Hospital.* I read the article in *The Hollywood Reporter.* Halsey Bates bought your story."

"Yeah, Halsey's a great guy," Terry said. "We had dinner with him last night. First we caught the opening of his new movie, *I.C.U.* They're hoping it opens at fifty million. I'm thinking sixty."

The movie business is filled with assholes. Terry has the potential to be their king.

Hairston's pupils were starting to dilate and his mouth was half open. He had a new idol. And Terry had a new audience.

"Gentlemen," I said. "I hate to interrupt, but we have a corpse and a truckload of garbage, both of which are festering in the heat." I gave Hairston my card. "Otis, if you think of anything, call us. We're at the Hollywood station on Wilcox."

"One more question," Hairston said. "Are you guys shooting your movie yet?"

"We're in pre-production," Terry said. "Mike and I both have producer credits. Right, partner?"

"Right, I can't wait to see my name on the screen." We had been in the movie business for a minute and a half and already we were lying to the public.

"So you're still casting," Hairston said, more excited about meeting a live Hollywood producer than finding a dead one. "Let me get you my wife's headshot and résumé. Her name is Melissa Little. I'm sure you've seen her on TV."

He started for the truck. In LA, even the garbageman has a spec script or his wife's headshot available at all times. Then he stopped and turned back to us. "But you haven't shot anything yet, right? Nothing's in the can."

Terry looked back at the big black can that contained the rigid remains of the late Barry Gerber. Then he turned back to me to make sure I caught the euphoric grin plastered across his ugly mug.

"No, Otis," he said. "Nothing's in the can. Nothing we can use anyway."

CHAPTER TEN

When people have a problem, they call the cops. When they have a problem with the cops, they call the fire department.

"What now?" Terry said when we heard the sirens.

Two fire engines and a chief's car made their way up the hill and then had to stop. El Contento had become a sprawling parking lot.

Terry and I were a few hundred feet away, but I could see that the men in the trucks were dressed for battle—bunker coats, helmets, full turnout gear. Then the guy on the passenger side of the chief's car got out. He had on his dress blues, a white shirt, tie, and one of those little conductor's caps with a badge on it that gleamed in the sun.

In his right hand he had a bullhorn, which he lifted to his face.

"Asshole alert," Terry said.

The bullhorn crackled, then spoke. "Who's running this show?"

"Don't look at me, Lomax," Terry said. "I'm just here working off my community service."

I'm a Detective II, so I have a grade on Terry. I headed toward the chief's car. He looked like he had more of an attitude than an emergency, so I walked. I don't know how many TV cameras were on the scene, but I'd bet they were all pointed my way and rolling.

As I got closer he put his bullhorn on the ground and yelled out, "I knew some dumb white boy cop had to be in charge. If it isn't Mike Fucking Lomax."

He took off his cap.

"George Fucking Fong," I said. "I knew this had to be a dumb Chinese fire drill, but I didn't realize they were going to send an actual dumb Chinaman."

We shook hands, and I took a deep breath and let it out. If this was going to be an interdepartmental pissing contest, at least I was dealing with someone I knew, respected, and had pissed with before.

"Don't tell me there's a fire up there," I said.

"Not yet," he said. "But if there is, those people would be toast. You're blocking our way up and you're blocking their way out."

"George, I got a dead celebrity in a garbage can. He's the one blocking the street. Why can't you just detour around him?"

"Obviously they don't send homicide cops to traffic school. This part of El Contento snakes around in a circle. There's only one road in and out and you're blocking it. People are trapped. A few of them called. They'd like to get down the hill to buy booze and rent dirty movies or whatever these rich folks who live in the Hills do on a Monday morning. But LAPD created a bottleneck. Technically I'd have to call it a fire hazard."

"So they called the fire department? Jesus, if people want to get out, why the hell didn't they just ask us to move some of these cars?"

"They did ask one of your cops but apparently he got a little nasty."

"Ed Sauer," I said. "He's trying hard to make us look bad."

"It's working. And it looks like you'll be looking bad on the five o'clock news." He pointed at the media vans. "Smile, you're on *Candid Camera*."

"Fong you, George. I got a high-profile murder to solve. You know what 'high-profile' means when you're a homicide detective?"

"Same as it means in the FD. Brass. Brass looking over your shoulder, brass breathing down your neck, brass up your ass."

"And the first thing LAPD does to show how competent we are is to create a fire hazard. Did you have to bring two engines to tell me to move a few parked cars?"

"I would have come up here alone, but one of the callers said he may have smelled smoke. I figure it's bullshit, but I read in a fortune cookie once that where there's smoke, there's fire, so bring hoses and big red trucks. Now, if you can get your boys to move these vehicles, I can go back to the firehouse and watch Regis and Kelly till the bell rings again."

He bent down and picked up his bullhorn. "You want to try this? All the movie cops use one."

"No thanks. Good to see you again, George. As long as we're on TV, why don't you shake my hand and pretend you like me. That way I won't look like a total idiot, and it'll be good for inter-departmental public relations."

He gave me a warm handshake and a pat on the back. "I do like you, Mike. Right about now, I just wouldn't want to be you."

Right about now I didn't want to be me either.

I had two cops move the vehicles, and stationed two more to direct traffic. We spent the next three hours canvassing. We couldn't find anything that could even pass for a weapon. And despite the fact that we had six cops questioning homeowners, maids, gardeners, and the FedEx delivery guy, we got the classic answer from our guys in uniform.

Nobody saw nothing.

CHAPTER ELEVEN

A team of detectives went to UCLA Medical Center and interviewed the man who owned the house where Barry was dumped. Ali Hammoud was a prominent Lebanese cardiologist and not, as Sauer had suggested, an Arab terrorist.

His wife Jennifer was in Denver on business. According to the doctor's statement, he took the garbage out the night before, left for work before the truck arrived, and never noticed the extra can.

"Did he know the victim?" Terry asked when I filled him in.

"No. Never even heard of him."

"I'd rule him out as a suspect, but it should at least be a misdemeanor to live in LA and not know all your major movie producers."

By one o'clock we had wrapped up at the scene, stopped at a Taco Bell for a couple of Gordita Supremes, which I'm convinced kill more cops than bullets, and were back in the car on the way to see Barry Gerber's widow.

"Take a look at this," Terry said, handing me the eight-by-ten glossy Otis Hairston had given him. "Melissa Little, the garbageman's wife."

"She's white," I said.

"And blonde. And beautiful. And just look at her résumé. Besides the soap, she's done commercials for Budweiser, Honda, and Tampax. I actually remember her from the Budweiser ad."

"You mean you don't watch Tampax commercials?"

"Mike, my whole life is a Tampax commercial. I live with Marilyn and three teenage girls on the corner of Estrogen Avenue and Drama Queen Boulevard. Rebecca spent the entire month of April crying because some boy told her that her nose was too big. If the freaking house were burning down, Sarah would have to change her shoes at least five times before she could make a run for it. Emily is only fifteen and she wants to have a huge hunk of shrapnel installed in her belly button and a tattoo of the solar system on her butt. And Al Gore called to say that it has been confirmed by the National Oceanic and Atmospheric Administration that Marilyn's hot flashes are the real cause of global warming."

I was laughing hard now, but he didn't let up.

"And I swear to God, Mike...I swear to God in heaven, that if I ever come home and find the toilet seat up, I will break down and weep. And then I'll take my gun and start firing into the closets, because you gotta know that one of those crazy hormonal women has to be hiding a man in there."

I applauded. "That's good stuff. You should really do one of those open mic nights at a comedy club and try it out."

"No. I'm still working on my material. I'm not ready to do stand-up in public. Even with just you and me in the car, I did it sitting down."

"Should I file Melissa's picture in the murder book with the rest of our case files?" I said.

"No, I'm giving it to Halsey. She's going to be in our movie."

"Terry, at the risk of penetrating your impenetrable denial system, I'd like to remind you that we don't have a movie. And the producer from last night—the one you thought was just a little late—he is now officially the extremely late Barry Gerber."

"You're always seeing the glass half-empty."

"Terry, he's dead. I'm seeing the glass as completely empty."

"Did you see the movie *The Player*?"

"No."

"Robert Altman. It's a classic. Tim Robbins is this hotshot studio executive and he calls someone from his car phone and says, 'I'll see you after my AA meeting.' And the guy says, 'I didn't realize you had a drinking problem.' And Tim says 'I don't, but that's where all the deals are being made these days.'"

"Is there a point to this?" I said.

"I know Barry is dead. But who's investigating his murder? You and me, babe. That's a whole lot of show-biz contacts we'll be making."

"We're not supposed to be making deals. In case you forgot, we've been recruited to solve a homicide, babe. Or should I call you Detective Babe?"

"To hell with the homicide. This is our big break. We'll be hanging with the Hollywood heavies, taking meetings, doing lunch at Spago. And if some producer doesn't like our movie pitch, we'll put the rubber hose to him."

And that's when I punched him. Not hard enough to make him lose control of the wheel. Just a swift knuckle sandwich to the shoulder. "You bastard. You ball-busting, chain-yanking bastard."

Terry's laugh is permanently set on Extra Loud. This time it was even louder. "Gotcha," he said, pounding on the steering wheel. "You should've seen the look on your face. Like Danny Glover in *Lethal Weapon* when he realizes that Mel Gibson is totally certifiable."

"You want to know why it was so easy for you to yank my chain?" I said. "Because you've been totally certifiable yourself." I waved the picture of the garbageman's wife at him. "*We're in pre-production?*"

"I might have exaggerated a little."

"Terry, you know I love you," I said.

"You're starting to sound like Marilyn. The next word is usually *but*."

"But," I said. "I can't deal with this show business shit. I know you're working on Plan B. I know you want to be the next Will Ferrell or Conan O'Brien or, or…"

"Weird Al Yankovic."

"Whatever. But when I'm on the job, I want to work with a smart cop, not a Hollywood asshole."

"You're right," he said. "I'm sorry."

"I wasn't fishing for an apology, just an agreement."

"Then I retract the apology and I agree. I realize I've been pushing it lately. I'll be a little less Hollywood asshole."

"A lot less."

"Jesus, I didn't realize I was pushing it that hard," he said. "Okay, I'll be ninety percent less Hollywood asshole."

"A hundred percent."

"Ninety-seven. I need the three percent wiggle room, or it's a deal breaker. Take it or leave it."

"I'll take it. Thank you."

"But I can still be funny, right?"

"That's a requirement," I said. "If you weren't funny, I'd have shot you years ago."

"Whoa," he said. "Now you're really starting to sound like Marilyn."

CHAPTER TWELVE

"I did a little research on Barry Gerber," Terry said as we made our way toward Bel Air.

"When?"

"Last week when I thought we might go into business with him. He's got some sketchy shit in his past."

"I'm a big fan of sketchy shit," I said. "How come you never told me?"

"I wanted to see what your take was on him, minus the dirt I dug up."

"And where did you dig up all this dirt?" I said.

"Google." He grinned. I knew he was lying, and he knew I knew.

"As long as you used the Internet," I said. "Because we both know it's a felony for a cop to tap into NCIC or the LAPD database for personal stuff."

"Actually, it's only a felony if you get caught, indicted, and convicted. But you know me. If I ever used department resources to further my movie career, I wouldn't be able to live with myself."

"So what did Google have to say about Barry Gerber?"

"His cars seem to get broken into, vandalized, or stolen in some real bad neighborhoods. Seven incidents in ten years."

"His insurance company probably dumped him on the third claim."

"He never filed. Every one of them was picked up by the cops. One time they find a brand-new Mercedes coupe all chopped up in South Central. They trace it to Barry, and he says, 'I'll be darned, Officer. I didn't know it was missing.' The cops who interviewed him didn't believe him, but they don't give a shit. If LAPD didn't find the car, it never would have been in our files."

"Google's files," I reminded him.

"Right. The other incidents happened in East LA, Hollywood—never in any of your upscale zip codes. He either had bad car karma or a very dark side."

"Remember what Baker-Broome said about him?" I said. "'He's probably got his nose in some blow and his dick in some underage coke whore.' And Halsey said he preferred street trash over the high-priced spread. What else do you have on him?"

"The usual trade mag stuff. He's done a shitload of movies and TV. Worth about four hundred million. He's married to a drop-dead gorgeous model from Trinidad. Her name is Royal Summerhaven."

"I'm just playing detective here," I said, "but with a name like Royal Summerhaven, I'm guessing there could be a disparity in their ages."

"She's twenty-seven. Exactly half his age."

"True love knows no bounds when a beautiful, brown-skinned, exotic woman meets a fat, dumpy, Jewish producer with four hundred mil in the bank."

"Depending on which website you believe," Terry said, "his house in Bel Air is either the third or fourth most expensive house in LA. It's called Park Place, like the expensive property in Monopoly."

"The one next to it is even more expensive," I said. "How come he didn't call it Boardwalk?"

"That's what he calls his house in Malibu."

CHAPTER THIRTEEN

I f you've seen one fifty-million-dollar house, you've seen
them all. Terry usually drools, but it's too far removed from
my reality for me to even care.

The Gerber estate covered two acres on St. Cloud Road in Bel
Air. We went through the ritual of stopping at the front gate,
flashing our IDs at the closed-circuit camera, poking along the
winding driveway at the posted 5 mph, parking in a designated
visitor spot, and climbing the front steps.

Terry stopped to take it all in. "It's amazing how much bad
taste you can buy if you've got enough money," he said.

"I thought you like houses you can't afford to own," I said.

"Not this one. Doric columns with gargoyles? It's like the
architect couldn't decide between a plantation or a castle in Tran-
sylvania, so he built them both. Let's see who answers the doorbell, Scarlett O'Hara or Count Dracula."

"I've got five bucks that says Mexican maid," I said.

I was right. A short woman in a gray maid's uniform
answered the door. Her name, Carmen, was stitched on her left

pocket. We identified ourselves, and got the same nervous look we usually get from immigrant help. Even if they're not hiding six cousins at home from the INS, they're just not comfortable with the gringo police. She asked us to wait.

A minute later, a tall elegant woman with bronze skin and silver hair came to the door. She wore a red and blue floral print dress that looked like it might be silk. "I'm Katryn," she said. "Royal Summerhaven's mother."

"Mrs. Summerhaven, I'm Detective Mike Lomax with LAPD. I'm sorry for your loss."

"What loss?" she said.

Oh, shit. We were told that the family had been notified. "Mrs. Summerhaven, I apologize," I said. "I thought you knew. Your daughter's husband was found dead this morning."

"Of course I knew. The police were here. But it's no loss to me. And my name isn't Summerhaven. That's my foolish daughter's make-believe name. You may call me Katryn."

She had such a lilting Caribbean accent that every nasty word out of her mouth sounded like sweet music.

"Catherine," I said, "we're here to…"

"Katryn. No *H*." She spelled it for me. "And who's your partner, Mr. Lomax? The one smirking."

I looked over at Terry, who was obviously enjoying my little run-in with Barry Gerber's mother-in-law from hell.

"Detective Terry Biggs, ma'am," he said. "And that's not a smirk. It's my natural joyful exterior. You know, don't worry, be happy."

Jesus H. Christ. He had looked her right in the eye and done a lame imitation of Bobby McFerrin. *Don't worry, be happy?* It was just a bad joke, but I was sure she was going to look right back at him and say, *I'm calling your boss, you goddamn racist.*

She laughed. "I like your partner," she said to me. "He has a sense of humor. Follow me."

We walked from the entryway into a large room that had enough books from floor to ceiling to be considered a library, but there was a glossy white grand piano in one corner of the room, and from what I remember about libraries, piano playing is not encouraged.

"My daughter is in here," Katryn said as we passed through an arch into an even larger room. If it hadn't been furnished it would have been perfect for arena football. Royal Summerhaven was sitting on a tufted white sofa on the fifty-yard line.

I have no idea how much of a loss it is for a beautiful young cover girl to have her coke-snorting, crack-whore-chasing, twice-her-age husband suddenly ripped from her life, but if Royal Summerhaven were grief-stricken, it did not in any way detract from her beauty.

She was wearing creamy white pants, a white blouse, a royal blue sash around her waist, and a rock around her neck the size of Minneapolis. Its twin, St. Paul, was set in platinum and parked on the third finger of her right hand.

Terry and I introduced ourselves and extended our condolences. Unlike her mother, Royal accepted them graciously. We chatted for a while about nothing, because it's not polite to ask the widow right off the bat if she has an alibi for the time of her husband's death.

According to Royal, they had been married three years and were deeply in love. Mama snorted but we all ignored her.

"When was the last time you saw your husband?" I asked.

"Yesterday morning," she said. "I was doing laps in the pool, and he came out to tell me he was going to visit Snow Way."

"What or where is Snow Way?" I asked.

"Snow Way is Barry's racehorse. She's stabled at the Pomona Fairplex. He adores her." She stopped to correct herself. "Adored. He adored her."

"And then?"

"I was still swimming, so he blew me a kiss, and he left."

"At what point did you realize he was missing?"

"I didn't," she said. "Barry doesn't call me during the day. He's always busy. And I knew he had a premiere to go to last night."

"And wouldn't you have attended the premiere with him?" I said.

"I've sat through that movie three times in our screening room," she said. "Some people think it's glamorous to get dressed up, walk down the red carpet with the paparazzi screaming at you, then sit in a crowded theater and watch a movie you've seen too many times already, but I think it sucks. It's what Barry does…did. Not me. Does your wife follow you to the office and watch you work, Detective?"

"I'm not married," I said, leaving out the my-wife-is-dead factoid that might have gotten hard-hearted Katryn to cut me some slack. "But I see your point. So you didn't expect to see him yesterday. What happened when your husband wasn't here this morning?"

"Excuse me, Detective." Mama Bear to the rescue. "My daughter and her husband have separate bedrooms. He only came to her bedroom or dragged her to parties when it suited him."

The doorbell rang.

"I'll get it," Katryn said. "Please be so kind as to hold all your questions until I get back." Her heels click-clacked on the marble floor as she left the room.

"My mother is upset about Barry," Royal said. "Well, not exactly about Barry, but how it will affect me. Can I have Carmen get you something to drink? Iced tea? Coffee? Coke?"

Our standard answer is no.

"Iced tea," I said quickly.

"A Coke would be great," Terry said, right on my heels.

Obviously we were on the same wavelength. We both wanted to get another look at the maid.

There was a telephone table next to the sofa. Royal picked up the phone, pushed a button, and called in our drink orders.

After about a minute, I could hear Katryn coming back. The staccato of high heels was much faster this time. What's her hurry I thought, as she breezed back into the room.

And then I got my answer. There, right behind her, was Lt. Brendan Kilcullen, and Katryn just couldn't wait to bust our balls.

"Gentlemen," she said, giving us a big, fat, don't-worry-be-happy smile, "your boss is here to check up on you."

CHAPTER FOURTEEN

Kilcullen was dressed for success. Dark-blue tailored suit, white shirt, subtle red tie. Same outfit the president wears for the State of the Union address.

"Believe me, I am not here to check up on my detectives," he said. "I'm actually here to check up on Ms. Summerhaven."

He took Royal's hand and shook it gently. "I'm Lieutenant Brendan Kilcullen, LAPD. I'm so sorry to meet you under these circumstances. The mayor asked me to personally extend his condolences."

"Thank you for coming," she said. "Please tell the mayor that I'm doing as well as can be expected."

"Whatever the city can do for you and your family, don't hesitate to call him on his direct line," Kilcullen said, pressing a business card into her hand. "Or me." He gave her a second card.

"The only thing I want from this city is for you to catch my husband's killer."

"These two detectives are the best in the entire department," I heard him say for the first time ever. "Last year they cracked the biggest series of homicides we've had in decades. This is an industry town and your husband was a giant in the industry. These men will find his killer quickly and bring him to justice."

The smirk had returned to Terry's face. He was cracking himself up, but he was smart enough not to share it with the grieving widow, the man-eating mother-in-law, or our ass-kissing boss.

Carmen arrived with our beverages.

"Thank you," Royal said, as the little Mexican woman set our drinks down, then backed out without making eye contact with a single cop.

"Would you like something to drink, Lieutenant?" Royal asked.

"No thanks," he said. "But I need to have a quick word with Detectives Lomax and Biggs. Can we step into the other room for a moment?"

Kilcullen is a tough cop with nineteen years under his belt, but he has slid seamlessly into the bullshit politics that go with rank. The fact that he showed up at an investigation could only mean one thing. Somebody was leaning on him.

We followed him into the room with the white piano.

"Rumor has it that you had a dick-waving contest at the crime scene with the fire department," he said.

"Not true," I said. "No dicks were waved."

"And there's no embarrassing video of some high-ranking fireman yelling at you with a bullhorn?"

"There's a heartwarming video of me shaking hands with my fireman buddy, George Fong. I'd be glad to have copies made for the Captain, the Commander, the Deputy Chief, and anyone else up the chain of command who thinks I might have embarrassed the department."

"So I don't have to worry about the Captain ripping me a new asshole?"

"Or the Commander," I said. "Or the Deputy Chief."

"They want this case solved fast," Kilcullen said. "You heard what I said to the widow about her husband being a giant in the industry. And a Jewish giant to boot. So they're all over me. Right up to the Mayor."

"We just got started," Terry said.

"Oh, you just got started. Why don't I tell that to the Mayor?" Kilcullen said. "And you know what he'll tell me? Barry Gerber was a dear friend of mine. And a generous contributor to my election campaign—"

"And if you don't catch his killer fast," Terry said interrupting, "a lot of big time Jewish producers who also make donations will be very upset."

Kilcullen smiled. "You got it. You finally understand politics."

"I thought my job was police work," Terry said.

"It is," Kilcullen said. "But my job is politics, and if you don't solve this thing fast, I'm the guy who is gonna rip *you* a new asshole. You wouldn't want that to happen, would you, Biggs?"

"No sir," Terry said. "The last thing this department needs is another asshole."

We rejoined the womenfolk. Kilcullen lowered himself onto the sofa next to Royal. "Why don't I just sit quietly and listen while these two detectives finish their interview. Sometimes the smallest things you can think of are all we need to crack a case wide open."

He nodded at me. "Carry on, Detective."

"Ms. Summerhaven, did your husband have any enemies?" I asked.

"Hah!" It came from Katryn. She opened a drawer in the telephone table, pulled out a Los Angeles directory and dropped it on the glass coffee table in front of the sofa. "This ought to get you started."

"Famous people often have their detractors," said the lieutenant who was just going to sit quietly and listen. "Can you think of someone who knew him personally and might have wanted to kill him?"

"Everyone who knew him wanted to kill him," Katryn said. "And you can put my name at the top of the list. I wished him dead every day, and now that he is, I hope he burns in hell."

"Mama," Royal said. "He was my husband, and you're in our house. Have some respect for the dead."

"Respect? The man was a tyrant, a drug addict, and a womanizer, and you were the ebony trophy wife. As far as I'm concerned, you're better off now that he's dead."

"Exactly how much better off will she be?" Terry asked.

Kilcullen started to get up off the sofa, but stopped himself. Before he was a cop-slash-politician, he was a homicide detective. He knows that everyone is a suspect. Especially the beautiful young widow-slash-beneficiary. And sometimes the cops asking the questions just have to drop a bomb. In this case, Terry was the bombardier.

Katryn, of course, was about to go mental, but Royal stopped her cold. "Let me deal with this," she said, turning to Terry. "Barry and I had a pre-nup. In the event of his death I get three million dollars, which may sound like a lot of money, but it's less than I earn in a single year as a model."

"Who gets the rest of his estate?" Terry asked.

"He has two ex-wives. They'll get a little. He has no siblings, no children. His parents get the rest. They're in their eighties. They still live in the same house in Queens where he grew up. They'll probably leave everything to charity when they die."

"Thank you," Terry said. "It's an ugly question. I'm sorry if I asked it in an ugly way."

"I understand," she said. "You're thorough. That's good."

It was time to bail. "Ms. Summerhaven, we realize this is a stressful time for you, and we understand there were some family tensions between your mother and your husband, so one more question before we go. What can you tell us about the other people in your husband's life—business relationships, personal contacts, things like that? Was he at odds with anyone? For instance, we know he had some kind of a falling out with Damian Hedge."

"I'm sorry," she said. "I don't really know. Barry was never very forthcoming about any of his business deals or his...his personal life outside our home. T.B. would be the best person to talk to."

"T.B." I said. "That would be Tyler Baker-Broome?"

"Yes."

Kilcullen's eyes widened, no doubt wondering how I put such a convoluted name to a two-letter clue. Maybe Terry and I actually were the two best detectives in the entire department.

"Thank you," I said. "I know where to find him."

Kilcullen extended his Look of Approval. Why spoil the magic by explaining to him that only last night T.B. had given me his business card?

"Can we talk to the maid and any other household staff briefly before we go?" I asked. "You never know what they might have seen or heard."

"There's four people," Katryn said. "I'll have them meet you in the kitchen."

Royal waited for her mother to leave the room.

"Mama is right," she said. "I was there when Barry needed eye candy. It was much more of a business arrangement than a marriage. Models have a short shelf life. Barry was going to help me start an acting career. I know he has a reputation for being..." She hesitated. "I was going to say 'difficult,' but he was a heartless bastard. Especially in business. But he could also be a very sweet, generous man. I'm very sad that someone murdered him, and I'd like you to do everything you can to find out who killed him."

Kilcullen stood. "Ms. Summerhaven, you have my personal guarantee. This department will not rest until the man who killed your husband is behind bars." He turned to me. "Am I right, Detective?"

"You're always right, sir," I said, recalling the inscrutable wisdom of my firefighter friend George Fong.

Brass up your ass.

CHAPTER SIXTEEN

Terry and I met with the help. They were no help.

Besides Carmen there were three others: see no evil, hear no evil, and speak no evil.

They were all appropriately upset about the death of Señor Barry, but nobody had any questions. Or answers. Just vacant stares.

We gave them our cards and told them to call if they thought of anything.

"Just dial 1-800-GESTAPO," Terry said.

They didn't laugh. "Language barrier," Terry said.

Kilcullen was still talking to Royal when we left the house. Katryn escorted us to the door. She didn't say anything. She probably just wanted to make sure we left.

"That was special," I said as we headed east on Sunset. "How generous of Lieutenant Kilcullen to stop by."

"Who says cops can't learn to micromanage," Terry said. "He did everything but recite the department credo. Neither snow, nor rain, nor heat, nor gloom of night, blah, blah, blah."

"I believe that's for postal workers," I said.

"Post office, police department," Terry said. "What's the difference? We're all just guys in uniforms toting guns."

Barry's company, Pita Productions, had their offices at Raleigh Studios on Melrose. I called Tyler Baker-Broome to make sure he was there. "We'll need a drive-on," I said.

He laughed. "Can't you guys just flash your badges at the front gate?"

"We could use lights and sirens if you don't mind everyone on the lot knowing that the cops are after you."

"You're right," he said. "I'm not thinking straight today. Barry's murder is a big shock to everyone at Pita."

I told him we'd be there in twenty and hung up.

"Pita bread is what they use to make falafel sandwiches," I said to Terry. "Pita Productions sounds like a Middle Eastern bakery. Couldn't he come up with something a little more creative?"

"Ah, grasshopper," Terry said. "You know so little of the ways of show business. 'Pita' is a blend of his parents' names. His father is Pinchas. His mother is Tanya. P-I-T-A. People who work there say it stands for Pain In The Ass."

"You are a treasure trove of Hollywood folklore," I said.

"It makes up for my shortcomings as a cop."

Terry's cell rang. He checked the caller ID and smiled. His kids don't call this early, so it had to be Marilyn. "Hey, babe," he said. "Have I *heard* about it? Mike and I caught the case. Yeah, we were just at Gerber's house in Bel Air. No, it doesn't change anything. We'll just have to look for another producer. They're like hydras. One dies, two more pop up. What? Are you kidding?"

He turned to me. "Marilyn said if we question Damian Hedge

she'd like us to get her his autograph."

"Tell her no problem," I said loud enough so she'd hear me. "We'll get you his prints and a mug shot too."

"Sorry, babe," Terry said into the phone. "Mike's a purist. Does everything by the book. I can't even get him to take bribes. Love you too. Bye."

We turned right on Bronson and pulled up to the studio gate. Terry rolled down the window. Before he could say a word, the security guard spread his arms out wide and said, "Detectives Lomax and Biggs. How the hell are you?"

Sergeant Rich Agins, recently retired from LAPD. So much for keeping a low profile.

"Rich," Terry said. "I heard you took a security job. How do you like it?"

"Are you kidding?" Agins said. "This booth is smaller than a gerbil's ass, the pay couldn't buy rice and beans for an anorexic Mexican, the Hollywood assholes who drive through here treat me like I'm a retard, and this uniform is so tight that my crotch has been chafed since my third day on the job. But hey man, I'm in show business. I love it."

"Another retired cop living the dream," Terry said.

"Sarge, good to see you," I said. "You got a drive-on for us?"

"Yeah, the girl at Pita left a drive-on for a *Mister* Lomax. Mister my ass. I figured somebody murders Barry Gerber, LAPD would be sending Starsky and Hutch. And here you are. You got a list of suspects yet?"

"Long as your arm."

"You can add my name to it. He was a hateful little toad."

Agins slid a parking pass onto our dashboard. "Make a right, drive down to the Clinton Building. Pita is on the second floor."

"Park anywhere, Sarge?" Terry said.

"Actually, there's an empty space right in front of the building." Agins gave us a broad grin and a mock salute. "It says, 'Reserved for Barry Gerber.'"

CHAPTER SEVENTEEN

We pulled up to the Clinton Building, which was not named after our colorful forty-second president. It borders on Clinton Street, so the name is strictly functional. The space itself is equally uninspired. Not a nickel was wasted on glitz or glamour for any of the executive suites. Baker-Broome's office was as exciting as a page out of a Staples catalog.

"We meet again," he said.

He looked better than he did last night. Less rumpled, less harried, and, of course, his boss was no longer missing.

He skipped the foreplay and machine-gunned us with questions: *How did Barry die? Was he already dead last night when we were waiting for him at the premiere? Did you talk to Royal yet? How is she taking it? Do you have any leads? Do you think you'll catch the guy?*

Our job is to ask questions, not answer them, so we fired back monosyllabic, noncommittal responses. But we do have a certain charm, and he seemed satisfied with our non-answers.

"Mr. Baker-Broome," I said, "we know you and Barry worked

together a long time. We're sorry for your loss."

"Call me T.B. I may be the only person in the world who actually liked him. And even then, not every day. Sixteen and a half years is a long time to work for a guy who has the reputation for firing everyone around him."

"You mean like Damian Hedge," I said.

"Damian is the tip of the iceberg. He's a big star, so the fallout got a lot of press. But Barry would fire writers, actors, directors, carpenters, gaffers, extras…did you ever hear about his famous barnyard massacre?"

"No," I said. "But anything with the word 'massacre' in it fascinates us."

"We were shooting on a farm. The animal trainer brings in a dozen chickens. They're supposed to flap their wings and scatter when the camera moves through the flock. But they didn't do it the way Barry was expecting, so after three takes he starts screaming at the trainer that these fat, lazy, union chickens can't act for shit. They're fired. The trainer says fuck you."

"Missed opportunity," Terry said. "I would have gone with cluck you."

"Well, nobody talks back to Barry on the set, so he goes ballistic. He says any idiot could train poultry better than you. In fact, I'll prove it. I'll buy them from you. How much do you want? The trainer blurts out a thousand bucks a bird. Barry yells sold and tells me to write a check on the spot."

"Twelve thousand dollars," I said. "For chickens."

"Yes, sir. And the next day those cluckers were back on the set. On platters. Barry fed them to the cast and crew for lunch."

"I had heard that story," Terry said, "but I thought it was an urban myth."

"It's true. There's still a picture in Barry's office of him and the two stars chomping on drumsticks. The man was legend. The ultimate control freak."

"How did you manage to work for this guy for so long?" I said.

"I guess I have the personality he needed. Unquestioned loyalty. Blind obedience. Willing to do whatever he asked and take all his secrets to the grave."

"This would be a good time for you to part with some of those secrets," I said. "What are the facts behind the feud with Damian?"

He shook his head, maybe out of panic. I took it as a no.

"Hey, we're not selling it to the tabloids. We're investigating a murder. Obstruction of justice is a crime, and you've probably shot enough prison movies to know what happens to guys who withhold information from the police."

He gave it about three seconds before he caved. "It all started last New Year's Day. I got a call from Barry at six in the morning. He tells me he just fired Damian from the movie we were prepping."

"*I.C.U.*"

"No, we shot that last year. We were getting ready to go to the U.K. to shoot a Knights of the Round Table movie. Damian was supposed to star. I told Barry that Damian had a play-or-pay contract. You know what that is?"

"If the movie doesn't get made, the actor still gets paid," I said. Terry's not the only one who knows this crap. "How much are we talking about?"

"Ten million. Barry didn't even blink. He just said he's fired. Pay it."

"So he fired Damian at 6 a.m. on January 1," I said. "I'm

guessing they were at the same New Year's Eve party."

He looked impressed that I had figured that out, but it was an easy connection. January 1 is a busy day for homicide cops.

"The party was at Barry's house. You know how the media loves to play up the decadent Hollywood lifestyle. Drugs, alcohol, sex. It's true. Barry woke up, went to Royal's bedroom, and there was Damian shagging the boss's wife."

"And that pissed him off," I said. "Even though he has a reputation of being a whoremonger himself."

"King Barry," T.B. said. "The rules that apply to him don't apply to anyone else. He fired Damian before the guy could get his Calvins on."

"And Damian got ten million dollars for not shooting a movie," I said. "That doesn't exactly sound like a motive for murder."

"Not until Barry started bad-mouthing him to the press. Said he needed an actor to play Sir Lancelot who could actually get his lance up."

"So was that his pattern?" Terry said. "Get in someone's face, can them, and then pay them off?"

"A lot of the time but not always. Sometimes he would do just the opposite. You're fired, and you're not getting a penny."

"And who stands out in that category?" I said.

"Steve Kronowitz. He's a trauma surgeon. Barry hired him to work on *I.C.U.* to train Damian and the other actors so they'd look believable. But the doc started bitching that Barry was too demanding, and he asked for more money. Barry said no. They argued on the set, and Barry threw a bedpan at Kronowitz's head. The guy needed thirty stitches. He's suing."

"We'll need his address and phone number," I said.

"Kronowitz has been at a medical conference in Vienna all week," T.B. said. "I know because our lawyers were trying to set up a deposition with him."

"Let's talk about some of those perverse habits you mentioned last night," I said. "Did he have any run-ins with the hookers or the pimps?"

"No. His car was trashed a few times, but that's because he would leave it in a bad neighborhood for hours, sometimes for the whole weekend."

"What about drugs? Barry's mother-in-law says he's an addict."

"That woman thinks anyone who smokes weed or does a little blow should be locked up. Recreational drugs are part of our culture. And not just the movie business. Tell me you don't know any cops or dentists or schoolteachers who light up a joint at the end of a tough day."

"And who does Barry buy his drugs from?" Terry asked.

"I wouldn't know."

"Bullshit," Terry said. "You know everything. Now answer the question. Who supplied Barry with his recreational weed so he could light up at the end of a tough day?"

"I don't know. And if you don't like my answer, arrest me."

Translation: it was Baker Broome's job to run the drug pipeline for his boss, but he didn't want to incriminate himself. Reality: we work homicide, not narcotics. We can't solve all of LA's social issues. Terry moved on.

"Last night you said you spoke to Barry in the morning, but when you called him again at noon, there was no answer."

"You have a good memory."

"Where did Barry say he was going when you spoke to him?"

"He owns a racehorse, Snow Way. He was going to watch

him work out. But I called the stable yesterday when I was looking for him, and they said he never showed up." He smiled.

"You think of something funny, T.B.?" Terry said.

"It's just a cute Barry story. It's not important."

"I didn't think I'd ever hear you use 'cute' and 'Barry' in the same sentence," Terry said. "And it's not for you to decide what's important."

"When Barry bought Snow Way, I found out that the California Horse Racing Board requires all racehorse owners to be fingerprinted. Barry couldn't be bothered. I told him he had to physically appear and get printed, or he wouldn't be able to get a license to race. He said to me, 'You go. They can remove my prints from your neck.' That's the kind of guy he was. He knew his reputation for being the biggest prick in show business, and he loved it."

"Somebody didn't love it," Terry said.

We spent another hour talking about the people who hated Barry. Katryn wasn't far off when she told us to start with the LA phone directory.

It was hard to believe that yesterday Terry and I were on our way to meet Barry Gerber, and now we were sifting through the shitstorm of his life trying to figure out who was the lucky winner of the I Want to Murder Barry lottery.

After two hours we thanked Baker-Broome for his help. "By the way," I said as we started to leave, "where were you yesterday afternoon around four o'clock?"

"I was at the Pantages Theatre setting up. Before that I was with the caterer finalizing the details on the premiere party." He gave us a smug look. "I hope you enjoyed it."

"Fabbo," Terry said.

"Look, I know you have to ask," Baker-Broome said, "but I didn't kill him."

"I'm sure you didn't," I said. "But I'll bet you thought about it."

He laughed. "Every fucking day for the last sixteen and a half years."

CHAPTER EIGHTEEN

It was 6:30 by the time we finished interviewing Tyler Baker Broome. Damian Hedge would have to wait till tomorrow. We were about to call it a day when my cell rang. It was Halsey.

"We have to talk," he said. "Barry's dead."

"We sort of know that," I said.

"Don't tell me," he said. "You're investigating his murder."

"We're trying."

"Where are you guys?"

"Raleigh Studios."

"That's fantastic. I'm just across the street. I'm wrapping up a meeting at Paramount. Meet me at Fabiolus Café on Melrose and Van Ness in ten minutes."

"Hold on." I hit the mute button. "It's Halsey," I said to Terry. "He wants to talk."

"Cop business or show business?"

"Good question," I said. "Let's decide when we get there."

Terry and I arrived first. We asked for bread, olive oil, and a large bottle of Pellegrino.

"So," Terry said. "Straight or gay?"

"Who?"

"T.B."

"Does it matter?" I said. "I don't think he killed his boss. What do you care what he does with his pants off?"

"I thought I detected a certain something between him and Halsey last night. I'm just curious."

Halsey Bates entered the restaurant, spotted us, and headed our way.

"Here he is," I said. "Why don't you ask him?"

Halsey Bates sat down. "Ask me what?"

"About you and Tyler," Terry said.

"Well, he wasn't supposed to say anything yet," Halsey said. "But I guess with Barry gone, it's not as important to keep it hush-hush. If the deal goes through, it'll be in the trades next week."

"What deal?" Terry said.

"I'm talking to Paramount about a three-year, multi-picture deal. If it happens, Tyler was planning on leaving Barry and joining my company as head of development. I'm surprised he told you. He's usually pretty tight-lipped."

"Tyler didn't say anything about a deal or the fact that he was planning on leaving Barry. I was just wondering if he was gay, and if you and he..."

"Oh, God no," Halsey said. "First of all, he's straight, although he doesn't work very hard at his sex life. Much more interested in work than women. Second of all, even if he were gay, he is *so, so, so* not my type."

I tapped my forehead with two fingers. Cop code. Think

twice before you ask the next question, partner. Don't ask Halsey what is *so, so, so* his type.

Terry picked up on the signal. "But you and Tyler are thinking of going into business together," he said.

"More than thinking. We're having lunch on Thursday to iron out the details. Tyler is one of the most under-utilized people in the business. He has great instincts for what will resonate with the movie-going public, but Barry never trusted anybody's instincts but his own. So Tyler ended up being a very high-paid…what's the word I'm looking for…? Facilitator. That's what he was. Barry snapped his fingers, Tyler made it happen."

"What do you think will happen to Pita Productions?" I said.

"Pita has some great films in their archives plus projects in the pipeline with different studios, development people, global partners, and all kinds of production and distribution entities. The lawyers will fight over who gets what, but without Barry, Pita will be history in about three years."

"Do you have any thoughts on who killed him?"

"Am I a suspect?" he said, winking at me. I wondered if I were his type.

"Should you be?"

"Quite honestly, no. The man was very good to me. He kick-started my career when I got out of prison and for that I am truly grateful. I asked because this case could turn out to be as hot as the Lamaar murders. If I'm a suspect and I option the story, I could wind up being a character in my own film."

"If it makes you happy, feel free to call yourself a suspect," I said. "Now let me repeat the question. Who do you think might have done it?"

"How did he die?" Halsey asked.

"Too soon to tell," I said. "We won't know till after the autopsy."

"That's interesting," he said.

"What's interesting about it?"

"Well, if somebody shot him—bang, bang—you'd say somebody shot him. But if the cause of death has a little mystery to it...a little drama...I'd suspect someone with a sense of theater. And a motive. Damian Hedge comes to mind. He never forgave Barry for those comments about his sexual prowess. Did you know that the day after Barry said he couldn't get his lance up, the ad agency for Viagra offered Damian a five-million-dollar endorsement deal. Of course, he didn't take it. He makes a lot more money playing a super stud on-screen."

"Damian seems too smart to murder somebody he's feuding with in the national media," Terry said.

"Don't kid yourself, Detective," Halsey said. "Lots of people are smart. But if they put enough cocaine up their nose, they can do some very dumb things. How do you think I wound up in prison? I drank myself stupid, then decided that the smart way to get a drunk man home was to drive drunk myself. I spent three months working with Damian. On any given day he is definitely high enough to commit murder."

"Can I ask one last self-serving question?" Terry said.

Halsey smiled. "Ah, yes. Our Familyland film. Barry was just the first person on a long list of possible backers. If I go ahead with this Paramount deal, I'll pitch it to them. Believe me, we are going to make this movie. Does that answer your question?"

"Actually, I was going to ask if you mind if I take this last piece of bread. But I'm glad you filled us in on the project. Mike hates when I jabber on about show business." He tore the piece of bread in two. "Here you go, partner," he said, giving me half.

"If you're hungry, let's order," Halsey said. "The spaghetti carbonara is excellent."

"I'll skip the pasta," Terry said. "Ever since we left Tyler's office I've had a real hankering for chicken."

CHAPTER NINETEEN

The Hollywood station on North Wilcox is only twenty minutes from Diana's apartment. A lot less if it's 6:45 in the morning and you drive like a cop. It's one of the older station houses in LA, an orangey-red brick low-rise that you'd mistake for a school if it weren't for the LAPD signage and the parking lot full of black and whites. Oh, and the bail bondsman across the street.

I like walking in the front door. There are big stars on the sidewalk, just like on the Hollywood Walk of Fame around the corner. Only our stars bear the names of cops from our station who died in the line of duty. *To Those Who Stood Their Ground When in Harm's Way.*

A star is the least we could do.

The other good part about going through the front door is that there's usually a newbie cop sitting at the front desk, looking all fresh-faced and eager to help. Somebody on high must have decided that grizzly old sergeants don't make a great first impression, so our front desk tends to be manned by women. Pretty ones. Today was no different. Donna Parisi. Young, blonde, and altogether too damn perky for this hour of the morning.

"Good morning, Detective," she sang. "Your case is on page one of the *L.A. Times.*"

"Does it say if it's solved yet?"

She giggled. A giggling cop. What is this city coming to? I turned left and entered the detectives' squad room.

Our station has about 220 uniformed officers and thirty-five detectives. Uniforms work around the clock. Detectives work a single shift, some coming in as early as six if they're pulling a ten-hour day.

The first ones to rag on me were three guys Terry and I play poker with, Eliot Ganek and Bob Kanarick from Autos, and Steve Venokur from Burglary. Part of the cop bonding experience is to bust another cop's balls. Terry is a master at it. These guys aren't. There's never a funny cop around when you need one.

The coffee pot is near my desk, at the far end of the room. I poured myself a cup while they cracked lame jokes about dead celebrities and Chinese firemen. When they ran out of steam, I walked over to talk to Ganek and Kanarick.

"I need a little help from the Auto table," I said.

"Doesn't your agent handle that for you?" Kanarick said.

"My vic left the house yesterday morning in a 2005 black Toyota Land Cruiser. His body turned up in the Hills, but we have no whereabouts on the vehicle. I don't have the plates or the VIN, and I don't have time to go through the system. Can you locate it for me? Preferably with a clean set of prints from the guy who jacked him."

"If we find it, who plays us in the movie?" Ganek said.

"The Olsen twins."

I went back to my desk and called my father.

"Your name's in the paper," he said. "How you doing on this case?"

"It practically solves itself. What's Dennis's cell number?"

"Dennis? My driver?"

"Yeah, what's his number?"

"What do you need Dennis for?"

I knew this would happen. But I was ready for him.

"Dennis is an ex-cop. I may have a freelance security gig for him."

"In a pig's ass," Jim said. "You know that Dennis is driving Damian Hedge around and you want to question Hedge. Calling me is the easiest way to track him down."

"You're wrong," I said. "Forget it. I gotta go."

I hung up. Boy, had I handled that badly.

The phone rang. It was Jim. He gave me Dennis's cell number and the location they were shooting at today. "And next time you want a favor, ask for it straight-out," he said. "Freelance gig...you think I'm stupid?"

"No, I'm stupid to think that I could ask my own father a simple favor and not be grilled with who, what, when, where, why, and how. Whatever happened to no questions asked?"

"Get me two Mexican hookers, a quart of tequila, and a bathtub full of lime Jell-O—that's a simple no-questions-asked favor a father could do for his son," he said. "But if you want me to help you find *your* homicide suspect, who's riding around in *my* car, I think I'm entitled to a couple of straight answers."

"Damian Hedge is not a suspect," I said.

"Why the hell not? He was schtupping Barry's old lady."

I was floored. "You knew that?" I said.

"Hello, Detective…I'm a teamster on a movie set. You think I just sit around soaking up the ambience? I'm like Central Intelligence. Did you forget who you came to for help on the Familyland murders?"

"Oh, right. It completely slipped my mind. You're the guy who solved that case. And who do you want to play you in the movie?"

"I'm playing me," he said. "Nobody plays Big Jim Lomax but Big Jim Lomax. And if you need his insider information on this case, you know his number."

"Thanks. If I ever need a 300-pound fly on the wall who talks about himself in the third person, I'll send for you."

"Two eighty-seven," he said. "And my cholesterol is down to—"

"Dad, I gotta go. Terry just walked in."

I hung up. Terry was not alone.

"Look who I found," he said. "She was parked across the street, deciding whether or not to come in and talk to us. I spotted her and helped her make the right decision."

The woman with him looked petrified.

It was Carmen, Barry's maid.

CHAPTER TWENTY

We took Carmen into an interview room. Terry wanted to make her feel comfortable, so naturally he went for a laugh.

"Miguel," he said to me, "get Carmen some café, por favor."

The joke sailed right over her head. "No, no," she said, horrified that a cop was being asked to fetch coffee for a maid.

I stepped in. "Carmen, what can you tell us about Barry Gerber?"

"I go to confession this morning. Father Bill say go to police."

"Father Bill is right," I said. "What did you say to him?"

"I say I'm sorry. I need the money. I'm sorry."

"What are you sorry about?"

"La basura," she said. And then the dam broke. First a flood of Spanish. Then the universal language all men understand. Tears.

"A hysterical woman," Terry said. "I feel right at home."

"Un momento," I said, and headed to the squad room for reinforcements.

Detective Elizabeth Estupinan was at her desk. She was perfect for the job at hand. Three years in homicide, thirty-four years as a Spanish-speaking woman. It took me five momentos to give her the background on Carmen.

Elizabeth went into the interview room, leaving the door open so we could listen. We didn't understand a word of it, but we could hear Carmen calming down. Finally, we were invited back.

"She thinks it's her fault that her boss got killed," Elizabeth said. "Last week a woman approached her at the farmers' market, said she was a reporter, and offered to pay Carmen two hundred bucks for the trash from Gerber's wastebasket. It's pretty common in Hollywood. Maids can supplement their income by trafficking in celebrity garbage."

"And she agreed to do it?"

"Not at first, but the woman upped the ante to five hundred, and said it's harmless because it's just crap he throws away anyway. She said if Carmen didn't help, she'd just hire some kids to go through the trash cans on garbage day, and Carmen would lose out on the money."

"So she did it," I said.

"It made sense, and five hundred is a lot of money in her tax bracket."

"Did she give you a description of the woman?" Terry asked.

"White, about five-five, somewhere between fifty and sixty years old, same color hair as Carmen's."

"Mousy gray," Terry said.

Elizabeth laughed. "Not gray. She says her hair is plata. Silver."

"Fine," Terry said. "Mousy plata."

"How does she get in touch with this woman again?" I said.

"It was a one-way street," Elizabeth said. "She never gave Carmen her number. A real reporter would have, because she'd want to keep Carmen on as a source. The woman approached her last Monday at the farmers' market and picked up the trash on Friday at the same location."

"Smart place to do it," I said. "No surveillance cameras."

"Ask her what went on between Royal Summerhaven and Damian Hedge," Terry said.

Elizabeth didn't have to say a word. Carmen caught the important part and shook her head. "No sé nada sobre Damian Hedge," she said.

Elizabeth started to translate.

"I caught the 'nada' part," I said.

"Tell her we're calling Father Bill, and if she doesn't answer the question, her soul will rot in hell for all eternity," Terry said.

"Somebody had a traumatic Catholic childhood," Elizabeth said.

"I had two aunts who were nuns," Terry said. "I'm scarred for life."

"Let me try something short of eternal damnation," Elizabeth said, resting her hand on Carmen's gnarled knuckles. "Señora, por favor. Es importante."

'Importante' must have been the magic word. Or maybe it was 'por favor,' because Carmen gave it up. Damian and Royal had been sneaking around for months, but even in a house as big as Park Place, you can't sneak steaming hot sex past the woman who does your laundry. Carmen knew. And she was there the day Gerber found out. Apparently Señor Barry was muy pissed off.

Terry made a fist with his left hand. "Ask her if Royal and Damian are still…" He took his right forefinger and began sliding it in and out of his fist.

Carmen shrugged. "Quién sabe?"

A few questions later, and we decided we'd gotten all we could. We told her she might have to come back for an ID if we ever found the bogus reporter.

"This poor woman feels very guilty about that," Elizabeth said. "I wish I knew how to help her."

"Send her home," Terry said. "Tell her to say ten Hail Marys, give the five hundred bucks to the church, and all will be forgiven."

Elizabeth looked at me. "I guess he wasn't kidding when he said he was scarred for life."

CHAPTER TWENTY-ONE

W e had only been in the interview room for half an hour, but when I got back to my desk there were five messages.

The first was from Wendy Burns. She's a Detective III, and she's the supervisor who assigns cases to the homicide teams and oversees a lot of what we do. Technically she's our boss, but she doesn't act bossy, because we all report to an even bigger boss— Lt. Brendan Kilcullen. And as Wendy says, when you have Kilcullen looking over your shoulder, you already have more control freaks than you need.

Wendy's desk is catty-corner to mine. She could easily have waited till I got back and told me that the morgue had scheduled Gerber's autopsy. But like a lot of good cops, she deals with the dark side of the job by making light of it.

She left a note. *Barry Gerber cordially invites you to his Final Opening. Tuesday May 8 at 11 a.m. 1104 North Mission Road, Los Angeles. Black tie optional. Masks and shoe covers mandatory.*

The next message was from the guys in Autos. *Found your*

vehicle. It's at the impound lot on Mansfield. You owe us. Love, Mary Kate and Ashley.

The last three were from Kilcullen. The first said, *My office. Now.* The second said, *Bring your wiseass partner.* And finally, *Stop reading your fucking messages and haul ass.* If Terry or Wendy had left a note like that, I'd smile. With Kilcullen, you know he's not kidding around.

I stopped reading my fucking messages, got my wiseass partner, and hauled ass to Kilcullen's office.

"Good morning, gentlemen," he said, smiling broadly.

Terry tossed me a look. We know how to deal with the angry Kilcullen, but the chipper version can be lethal. We said good morning.

"Look what I'm reading," he said, holding up a paperback book. "It's called *Secrets of Successful Speakers: How You Can Motivate, Captivate, and Persuade* by Lilly Waters. Did you know that psychological studies show that the average person is more afraid of public speaking than of dying?"

"Actually, I knew that, sir," Terry said. "Seinfeld used that as a setup for a bit once. Then he says, 'So when you go to a funeral, most of the people there would rather be lying in the box than standing at the podium giving the eulogy.'"

"Shut up, Biggs. I'm in the middle of a motivational speech."

"Yes, sir," Terry said. "And God knows you're good at it."

"I'm not like the average person," Kilcullen said. "I'm not afraid to open my mouth. My fear is that I won't be heard. Or I'll be heard and my message won't be processed. So let me elaborate on what I said yesterday. You don't have a life. You have a homicide. I understand that Mr. Gerber was a coke-snorting, pussy-chasing, big time Hollywood producer. But the key words here are 'big time,' 'Hollywood,' and 'producer.' LA is an industry town, and lest you forget, this is the Hollywood station. We have relationships with all the studios in our area. We get more media coverage than the other divisions, because we live right here in 90028. And as we all know, there are two kinds of media coverage. The first is called good. And what's the second one called, Biggs?"

"I don't know the technical term, sir, but I think it may have the words 'Lomax,' 'Biggs,' and 'traffic detail' in it."

"You're a smart man, Detective Biggs. Are you smart enough to solve the heinous murder of one of this town's most valued citizens?"

"Absolutely, sir."

"So then, the two of you are motivated."

"I speak for my partner, sir," Terry said, "when I say that we are motivated within an inch of our jobs."

"Good. I'll have to write to Miss Lilly Waters and let her know that her book is extremely effective. Now fill me in."

We did.

"What about this Damian Hedge? Have you interviewed him yet?"

"First we have an autopsy," Terry said, "then we meet with crime lab and go over the victim's car, then Hedge."

"So you won't have time to do lunch with your Hollywood asshole friends?" Kilcullen said.

"Only the ones who are suspects, sir," Terry said.

"Lomax, get your wiseass partner out of here and get back to work."

"Yes, sir," I said and headed toward the door.

I'm not one of those dogs who has to be motivated by fear,

but every time we catch a big case, Kilcullen loves to remind us that police work and politics go hand in hand, and that some victims are more important than others. I hate being browbeaten, but I don't say much. I internalize.

Terry, on the other hand, sees it as part of the game. Tag, you get your balls busted. Tag, you bust back. Sometimes I love it when he busts back. This time, I was counting on it. We were almost out the door when he came through.

"Hey, Loo," he said.

Kilcullen looked up. "What?"

Terry blew him a kiss. "Ciao."

CHAPTER TWENTY-TWO

Los Angeles has the busiest morgue in the country. New York City gets more dead bodies but they spread the wealth across four different facilities. LA puts all its dead in one basket.

According to the coroner's daily inventory sheet, Barry Gerber was 1 of 129 bodies waiting to be processed. Just another average day at the morgue. As Craig Harvey, Chief of Operations, likes to say, "That's how we keep our prices so low. Volume."

Not all of the dearly departed are crime victims. They die in car wrecks, kitchen fires, or alone in motel rooms with an empty pill bottle on the night table. But unless they die under the watchful eye of a doctor, the cause and manner of death must be determined by a forensic specialist. And when the death is a homicide, the cops investigating the murder have to be there too.

Anybody who's ever seen a TV cop show thinks they know what a morgue looks like. A stark, sterile room. A wall of stainless steel drawers. A somber attendant slides one drawer open and unzips a black body bag.

"Yes," the next of kin says, "that's Grandma. I knew I should never have let her go to that monster truck rally after she drank all that eggnog."

The body bag is zipped up, and the drawer closes with a metallic thunk.

That's a movie morgue.

In real life, the morgue looks more like something out of Edgar Allen Poe. No steel drawers, just gurneys. And no body bags. They cost too much. The cadavers are wrapped in sheets, heads and feet sticking out at either end.

The air is ripe with the smell of disinfectant, formaldehyde, and decomposing humanity. The recently deceased don't smell so bad. But if Granny died in bed July Fourth and nobody found her till Labor Day, she's gonna stink to high heaven.

Gurneys are parked everywhere. On the loading dock, at the admissions desk, in the hallways, waiting to be weighed, finger-printed, sliced, diced, and gutted. At times you can't walk ten feet without seeing a toe tag. It's one big, crowded, waiting room. Everyone's waiting for the doctor.

It's not a pretty place. Which is why next of kin are not invited—not even to identify a body. Instead they get to look at Polaroids.

There is one place the public can visit. On the second floor, there's a gift shop. Really. They sell T-shirts, windbreakers, coffee mugs, and all kinds of fun stuff with the coroner's logo on it. And if you're a little creeped out about driving to the morgue to do your holiday shopping, they have a website. The profits help fund their Youthful Drunk Driver Visitation Program. When a young kid gets arrested for driving drunk, the court can sen-tence him to spend three hours in the morgue, where he'll get an education he'll never forget.

Terry and I got there at 10:45 and pulled the car around to the loading dock. A transport van was backed in, with its rear doors wide open. The driver stepped out of the back. He had a mop in one hand. He waved with the other.

"Yo, Mike, Terry. How's it going?"

It was Victor Shea, our favorite hyphenate.

LA is full of hyphenates. A rarified few are writer-hyphen-directors or actor-hyphen-producers. The rest are actress-hyphen-Gap salesgirls, cinematographer-hyphen-pizza delivery guys, or some other career combo with a dream on one end of the hyphen and a dead-end job on the other.

Victor is different. After four years of waiting on tables, driving a cab, and pushing a mail cart up and down the halls of a law firm, he realized that working his ass off for the Man ten hours a day was never going to advance his screenwriting career. So he quit his day job and found something that would.

The money is piss poor, but the job is just what he needed to get his creative juices flowing. Even better, it gives him plenty of time to write. Victor Shea is a writer-hyphen-LA County morgue attendant.

He's five-foot-six, chubby by at least forty pounds, with curly brown hair that's crying out for Rogaine. He's the kind of kid who probably got a lot of wedgies in grade school, but at twenty-seven he's just a likable loser from Allentown, Pennsylvania who's braving the smog, the earthquakes, and the drive-by shootings for a shot at fame and fortune as a Hollywood screenwriter.

"Vic," Terry said. "You sell anything to Quentin Tarantino yet?"

"No, but I gave a copy of my latest script to Barry Gerber this morning, and he must love it, because I can't pry it loose from his cold, dead hand."

"Small world," Terry said. "We have a meeting with Mr. Gerber ourselves. Last time we met we couldn't coax him out of his shell."

"We cut the garbage can," Victor said, "but he was in full-blown rigor, so he was about only three feet high when we pried him loose. It took hours to get him to lie flat. Why don't you suit up. Dr. Hand is doing the postmortem."

Talk about hyphenates. Eli Hand is a brilliant pathologist-hyphen-lapsed rabbi. He went to rabbinical school, was ordained, then realized he had one major shortcoming that got in the way of doing his job. He doesn't like people.

"Especially the ones that kvetch," he told me. "And when you're a rabbi, that's all you get. Complainers."

So he went to med school. Not to learn to administer to the sick, but to work with the dead. Less complainers. He's rumored to be seventy-five years old, but he could pass for fifty. He's five-three, athletic, sinewy, and looks like he'd be right at home coming around the far turn at Santa Anita. A geriatric Jewish jockey.

I'm not a big fan of autopsies, but if you have to spend three hours watching someone cut up a dead body, Eli is the best person to do it with. He keeps it light and breezy, and he likes trading zingers with Terry. He's also the most respected doc in the building, so I'm sure it was no accident that the coroner assigned him to work on their most famous dead guy.

Terry and I went to the supply room for basic autopsy protection gear: face masks, rubber gloves, head and shoe covers. Then we walked down the hall to the autopsy room. Dr. Hand was already there.

"Ah, good," he said. "We have a *minyan*. We can start."

Eli loves his heritage and peppers the conversation with Yiddish words. And because Diana Trantanella, my Italian-sounding girlfriend, is actually Jewish, I get to use a few of them at home.

Eli starts every procedure the same way; today was no different.

"*Barrala*," he said, addressing the naked man on the table in front of him. "My name is Eli and I'm going to cut you apart. The good news is that I will do everything in my power to determine exactly what foul deed has befallen you, so that these two gentlemen can find your killer and bring him to justice. The bad news, kiddo...I'm afraid this is going to be your last Hand job."

CHAPTER TWENTY-THREE

"He's the whitest white man I've ever seen," Terry said. "He's like an albino."

"Not quite," Hand said. "An albino's lips and nails would be pink. This fellow is completely absent of color."

"Loss of blood was Jessica's take on it," I said.

"Yes, I read CSI Keating's field notes," Hand said. "Extreme pallor, waxy, no visible wounds, but victim shows signs of massive blood loss. Good call. Where is Keating anyway? Doesn't she enjoy my autopsies anymore?"

"She's pregnant," I said. "Her doc said she could only visit the morgue if she promises not to inhale."

"Bullshit," Hand said. "You think the air down here is any worse than the rest of Los Angeles? Tell her I've been breathing it most of my life, and I'm healthier than ninety-five percent of the people out there on those gurneys."

"I'm sure she'll be thrilled to hear it," I said.

"Also tell her that considering the fact that Mr. Gerber was folded up like a concertina, she made a very keen observation. This man appears to have lost a lot of blood. I wouldn't be surprised if we open him up and find he's five pints low. And yet, there are no obvious wounds to account for such dramatic blood loss."

"But there are obvious ligature marks," Terry said.

Hand cleared his throat and slipped into his authoritative pathologist voice for the audiotape, "The decedent appears to have been restrained. There are marks on the tops of his wrists and his ankles and across his chest. But no such marks on the underside of his extremities or on his back. This would indicate that he was strapped to a bed, a table, or some flat surface. And I say 'strapped,' because these are not rope burns. They're more like belt marks."

"If somebody tried to strap me down like that," Terry said, "I'd put up a fight. It doesn't look like he did."

"He could have been held at gunpoint," I said.

"Or drugged," Hand said. "We'll take tissue samples and see what we can find."

"The man had a kinky side," Terry said. "He could have paid extra for the bondage."

"The ligature marks are not the cause of death. I'm more interested in the blood loss," Hand said. "I was speaking with the decedent before you got here, and I said, Barry, why do I find no evidence of a wound?"

"Did he answer?" Terry said.

"Of course not, you idiot. He's dead. I'm the one who has to figure it out." Hand loves nailing Terry, and his mask could not hide the grin on his face. "But I do have a hypothesis. Give me more light down here by the pubic area."

Victor adjusted the lights, and the doc pointed at Barry's shriveled genitalia. "You see that little wrinkled bit of skin on the right side of his groin?"

I stared at the folds and creases around Gerber's ball sac. "Doc, it's all wrinkled," I said.

"Look closely at this one," he said, holding up a magnifier. "It looks like a paper cut. It's the kind of thing I wouldn't notice unless I were looking for where the blood came from. But since it's in the neighborhood of his femoral vein, I'm curious if it could be a tiny incision."

He took a probe, touched it to the wrinkle. It parted. He spoke up for the audio, "It's a slit in the skin, approximately three millimeters." He pushed the probe in. "I've inserted a probe about seven millimeters into the opening. We'll leave it there and see what we can see from the inside."

Eli cut into Barry's chest, chatting as he worked. "Terry, did I mention that I was a guest lecturer at the Keck School of Medicine at USC last week? Victor made an audio montage of some of my more interesting autopsies and I played it for my students. They want to meet you."

"Great," Terry said. "More people who want to cut my heart out."

"I played the tape of that homeless woman who was chopped up and left in separate dumpsters."

"Backstreet Betsy," Terry said.

"Yes," Eli said. "The students got a big laugh out of your comments."

Terry shrugged. "Refresh my memory. I don't remember half the things I say under the influence of formaldehyde."

"Well, I said she may have been a bag lady, but by the time the funeral home gets her maquillaged and coiffed, she'll look like the Queen of England. And you said it couldn't hurt if they sewed her head back on. It'll cut down the odds of her tiara rolling off."

Eli removed Barry Gerber's heart from his chest and put it on the scale.

"Well, that solves one mystery," Terry said.

"What's that, Detective?"

"Producers do have hearts."

And so it went for three hours. Death and comedy. Finally, we got what we came for. "I think I know how Mr. Gerber died," Eli said.

He was working deep inside Barry's gut. "Here's the probe I inserted into the incision earlier, and it's clear from this angle that it leads directly into the femoral vein. I'd say he was cannulated by some type of vascular access device and then systematically exsanguinated."

"'Cannulated' and 'exsanguinated'?" Terry said. "I'm still working on 'maquillaged' and 'coiffed.' Can you give me the *Autopsies for Dummies* version?"

"You know how a phlebotomist draws your blood?" Hand said.

"Yeah. She takes a needle and taps a vein."

"This is similar. Only this time she didn't turn off the tap. My best guess is that somebody shoved a sixteen or an eighteen-gauge vascular access catheter into Barry Gerber's vein and drained the blood from his body."

"Exsanguination." It was Victor. "I don't believe it."

"Victor, to tell you the truth, I've been doing this for years, and I've never seen anything quite like it myself. I've seen every imaginable wound that causes people to bleed to death, but this man was bled out. And it's venous bleeding, not arterial, so it would have been a slow death."

"Define slow," I said.

"When you donate blood, how long does it take you to give a pint? Forty-five minutes? This man gave pint after pint after pint. And I doubt if he passed out. He'd be lightheaded from the blood loss, but he'd be conscious."

"I just want to make sure I have this right," Terry said. "This guy was strapped to a table and had to watch the blood being drained from his body."

"We'll run tissue samples through toxicology, but based on the physical evidence, I'm going to say the cause of death was exsanguination. And very professionally done, I might add."

"So it would take a doctor or a nurse to do this," I said.

"Doctor, nurse, paramedic, a good barber, an Eagle Scout. It's not brain surgery. Anyone with the right equipment and the right training could do it."

"How hard would it be to learn?" I asked.

"Relatively easy. You could learn in an hour," he said.

"Relatively easy," I repeated. "So a good trauma surgeon could teach me how to do it?"

"Oh yes," Hand said. "A good surgeon could teach a monkey to do it."

I looked over at Terry. He nodded at me. It was not the most subtle of cop communications. To our credit, we didn't jump up and down and yell, hey, that's a clue. Victor was oblivious, but the wise old doc took it all in.

"Thank you, Eli," I said. "As usual, you have inspired us."

"I thought I saw a light bulb go off," Hand said. "You think you boys might know who did it?"

"Not yet. But we definitely know which monkey we're talking to first."

CHAPTER TWENTY-FOUR

Barry Gerber's Land Cruiser had been parked two miles from his house, in a faculty-only zone on the North Campus of UCLA. The campus cops swung by every few hours and gave it another ticket. Finally, they had it towed.

It had been logged into LAPD's database about twelve hours before we got around to asking Ganek and Kanarick to help us look for it. A minor screw-up on our part. I was hoping that Kilcullen would be too busy to do the math.

Keating and her team were going over the car when Terry and I got there.

"Kudos from Dr. Hand," I said. "You were right about the blood loss."

"Well, he didn't lose it in the car," she said. "Not a drop. His briefcase and cell phone were on the floor. The keys were still in the ignition."

"We'll run his calls," I said. "Any prints?"

"Plenty. But I wouldn't get my hopes up. Whoever did this doesn't strike me as the type to make it that easy-breezy on us."

She held up an evidence bag. "This might help. It was on the neck rest of the front seat, passenger side. One gray hair."

"We'd be happier if you said plata," Terry said. "A white woman with silver hair paid Gerber's maid for all the garbage in his waste basket."

"It looks female. I'll do a gender and race ID in the lab."

"That's all you got for us?" Terry said. "One lousy hair?"

"The killer left a note with an address and phone number for you, but I seem to have misplaced it," she said. "Go back over the part where I was getting kudos from Dr. Hand and tell me what he put down for cause of death."

We told her.

"Holy shit." Her eyes lit up. "Exsanguination. How cool is that?"

"Yeah, it's really a cool way to die," Terry said. "We're all thrilled about it. With the possible exception of Barry, but hey, you can't please everyone."

"They cannulated the femoral vein and drained him dry," she said. "Your average person can't do that."

"Hand said with a little bit of training an Eagle Scout could do it," I said.

"When I was a Scout I got my badge in canoeing and bugling," Terry said. "Who knew you could go for exsanguination?"

"He's full of shit," I said to Keating. "He wasn't a Scout. He grew up in the Bronx. He ran numbers when he was ten years old."

"So I ran numbers," Terry said. "A lot of old ladies counted on me to get those numbers to their bookies. I was helpful, courteous, friendly, cheerful, and kind. And if they hit the number, I got a piece of the action."

Terry's cell phone rang.

"Damn," he said as he checked the caller ID. "And we were having such a fun time." He flipped it open. "Yes, Lieutenant. Yes, sir, we're going over the car now with the crime lab people. Cause of death was exsanguination. That's E-X-S-A-N-G—sorry, sir, just trying to help. Not yet, sir. I'll ask my partner."

He held the phone toward me. "When are we talking to Damian Hedge?"

Hedge was shooting on location. We'd been so busy I hadn't called Dennis yet to find out where. I certainly didn't know when. I shrugged.

Terry put the phone back to his face. "Mike says we've set up an interview for 5:30. Yes, sir, if anything breaks I'll call you immediately."

He hung up the phone. "Sure I'll call him," Terry said. "Right after I call my movie agent."

CHAPTER TWENTY-FIVE

I never worked with Dennis Hoag when he was on the job, but people who did say he was a damn good cop. He could have found a much more challenging retirement job than driving for my father, but like Rich Agins, who was raising and lowering gates at Raleigh Studios, Dennis wanted the second half of his life to be less stressful than the first. Driving celebrities around in a big-ass car fits that bill.

I called him at the cell number Big Jim gave me.

"Hey Mike," he said. "Your father said you'd be calling. He said you told him you have a security gig for me."

"I lied."

"Yeah, he told me that too. He said the real reason you called was because I'm driving around with a murder suspect, and I shouldn't turn my back on him. Is that dumb, or what? I'm driving the guy. I have my back to him the whole time."

"Terry and I want to talk to Hedge as soon as possible, and we have a lieutenant who wants us to talk to him sooner than that."

"Typical brass," Dennis said. "Busting balls. Did I ever tell you about the captain I worked with down in—"

"Dennis, I love war stories as much as the next cop, but where the hell are you, and is Damian Hedge still with you?"

"We're on Main Street just off Pico in Santa Monica," Dennis said. "They're just setting up the last shot of the day. How long till you get here?"

"It's rush hour," I said. "Thirty, forty minutes."

"And I'm guessing you don't want me to give Damian a heads-up that you're coming."

"Good call," I said. "We'd like it to be a surprise. Make sure he doesn't leave till we get there."

"Don't worry about it. This last shot is a biggie. They only get one take, and they've got like eight cameras covering it. They won't roll for at least a half hour. I'll see you when I see you."

"Hey, Dennis," I said. "I need one more favor."

"You name it," he said. "You need a limo ride with the girl-friend? What can your friendly neighborhood chauffeur do for you?"

"It's not a personal favor," I said. "It's more cop-to-cop."

"Go ahead," he said, losing the happy-go-lucky limo driver persona. "I'm listening."

"My father loves to stick his nose in my business," I said. "So I'm betting he told you to call him and tell him when I'm coming."

"Aw, come on, Mike. Don't put me in the middle of family shit."

"Am I right?"

Silence.

"Dennis, did Big Jim ask you to let him know when I'm

coming to the location to interview Hedge?"

"Yeah."

"Don't."

I waited.

"Word," he said.

CHAPTER TWENTY-SIX

I've been around movie-making my whole life. My mother was a stuntwoman. My teamster father has worked for every studio in town. So when someone asks how could anyone spend a hundred million dollars on a piece of shit movie like that, I know the answer.

Film budgets are like dicks. Big is good. Bigger is better. Granted, like dicks, movies have been known to flop. But, hey, they're still big. And in Hollywood, size matters.

Judging by the number of trucks, people, and equipment choking the streets of Santa Monica, Damian's movie had Big Dick written all over it. Six blocks before we got to Main, the street was closed and a motorcycle cop was detouring traffic.

I was about to put the Kojak light on the roof so we could get through, when Terry stopped me. "I know that guy," he said. "Let's have some fun."

Who am I to deny Terry his fun during a homicide investigation? I nodded, and he leaned on the car horn.

The biker cop pointed to his right. "That way, asshole."

Terry rolled down his window. "I'm a taxpayer," he yelled. "You can't close these streets for some dipshit movie. Move the barricade, dickwad." He rolled the window back up and honked the horn again.

At first the cop stared at us in disbelief. Then the look turned to resolve, almost joy. He began walking toward us. Swaggering actually.

"I just made his day," Terry said. "He's ready to whoop my ass."

"Just remember to flash your badge before he goes for his gun," I said.

The cop rapped on the window. Terry rolled it down and stuck his head out. "You don't scare me, copper."

"Biggs from Da Bronx," the cop said. "I shoulda known."

"How ya doin', Pags," Terry said. "Mike, you remember Paul Pagnozzi? He used to drive around in a squad car, but he decided he needed to get in touch with his inner Steve McQueen."

"And I love it," Pagnozzi said. "What are you guys doing here?"

"We're with the Damian Hedge fan club and we need a police escort to his trailer."

We followed Pagnozzi through a four-block-long corridor of camera trucks, wardrobe trailers, hair and makeup trailers, monster generators on flatbeds, motor homes, catering trucks, rolling bathroom facilities called honeywagons, a jimmy jib, and a technocrane for overheads.

"Looks pricey," Terry said. "Hard to believe they only charge ten bucks to show you the movie."

Finally, we got to Damian's trailers. Two of them. Both rented from my father. I had to smile when I saw his logo on the front panel. My mom had come up with the name. Star Truckers.

Damian's second trailer was filled with exercise equipment. As soon as the high-priced talent found out that the studios were paying for Schwarzenegger and Stallone to have rolling workout centers, they all demanded one. Naming it was easy. Big Jim's Big Gym.

We thanked Pags and met up with Dennis, who was standing in the doorway of the first trailer. "Good timing," he said. "They're going for the big money shot in about three minutes."

It turned out to be a Hollywood three minutes, which dragged on into forty-seven. I tried to calculate how much money was being poured down the drain. A hundred people stood around with their thumbs up their asses while two guys dicked around with the lights. One light, actually. But even if there were a hundred light bulbs to change, the hundred people with nothing to do couldn't have helped. They could only stand around and wait for the union electricians to do the job.

It's not the most efficient system in the world, but since the teamsters union helped pay for everything from my potty training to my college education, I've never been one to complain about the pace of organized labor.

Dennis is an ex-cop, but he's not your silent-but-deadly Clint Eastwood type. He's a talker. So while we waited, he nattered. "Do you guys remember those two blondes in nurses' outfits that drove up in the ambulance with Damian at the premiere?"

"Long legs, pouty lips, big tits?" Terry said.

"Them's the ones," Dennis said.

"Didn't notice them."

"Damian told me he took them home for the night," Dennis said, trying to dazzle us with his new Hollywood-insider status. "And guess what he paid them?"

We didn't guess, but that didn't stop Dennis. "Three grand apiece," he said. "Can you believe that? Six grand for two chicks in nurses' uniforms."

"You'd think that would've been covered by medical insurance," Terry said.

Finally, lights came on, bullhorns screamed for quiet, cameras rolled, and the director yelled, "Action."

They were shooting a car chase. Thirty cars, each with stunt drivers, were strung out along Pico Boulevard. A helicopter caught it all from the sky. A red van, obviously the bad guys, weaved in and out of the traffic, followed by an LAPD cop car. Our boy Damian was driving. When the van got to its preset mark, Damian leaned out of his window and fired his gun.

"Oh yeah, that's real believable cop shit," Terry said. "Shooting at a speeding vehicle in heavy traffic."

"Left-handed," I pointed out.

He must have been a fantastic shot, because he apparently hit the rear tire of the van, which spun out of control, barreled through an outdoor café, and—with a little help from an unseen ramp—lofted up in the air and crashed through a liquor store window.

Damian's black and white had barely stopped rolling when he jumped out, gun in hand. Right hand this time. He ran toward the wrecked van and yelled, "Freeze, motherfucker."

"Snappy dialogue," Terry said. "I may steal that next time I drive a bad guy through a plate glass window."

The director, a lanky Brit with a blond ponytail, was ecstatic. "Cut!" he bellowed into a bullhorn. "Brilliant, Damian! Bloody fucking brilliant. Ladies and gentlemen, it's a wrap."

There were no cheers from the hundred ladies and gentlemen

involved in the bloody fucking brilliant production. It may look glamorous when you watch the rich and the beautiful clutching their Oscars on award night, but for the people who make the movies day in, day out, in the drenching rain, the staggering heat, and the bone-chilling cold, the glamour wears thin. Then it's just another bloody fucking job.

And then there are people like Damian who believe all the make-believe. He's not one of those guys who goes home to a cold beer, a large pizza, math homework with the kids, reality television with the wife, then before bed, fills out the Publishers Clearing House letter, because, hey…you never know.

Damian Hedge has a different reality. Screaming fans, swarming paparazzi, eight-figure paychecks, revolving hookers, a gym on wheels, a nasty affair with the boss's wife, and an ego that has its own zip code.

I was looking forward to giving Mr. Hedge a reality check.

CHAPTER TWENTY-SEVEN

I'd not only seen Damian's trailer before, I'd made love in it. For years my wife Joanie and I had tried desperately to have a baby. But after we struck out with progesterone shots, intrauterine insemination, gamete intrafallopian transfer, and in vitro fertilization, Joanie decided the fertility gods might respond to something more romantic.

Like spending the night in that star trailer.

It's a forty-three footer with three slide-out compartments; a lot of big name actors have made it their home away from home.

"Including Bruce Willis and Demi Moore," Joanie informed me. "And who has had the most famous pregnancy ever?"

"The Virgin Mary," I said.

"I'm talking LA pregnancies, Michael. Besides, my chances of an immaculate conception were over long before I met you. Demi Moore posed nude for the cover of *Vanity Fair* when she was in her seventh month. It was awesome. She's the poster girl for expectant motherhood. We owe it to our unborn child to try to conceive where the Famously Pregnant have gone before."

We tried. We failed.

That was eight years ago. Sadly, Bruce and Demi are no longer a couple. Neither are Mike and Joanie.

Terry and I walked through the door of Damian's trailer. Except for the predictable gallery of photos of himself, he hadn't done much to change the decor. The curtains, the carpeting, the furniture, all had that Very Best of Winnebago commercial sameness that I remembered. It looked just the way it had that night, and I could feel Joanie's presence. I forced myself to shake it off. This was a homicide investigation, not a séance.

We decided that Terry would ask the questions. Damian was an actor. He gets paid to lie well. If one of us did the talking, the other could focus on the suspect's body language and voice patterns for tells. Terry would be the interrogator; I'd be the shit sorter.

"Can I get you something to drink?" Damian said. He was still wearing his LAPD uniform.

"No," Terry said, "but you can unholster that gun."

"Relax," Damian said. "It's a prop. They call it a non-gun."

"It's a non-issue," Terry said. "Take the gun out of the holster and put it where I can see it."

Damian flashed a multi-picture-deal smile. "Well, since you outrank me, Detective, I'd be glad to put it away."

He unbuckled his gun belt and tossed it on the counter. Then he opened the refrigerator and took out a beer. "From Australia," he said. "But not that weasel piss they sell here. The studio has this stuff flown in fresh for me." He opened it and took a swig. "Ask away."

"Why did Barry Gerber fire you?" Terry said.

He shrugged. "Don't know."

"Where were you this past New Year's Eve?"

He shook his head. "Don't remember."

"I bet the paparazzi remember," Terry said. "Why don't you come to the station with us till we can find some photo hound who will jog your memory."

"Fine. I was at Barry's house."

"And there was trouble. Correct?"

"We had a falling out. That's show business."

"A business dispute on New Year's Eve?" Terry said. "Come on, Damian."

"Okay. A Royal dispute. He caught me kissing his wife."

"And kissing is a euphemism for what?"

The questions were far too insightful to be random. I watched as Hedge's self-involved brain began to open up to the fact that maybe this dumb ugly cop knew something.

"I'll repeat the question," Terry said. "Did Gerber catch you kissing his wife, or…"

"Humping. He caught us in bed."

"You were having an affair with Barry Gerber's wife?"

"I never said 'affair.' We were drunk. We thought Barry had tranked himself into a coma. We got naked. We got caught. What pisses me off is a guy like Gerber, he walks around with his fly open and he has the nerve to fire me for boning his old lady?"

Actors make choices. Hedge did his best to act indignant.

"So it was more than a Royal dispute," Terry said. "It was a Royal Screwing."

"Hey, all I did was bang the guy's wife. I didn't kill him. I have an alibi."

"How can you have an alibi if I didn't give you the time of death?"

"It doesn't matter," Hedge said. "I was on the set all day, and those low-life paparazzi you're talking about follow me all night. I'm sure they'll sell you the pictures to back up my story."

"He was murdered on Sunday," Terry said. "You were shooting on Sunday?"

Hedge didn't answer. He was trying to think. I could tell it was not a process that came natural.

"Were you shooting Sunday afternoon at four o'clock?" Terry said.

"No, I was getting ready to go to the premiere at the Pantages."

"Getting ready with witnesses?"

"I was home alone. It was Sunday afternoon. I might have done a few lines. You still arrest people for that in this town?"

"No, other cops do that. We arrest people for murder, and right now all I can see is you have no alibi and you were really pissed off at the victim, because he didn't buy into your thinking that ringing in the New Year with his wife was no big deal."

"So am I under arrest?"

"No, you're under suspicion," Terry said. "And if we do arrest you, you're going to have to change out of that uniform. When was the last time you saw Barry Gerber?"

"I haven't seen or talked to that asshole in months."

"How about his wife?

Hedge laughed. "No, I haven't seen that skinny black bitch either. News flash, Detective: there are plenty of other women in Hollywood. And if I find the right one, her husband won't even care if I'm doing her."

"Yeah, I'm sure there's a line of guys outside your trailer just begging you to loot their villages and screw their womenfolk."

There was a knock at the door.

"And there they are now," Terry said. "Right on cue."

"Come in," Damian yelled.

A young woman opened the door. Early twenties, pretty face, good body, clipboard in hand, glasses tipped up on top of her head. I knew the type. The classic production assistant. This town is full of them. They come in two flavors: male and female. Young kids who want to be directors, producers, writers, and movie stars, who show up in LA looking for their first big break.

The better-looking ones, especially the girls, get invited to the industry parties, so the people who are already directors, producers, writers, and movie stars can check out the fresh meat. If a girl is lucky, she'll be ignored, give up, go back to Peoria, marry the produce manager at the Kroger's Market, and live happily ever after.

The unlucky ones get a line like, "I don't have any acting jobs but we need a PA. The job pays $450 a week, the hours suck, and nobody appreciates anything you do."

She's thrilled. She grabs it. She's thinking all she has to do is order a few lunches, send a few faxes, whip up a few cappuccinos, and she's the next Reese Witherspoon.

More likely she's running film canisters to the processing lab, trekking out to some remote location with a pair of sunglasses that the director forgot at home, moving furniture for the producer's wife, or driving from Malibu to Diamond Bar delivering middle-of-the-night script revisions to the entire cast.

This one was extra unlucky. She was doing servitude for Damian Hedge.

"Sorry to interrupt," she said. "Here's the call sheet for tomorrow. You're in makeup at 6:30." She smiled politely at me and Terry. "Hi. I'm Robyn."

"These are cops," Damian said quickly. "This one is Detective Briggs. I think the other one is just an extra. He doesn't seem to have a speaking part."

"Nice to meet you Detective Briggs," Robyn said.

"It's Biggs. Nice to meet you, Robyn."

"Yeah, if you're ever in a jam, just call these guys," Damian said. "They're my new best friends."

"I have to drive out to Western Costume," she said. "Do you need anything before I go?"

"The second draft of that script was supposed to be here yesterday."

"He said it won't be ready till tomorrow morning. I'll pick it up first thing. If there's nothing else, I'm gonna run. Nice meeting you all."

She started out the door.

"Keep your cell charged," Damian yelled.

She turned and looked at him, the devoted look of a personal slave. "Don't I always?"

The door shut and Terry let fly the next question. "Do you know Steve Kronowitz?"

"Who?" Hedge looked genuinely confused.

"Dr. Steven Kronowitz," Terry said. "He was your technical advisor on *I.C.U.*"

"Oh, Dr. K. Yeah, he taught me lots of doctor shit for the movie."

"Doctor shit," Terry said. "So that means you can give shots, draw blood...simple medical procedures."

"That's cake," Damian said. "I can do better than simple stuff. I'll tell you what, Detective, if you ever need a vasectomy, give me a call. No charge."

Before Terry could give it back, we were interrupted by the sound of a string orchestra playing "Ave Maria." It was a ringtone. Damian's cell phone.

He answered, "Yo." He listened for a few seconds, then turned to Terry. "Are we done here? I got a life."

Terry looked at his watch. "Guess what? So do I. Yeah, we're done. For now."

Damian put his hand over the phone's mouthpiece and moved a few feet closer to Terry. "I don't care what it looks like. I hated him, I fucked his wife, I took his money, but I didn't kill him. Thanks for stopping by."

He turned his back on us and started talking into the phone.

Terry and I walked out of the trailer and stepped onto the street. Dennis was still outside.

"How'd it go with Damian?" he said.

"It went great," Terry said. "He offered me and Mike six grand if we'd spend the night with him."

CHAPTER TWENTY-EIGHT

I miss my dog. Andre is a black standard French poodle that Joanie and I brought home seven years ago. After she died I did the best I could to take care of him, but it's not easy being a single parent, especially when you work cop hours. A dog can only keep his legs crossed for so long.

When I started bouncing back and forth between Diana's place and mine, Andre got caught up in the shuffle. So I recruited my carpenter buddy Kemp Loekle to dog-sit when I couldn't be there. Three months ago Kemp quit.

"I'm moving to Oregon to pan for gold," he said.

"I never heard that one before," I said. "What is that, some kind of metaphor for finding a new girlfriend or getting a new job?"

Kemp laughed. "No, it means I staked a claim up at the Klamath River. I got a pan and a sluice box and a metal detector, and I'm going to pull gold nuggets out of the water and sell them for six hundred bucks an ounce. A lot of my friends are moving up there. It's like the gold rush of 1849."

"I pay you by the hour," I said. "I've never known you to be in a rush. You really think you can make a living at this?"

"On a good day panning, I can make more than I do in a week hammering nails. Plus you set your own hours, there's great fishing, lots of women, and no freeway traffic."

It was hard to argue with him. Kemp is a bit of an oddball, but his latest life plan sounded pretty damn good to me.

So Andre got shipped off to Big Jim's. But one of Jim's dogs, Jett, the black Lab, apparently doesn't like the French. "I can't keep them both in the yard," Jim said. "They're barking at each other 24/7. It's driving Angel nuts."

Terry to the rescue. His youngest daughter Emily had always wanted a puppy, but Marilyn had always refused. "She's totally against it," Terry told me. "She invoked the No Puppy Clause in our pre-nup."

So Terry suggested they adopt Andre. But when Emily went to Big Jim's to meet the poodle, she fell in love with the Lab.

"If you love Jett that much," Big Jim said, "take her home with you. Just promise me you'll take real good care of her."

Emily was thrilled. She promised at least a hundred times.

Now everyone is happy. Andre isn't cooped up at home all day. Marilyn and the three girls are crazy about Jett. Jett loves all the attention she's getting. And Terry, of course, gets to complain. "Just what I needed. Another damn female in the house who doesn't listen to a word I say."

Everyone's happy but me. In the game of musical dogs, I came up short.

I opened the front door to Diana's apartment. Blanche, her long-haired white cat, looked up, saw it was only me, and went back to doing what she does best. Shedding on the couch.

Diana was in the kitchen making dinner. "How was your day?" she said.

"It sucked," I said. "I spent a good chunk of it with a hundred and twenty-nine dead people in the morgue. How was yours?"

"Fantastic. There were only fourteen kids with cancer on the floor, and they all made it through the end of my shift."

"You win," I said.

When you play how-was-your-day with a nurse at a pediatric cancer ward, she always wins.

Dinner was whole-wheat fusilli, chicken, and broccoli rabe. "For a Jewish girl," I said, "you're a darn good Italian cook."

"When you have a mother-in-law everyone calls Mama Trantanella, you learn fast."

"Speaking of which, I learned another Jewish word today, but I don't know what it means. When Terry and I got to the morgue, Eli Hand, the pathologist said, 'We have a *minyan*. We can start.'"

"It's a quorum. When you gather in the synagogue for communal prayer, you're supposed to have ten adult Jewish males. That's a *minyan*. I doubt if you'll ever get a chance to use it in conversation."

"I'm hoping if I learn enough Jewish words your father might not hate me so much." Like Eli, Diana's father is also a rabbi. Only he's strictly kosher. He wasn't happy when she married an Italian Catholic, and he's just as unhappy with me.

"My father doesn't hate you. He likes you. He's just not as demonstrative as your father."

"Honey, nobody is as demonstrative as my father. It's the cross you have to bear for falling in love with his son."

We finished our dinner and a bottle of chianti. Diana made espresso and put out a plate of biscotti.

"I saw a ghost today," I said.

"Joanie?"

"Yeah." I told Diana about my visit to Damian's trailer.

"What did you feel?" she said.

"Guilty. All she wanted was a baby, and I couldn't give her one."

"How happy do you think that baby would be, growing up without a mother?" Diana said. "What happened to Joanie is tragic, but for me, it's a little less sad knowing she didn't leave any children behind."

"I guess you're right. Look what a piss-poor job I did with Andre." I gave her my most serious look. "Do you mind if I change the subject? There's something important that I need to ask you."

"You look like you're either going to dump me or ask me to make some kind of long-term commitment, neither of which I can deal with two weeks before my birthday. Can't it wait?"

"Sorry. It's gotta be now."

She picked up a biscotti, took a bite, and braced herself.

"Here goes," I said. "What do you know about bleeding someone to death?"

She threw the rest of the biscotti at me.

"Sorry," I said. "All that dead-wife talk. I needed to make you laugh."

"It wasn't that funny," she said, "but at least I got to remind you about my birthday. So who bled to death?"

I gave her the details of Barry Gerber's autopsy.

She was fascinated. "I draw blood every day. Who would have ever thought that you could…Oh, Mike, that's horrible."

"Eli says anyone can learn to do it. Do you agree?"

"Yes, it's simple to stick a needle in someone's vein, but I can't imagine what kind of person could just leave it in and drain another person's blood."

"Me either. Everybody wanted this guy dead, but I keep wondering why the person who actually did it went to all that trouble."

"If you wanted to kill someone," she said, "how would you do it?"

"I'd send him on a cross-country trip with my father. The poor bastard would probably blow his brains out before they got to Nebraska."

We turned in early. One of the key responsibilities of a homicide team is creating a Murder Book. It's a detailed report of everything connected with the case. The only way to do it right is to document everything as you go along. The longer you wait to write it all down, the more stuff will slip through the cracks.

We were only two days into Barry Gerber's murder, but Terry and I had already fallen behind. He was picking me up at six so we could spend a few hours catching up on paperwork, instead of catching Barry's killer.

I set the clock for 5:30. Another pre-dawn wake-up call.

Panning for gold was starting to sound better and better every day.

CHAPTER TWENTY-NINE

I had a rotten night's sleep. It was either that second cup of espresso, the pressure of a high-profile homicide, or the middle-of-the-night visit I had from the Ghost of Mrs. Lomax Past.

From 4:49 on, I just lay in bed, watching the numbers on the digital clock change. At 5:25 I turned off the alarm so it wouldn't wake Diana.

I was showered, dressed, and ready to go out the door when the phone rang.

"Mike?"

It was my father. He sounded like shit. "Dad, what's wrong?"

"They took Damian."

"What are you talking about?"

"I was picking Damian up at his house. I put him in the car, and this pickup pulled up, and they knocked me out. A stun gun. When I came to, Damian was gone. They kidnapped him."

"Did you call 911?"

"No, you're on my speed dial. It was faster."

"Where are you?"

"Damian's house on Wyton Drive, just west of Beverly Glen. I figure if you're at Diana's, you're only about three minutes away."

"I am. Where's Dennis?"

"I gave him the day off. He needed a break."

"You mean you needed to stick your nose in my case."

"I'm having trouble understanding you," he said. "Did you hear the part about your poor old father who has a bad heart getting zapped with a stun gun?"

"Oh shit," I said. Jim has atrial fibrillation, which means his heart can suddenly go out of rhythm. He has to get it back on track or he's a candidate for a stroke.

The first time it happened he wound up in the hospital. The cardiologist put the defibrillator paddles to his chest and shocked his heart right back into its normal rhythm. They kept him twenty-four hours, then sent him home. The second time, Jim simply went out to the barn, fired up his tractor, licked his fingers, and touched the spark plugs.

I went ballistic. "Are you out of your mind?"

"Hey, it worked," he said. "I didn't have to waste a day in the hospital and there's no co-pay. Don't tell an old trucker how to get something jump-started."

His doctor suggested a pacemaker, but Jim is afraid of surgery, so he has pills to take if he feels his heart start to flutter. I can't think of anything that would knock it out of whack faster than a stun gun.

"Do you have your meds with you?"

"They're at home. I wasn't expecting a prob—"

"Listen to me," I said. "Can you call Angel and Frankie?"

"Of course I can call them. It's my heart that's screwed up, not my dialing finger."

"Dad, I'm calling for paramedics. The closest hospital is UCLA Medical. Have Frankie and Angel meet you there in the ER."

"What about you?"

"I'm on my way. Stay where you are."

I hung up and called Wendy Burns at the station for backup and EMS. Then I called Terry.

"I'm just getting off the 405," he said. "I'll be there in two minutes. What's your take on this?"

"What do you mean?"

"Damian is our prime suspect," Terry said. "Suddenly he gets kidnapped. It could be a publicity stunt."

"Some scumbag stun-gunned my father and knocked his heart out of whack," I said. "If this kidnapping is a scam, that arrogant son-of-a-bitch Damian Hedge is going to be in a hell of a lot of trouble."

"Yeah," Terry said. "Of course if it's for real, he's in a hell of a lot more."

CHAPTER THIRTY

G od love Wendy. It only took a few minutes for us to get to the scene, but she had a patrol car with two uniforms pulling in just as we showed up.

"Dispatch said we got an abduction," the older cop said.

"Limo driver called it in," I said. "Pickup truck, possibly two perps, no descriptions. Victim is Damian Hedge."

"The movie star?" the younger cop said.

"Yeah, so it's gonna get ugly. Give me a double perimeter. I want an inner circle around this vehicle. Crime lab only. Then lock up Wyton from Beverly Glen to Loring and rope off a section for the brass, the press, and the adoring fans."

"My fiancée is one of them," the young cop said. "Me, I think he's a jerk."

"Well, now he's our jerk. Get moving."

They started stringing yellow crime scene tape, and Terry and I went over to the limo. Jim was sitting in the driver's seat with his door open and his feet on the ground. He looked a little shaky, but nothing a trip to the ER couldn't cure. I was relieved and pissed at the same time. Part of me wanted to hug him; part of me wanted to throttle him for meddling in my case.

"Please," I said. "Don't get up on our account."

"Man," he said. "I was so suckered."

"Shut up," I said. I put my fingers on his pulse. I gave it twenty seconds.

"How's he doing?" Terry said.

"His heart rate is perfect," I said. "For a twenty-two-year-old who just finished a triathlon. But for a 300-pound old fart who eats an entire box of Krispy Kremes in a single sitting—"

"Two eighty-seven," Jim said. "I told you I lost—"

"The two of you, cut it out," Terry said. "Jim, tell us what happened."

"Thank you, Detective Biggs. At least one cop isn't blaming the victim. Let me think…I got here at 5:45. I sat in the car about ten minutes, then Damian comes out of the house. He's yakking on his cell phone. He's got a coffee mug in the other hand. I jump out, open the back door, he gets in the car."

"Do you know who he was on the phone with?" Terry asked.

"I only picked up a few seconds of it, but it didn't sound like business. I heard something like, 'I love it when you do that baby,' so I'm guessing he was talking to some tomato he was banging."

"So you got him in the car," Terry said. "Then what?"

"I close the back door and I start to come around to my side. I heard this pickup truck come up behind me, but there was plenty of room, so I figured it was passing. I open my door and the pickup stops. My back is to him, but I hear a guy jump out of the passenger side."

"So there were at least two of them in the pickup."

"Had to be," Jim said. "The truck was still rolling when the guy got out. Next thing I know, I feel this incredible pain in my back, like a million needles shooting into me, and I fall face-down on the driver's seat. I'm seeing all these flashing colors behind my eyes, and I think I hear Damian yelling, but I'm paralyzed. I can't move. Then the pain starts to lift, and I hear a door slam, and then another voice says, 'Shoot him again.' I knew it was coming, and this time it was worse. It's like somebody ripping you open and touching every nerve in your body. I blacked out. By the time I could move, they were gone."

"I got a question for the victim," I said. "Why don't you keep your heart medication in the glove box?"

"Which glove box? I got at least fifty of them."

The ambulance and two more squad cars pulled up.

"He's in A-fib," I said to the paramedics.

One of them took his vitals while the other rattled off questions, which Big Jim answered reluctantly.

"Mr. Lomax," the paramedic said, "you're going for a ride in our limo. We need to get your heart back to normal sinus rhythm."

"If you open the hood of this Lincoln," Jim said, "I can do it myself."

"Why don't you just stick your tongue in the cigarette lighter?" I said.

"I'm fine. I don't need to go to the hospital. I'm the only living witness you got. You're better off if I stay here and answer questions."

"Okay," I said. "Answer this: how come you were driving Damian Hedge? And don't tell me Dennis needed the day off."

"I don't feel well enough to answer stupid questions," Jim said.

"Gentlemen," I said to the paramedics. "I'm the detective in charge. Take this man to the ER. If he doesn't go willingly, I'll cuff him."

They helped Jim stand up. "I'm calling my lawyer," he said to me.

"You charging me with police brutality?"

"No, I'm writing you out of my will."

By the time Jim was carted off to the hospital, the area had filled up with cop cars, media vans, and gawkers. Unlike the scene on El Contento, there wasn't much to gawk at. An empty limo and a bunch of cops looking for clues.

There was a broken coffee mug just outside the limo door. But the young guy whose fiancée was a fan of Damian's came up the big winner. He found a cell phone in a flower patch about thirty feet from the car.

"Looks like he tried to run," Terry said. "But he didn't get far."

Terry had just put Damian's cell phone in an evidence bag when Lt. Kilcullen showed up.

"And you boys thought you were overworked before," he said.

"We're homicide, Loo," Terry said. "Won't it be spreading us a little thin if you pile on a kidnapping?"

"Kidnapping, my fat Irish ass. It looks more like Damian Hedge is a viable murder suspect, and he took it on the lam. I already spoke to the Deputy Chief. There are no jurisdictional issues. This is all part of your case. What have you got so far?"

We caught him up on the session in Damian's trailer.

"So this guy Hedge hated the victim, has motive up the wazoo, is trained to draw blood, and has no alibi," Kilcullen said. "A good prosecutor could go pretty far with that."

"And lose," I said. "Everybody hated the victim, and drawing blood ain't brain surgery. A good defense lawyer would win with a two-word summation. Reasonable doubt."

"Yeah, well I got some reasonable doubt of my own," Kilcullen said. "The day after Hedge gets grilled by the cops, someone drives by his house, knocks out his limo driver, and kidnaps him? Pretty convenient, if you ask me. Kind of like a bad movie. This guy isn't kidnapped. He's skipping town. Find him."

Kilcullen is a giant pain in the ass, but he's a smart cop. Maybe his theory wasn't as dumb as it sounded. Maybe the whole kidnapping scenario was just an act. I remembered what Halsey said Monday night at the restaurant: *If it has a little mystery to it...a little drama...I'd suspect someone with a sense of theater. Damian Hedge comes to mind.*

CHAPTER THIRTY-ONE

"Wake him up," Roger said.

Aggie held the ammonium carbonate ampule under Damian's nostrils and snapped it between her fingers.

"Fuck me," Damian screamed as his brain was jolted into consciousness.

"Language, please," Roger said.

"Who the hell are you?"

"I'm Roger. This here's my wife, Aggie."

Damian tried to sit up. His chest pressed hard against the strap, but it didn't budge. He tried to raise his arms, his legs, but they, too, were lashed down tight. "What the fuck," he yelled. "Untie me."

Roger held the sickly-sweet-smelling bandana a few feet from Damian's nose. "Chloroform," he said. "No more yelling, no more cussing, or you go back to dreamland."

Damian twisted his head a few inches to the left to get away from the smell. He clamped his mouth shut. But inside he was screaming, *Who are these people? Where am I? What do they want? How long have I been here?*

"That's better," Roger said, tossing the red bandana to the side. "Relax for a few minutes. Aggie and I are still prepping."

Damian was flat on his back, looking up at the ceiling. The halogen light was harsh, so he cast his eyes down. There was a sheet draped over his body. He pressed down and felt the smooth metal surface under his butt. He was stripped naked and strapped to a metal table.

"Why are you doing this?" he said.

"Don't speak until you're spoken to," Roger said.

Damian squeezed his eyes shut and tried to think. *Stalkers. Crazies, holding me for ransom. That's probably what happened to Barry, but he was too stubborn to pay. I'll pay, they'll let me go, then I'll identify them. The idiot gave me his name. Roger. Probably a fake. But you can't fake a description. White guy, mid-fifties, salt-and-pepper hair, about six foot, jeans, cowboy shirt. The woman is five-four, gray hair, bony hands, looks like a bad casting director's idea of a farm wife. Well, you can kiss the farm good-bye, lady. When I get out of here, I will hire every private detective in LA. You and your cowboy husband are dead.*

"How much ransom money do you want?" Damian said.

"You just don't listen, do you?" Roger said. He picked up the bandana.

Damian strained to turn his head away. "I'm sorry, I'm sorry, I was just trying to make it easy on you."

Roger laughed. "You hear that, Aggie? He's just trying to make it easy on us." He put the bandana back down. "Go ahead, Mr. Hedge. Tell me how you're gonna make my life easy."

"Money," Damian said. "It's always about money. You kidnapped me. Naturally you expect the studio to pay ransom. But that's the thing about studios. Some tight-fisted, hook-nosed accountant does a cost analysis, and says this ain't worth the money. That's why so many movies suck. The money people cut the budgets."

"You're making no sense boy," Roger said. "We ain't making no movie."

"Okay, what I'm saying is, you can't count on the studio to pay the ransom. So I'll pay it. How much are we talking about here? A million bucks? That's the classic Hollywood ransom number. But, what the hell, what with inflation and the high price of gas, I'll give you two million."

"Save your money, Mr. Hedge. I ain't interested."

"Fine. What does it take? We all have a price. How much do you want?"

"You don't have enough money, boy."

"Do you know who I am?" Damian said. "I make more money for one picture than you two Beverly Hillbillies could spend in a lifetime."

"Roger, I'm all ready." It was the woman.

"Ready for what?" Damian said. "Tell her we're in negotiation here."

"Negotiations are over," Roger said, pulling the sheet off Damian's body.

Damian strained against the straps. "Is this how you get your kicks? You sick perverts. What the hell is that in her hand?"

"Needle," Roger said. "But it won't hurt. Aggie knows what she's doing. She's a professional."

"I'll get you ten million, twenty million." Damian was whimpering now. "Please."

"You might feel a little prick," Roger said.

Aggie reached down between Damian's legs and rubbed an alcohol swab on his femoral vein. "You talking to him," she said, laughing, "or me?"

CHAPTER THIRTY-TWO

By 9 a.m. the black limo with the yellow tape around it sitting on Wyton Drive had become the most popular tourist attraction in Southern California. Everyone who is anyone in LAPD made an appearance. Our Captain, the Commander, the Deputy Chief, right on up to the Top Cop himself.

"We got more brass than the Ohio State Marching Band," Terry said. "The good news is, they're keeping Kilcullen busy."

And, of course, the media was not to be denied. Put out the words "abduction," "Damian," and "Hedge" on a police scanner, and they will come. There were so many camera trucks two of them wound up in a fender-bender.

"Call the *Guinness Book of Records*," Terry said. "Your father's Lincoln is about to become the most photographed car since O.J.'s Bronco."

Damian's house was extremely modest for a man for whom modesty was not an option. We found out why by talking, or at least trying to talk, to Valeska, his housekeeper, a large Polish woman for whom English was not quite yet a second language.

"This house is for renting," she explained. "Mr. Damian buys big house with big gate on Mapleton. He's fixing up nice, so we live here a year, maybe later."

Valeska had preset the coffee pot to start brewing at 5 a.m. and hadn't heard Damian leave the house. She had no idea where he had been the night before, except she was pretty sure he hadn't brought anyone home with him. At least I was pretty sure she was pretty sure.

We searched, but the inside of the house was a dead end. Outside was a nightmare. Trying to avoid the reporters was like trying to avoid the horseflies when you're the horse shit.

We were working our way through the pack, ignoring the chorus of reporters yelling, "Detective, Detective, Detective," when a sweet voice called out "Mike."

It was Julie Burton, young, beautiful, talented, and lucky to be alive.

"Go ahead," I said to Terry. "I'll catch up."

I met Julie three years ago. She and my wife Joanie shared a common bond. They went through chemo together. Julie was just better at it. She survived.

Her camera was rolling, so there was no time for a hug and a quick recap of what we'd both been up to since we last saw each other. She kept it totally professional, shoving a microphone in my face.

"Julie Burton, KLAJ. Detective Lomax, can you tell me about the situation here? Word has it that Damian Hedge has been abducted."

"It's still under investigation," I said.

"But can you confirm that Mr. Hedge is missing?"

"Like I said, Julie, there's not much I can confirm right now."

"As you can see, the police have their hands full with this investigation," she said to the camera, "but KLAJ will stay on the scene until more information becomes available. This is Julie Burton, outside the home of actor Damian Hedge. Back to the studio."

"We're out," the cameraman yelled.

Julie handed the microphone to the soundman. "Mike," she said, giving me a hug. "It's so good to see you. How are you doing?"

"Moving on with my life. How about you?"

"I'm so healthy I'm baffling the medical experts." She held up her left hand and flashed a diamond ring at me. "And I'm engaged."

"Congratulations," I said. "If I'd have known, I'd have tried to give you a better sound bite."

"It was pretty toothless," she said, "but it gave me screen time with a good-looking cop."

"I wish I could help you out," I said, "but we really can't even call it an abduction until we know more."

"You think it's a publicity stunt?"

"We haven't ruled it out."

"What did you find inside Damian's house?"

"Rented furniture, sex toys, and a shitload of pictures of the alleged victim. Not exactly breaking news. Do me a favor," I said. "You see Lt. Kilcullen over there? Why don't you go annoy him for a while, so I can get back to—"

"Hold on." She covered her left ear and pressed her right earpiece tight so she could hear better. "We do?" she said. "Holy shit. Just a minute, I'll tell him. Mike, we have exclusive footage of the kidnapping."

"What are you talking about?"

"One of the paparazzi who follows Hedge caught it all on video. He brought it to the station and we bought it. We're about to go live with it."

"It's evidence of a crime," I said. "You can't do that."

"Apparently our lawyers think we can. They're taking the same stance you just took. It may just be a stunt. I'm going over to the truck to watch it. You're invited."

"I'll be right there."

I grabbed Terry and Kilcullen and told them what was going on.

"They can't run that," Kilcullen said. "They're going to show it to the public before they show it to us?"

"I hope the public takes notes," Terry said. "We're gonna need all the help we can get."

CHAPTER THIRTY-THREE

Julie was in front of the KLAJ truck getting her hair and makeup touched up. The live feed on the television monitor showed an anchorwoman in the studio, with a picture of Damian in the upper left-hand corner of the screen.

"Fifteen seconds," her producer said.

"Guys, thank you," Julie said. "I can't tell you what a coup it is to screen what could be a crime in progress for the detectives at the scene."

"Normally I'd wait for the DVD release," Terry said. "But this was too good to pass up."

"In five," the producer said and counted down.

"This is Julie Burton outside the home of movie star Damian Hedge, who was allegedly dragged from his limo earlier this morning by unknown assailants. KLAJ has obtained exclusive footage of this shocking abduction, which we are about to air for the first time to our audience and to the LAPD detectives investigating the fate of Mr. Hedge. Some of the images you are about to see are disturbing, so viewer discretion is advised."

We watched the monitor. It had been dark out when the video was shot, so we were looking at it in night-vision green. For the first few seconds all you could see was a grainy shot of Big Jim's car parked on the street. Then he got out of the driver's side and walked around the back.

The camera picked up Damian, carrying a coffee mug and talking on his cell. Jim held the door open, and Damian slid into the back seat. As Jim came around and re-opened the driver's door, a pickup truck came into frame. The next part was hard to make out, because the truck blocked most of the action. But I could see a man jump out of the truck. Then Jim fell.

The camera panned to the rear of the car. Damian was out the door and running. But the guy caught up and held something to Damian's nose. He struggled briefly, then went down.

"Chloroform," Kilcullen said.

The guy dragged Damian to the back of the pickup. The driver jumped out, dropped the tailgate, and the two of them hoisted Damian onto the bed of the truck. The driver gestured to the guy with the chloroform, who ran back to Jim. I couldn't see what happened to him, but this was probably when he got the second zap from the stun gun.

The driver got back in the cab. There were too many shadows to tell if it was a man or a woman. Stun gun man jumped in the rear with Damian, and the pickup peeled out.

The camera followed it till it disappeared, then panned back to the limo. Jim was lying motionless, his torso on the front seat, his legs hanging outside the door. It was all too real to have been staged.

The next picture was a live shot of me, Terry, and Julie. "Our viewers may remember Mike Lomax and Terry Biggs as the celebrated LAPD detectives who solved the infamous Lamaar Family-land murders last year," she said. "Detective Lomax, what are your thoughts on this disturbing, exclusive KLAJ footage?"

Once again, she shoved her microphone in my face. If it had been any other reporter, I would have said, what the hell do you think I think? Some money-hungry asshole videotaped a kidnapping, then instead of calling the cops, he sold it to your ratings-hungry TV station, who showed it to the world before they called the cops.

"Julie," I said, "it's too soon to tell."

She moved her microphone over to Terry. "Detective Biggs, what's your reaction?"

Before Terry could answer, we heard a string orchestra playing "Ave Maria." It was the cell phone Damian had dropped when he tried to escape. Terry reached into his jacket pocket and held it up, still sealed in plastic.

"Excuse me, Julie," Terry said. "My evidence bag is ringing."

CHAPTER THIRTY-FOUR

One of the things they teach you in cop school is how to make split-second decisions. You never know when you're going to have to decide to fire your weapon, use force, or in this case, answer a movie star's cell phone and pretend you're the star.

Terry didn't think twice. He walked out of camera range, pulled Damian's phone out of the plastic bag, and flipped it open.

"Yo," he said. Then he hit the speaker button. Kilcullen and I huddled around him so we could hear.

"Damian, it's Robyn. I know I'm late, but it's not my fault. I got to McDonald's at eight, but Carlos wasn't there. I was waiting and waiting, so I ordered one of those sausage McMuffin things, which was a big mistake because the food there is so gross."

Terry gave her a supportive grunt. Robyn went on.

"Carlos finally showed up over an hour late. I was racing back to give you the script revisions when a cop stopped me for speeding. I told him this would be my third ticket this year, and if I lose my license I'll lose my job, but he doesn't give a shit, and now he's in his car writing me a ticket. Damian, I'm really, really sorry."

"Hold," Terry said. He muted the phone and turned to me. "I don't know a lot about show business, but I don't think you pick up script revisions from a guy named Carlos at Mickey D's at eight in the morning."

"Drug deal," I said.

"Bingo. I don't know why I didn't pick up on it yesterday when he was asking her where the second draft was," Terry said. "Damian strikes me as the kind of actor who's more interested in a coke fix than a script fix."

"Get the cop on the phone and have him hold her," Kilcullen said. "You're not gonna get away with that lame Damian Hedge impression much longer."

"Too bad they didn't kidnap John Travolta," Terry said. "Him I got down pat." He unmuted the phone. "Hello, Robyn. Damian asked me to talk to you."

"Who is this?"

"Detective Terry Biggs, Damian's friend. We met yesterday in his trailer. Remember? He said if you're ever in a jam…Well it's lucky I just happened to be here hanging with him. I can help. When the police officer comes back, tell him I want to talk to him."

"I'll get him."

"No, no, don't. Cops don't like it if you get out of the car when they're writing a ticket. Just wait quietly till he comes to you."

We waited two minutes. Finally, we could hear her talk to the cop. "I work for Damian Hedge. A friend of his wants to talk to you."

"No, Robyn, no," Terry said. "He won't talk to me if you tell him I'm a friend of your famous actor boss. Tell him my name is Detective Terry Biggs from the Hollywood station, and the color of the day is turquoise."

"What does that mean?"

"It's cop code, honey. Please just tell him what I said."

It worked. The cop took the call.

"Officer, listen carefully," Terry said. "The girl you just stopped is a person of interest in a kidnapping. She also may be in possession of drugs. Don't search her car, and don't let her go."

"I hear you," the cop said, "and you knew the color of the day, but I need a little more. What's your boss's name and rank?"

"He's right here. He can tell you himself."

"This is Lt. Brendan Kilcullen. Who is this?"

"Officer Jason Wood."

"Aw, Jeez, Woody's boy? I worked with your dad back when we were both in the bag. How's he doing? And how's your Mom...Constance, right?"

"Yes, sir. They're both well, sir."

Terry took over. "You better be convinced, or he'll go through your whole family tree."

"I'm on board, sir. What can I do?"

Terry turned off the speaker and put the phone to his ear. "First where are you? Okay, we'll be there in fifteen. Tell her you can undo the speeding ticket, but Detective Biggs has to come and sign for it. Yeah, I know it's stupid. If you can make up something smarter, be my guest. Don't let her use the phone or listen to the radio, especially the news. And get a female officer on the scene."

He hung up. "Damn, we're good," he said.

"Where are we going?" Kilcullen said.

Terry looked at him. "We?"

"I thought I'd ride along with you. It's Woody's boy. I want to say hello in person."

"Oh sure, as long as it's not part of our motivational training."

"A murder, a kidnapping, and now a drug bust," Kilcullen said. "I'd say you're sufficiently motivated."

"Hell yeah," Terry said. "If we can catch an armed robbery before lunch, we got ourselves a Steven Seagal movie."

CHAPTER THIRTY-FIVE

The problem with being first on the scene is that your car gets boxed in by vehicles number two, three, ten, twenty, or in this case, even higher than that. While Terry was digging our car out, I ran back to talk to Julie.

"I want the name of the photographer who shot that video," I said, "and a copy of everything he shot, not just what you aired. And I want it now."

"Why ask me?" she said. "You might want to start out by calling—"

"Julie, I don't have time to call anybody, or get dicked around by your legal department, or get wrapped up in corporate red tape. Your station ran the video before they contacted LAPD, and I posed with you on camera while you got your scoop. Now I need payback. Tell the powers that be that if they don't name the photographer and hand over all the video he shot, they're withholding evidence, obstructing justice, and pissing off a cop who will make sure KLAJ doesn't get anymore news connected to this case unless they happen to see it on another channel."

"Mike, have you ever met my boss?" Julie said.

"No."

"Angela's a total bitch." Julie smiled. "Best boss I ever worked for. Threatening her with a news blackout is like shoving your chips to the middle of the table and saying all in. She won't cooperate. She won't even blink."

"I bet I know a few judges who could get her to blink."

"Do you want your evidence tied up in a court case?" she said. "Or would you like me to help you get everything you want in one short phone call?"

"B," I said.

"Good. I'll call her and tell her I cut a deal. We give you what we've got. You give us what you've got. Exclusive updates on the Damian Hedge case an hour before you release it to any other media."

"That's blackmail."

"That's business. I told you, Angela is one tough cookie."

"Alright. I'll give you the updates ten minutes ahead of everyone else."

"Make it thirty."

"Twenty," I said. "Deal or no deal."

"You drive a hard bargain. Deal." She took out her cell phone. "I'll call you with the photographer's name. Where do you want the tapes delivered?"

I gave her an address and took off.

To his credit, Kilcullen was sitting in the back of the car. "You sure you don't want to ride shotgun?" I said.

"Nope, this is your case. I'm just going along for the ride. Think of me as Lt. Low Profile."

"I spoke to Julie about getting that videotape to our crime

lab," I said.

"It's all taken care of," Kilcullen said.

"Meaning what?"

"I called the station," Lt. Low Profile said. "You know my motto. All for one and one for all."

"That's us," Terry said. "The three musketeers: Athos, Porthos, and Annette Funicello."

"Who did you talk to at the station?" I said.

"The station manager, Josh Kane. He's a good guy. Said his lawyers told him he could put it on the air, but he'd be glad to run copies over to the crime lab in an hour. He gave me the photographers' names too. Scott and Julian Beeby. They're brothers. Work as a team."

"Wait a minute, " I said. "I thought the boss was some woman named Angela."

"You mean Angela Martin?" Kilcullen said. "They fired her months ago. Total bitch. Got the station sued a couple of times. Started teaching the young kids who work there too many dirty tricks. She's history."

But her legacy lived on. I had just been outfoxed by Angela's star pupil.

CHAPTER THIRTY-SIX

Robyn's red Toyota was sandwiched between two squad cars on Venice Boulevard near Sycamore. The female officers from the second unit were doing their best to discourage rubberneckers from slowing down for the flashing lights.

Officer Wood had one hand resting on Robyn's open window, the other gesturing as they made conversation. His uniform said protector of the peace. His body language said looking for a piece.

Terry, Kilcullen, and I got out of the car, and Wood straightened up and walked over with Robyn's license.

"Robyn Tate," he said. "Upper Saddle River, New Jersey. Issued by the Jersey DMV two years ago. She never traded up to a California license, but her lead foot has earned her a few speeding tickets on our freeways. Otherwise, she's clean."

"Let's see about that," Terry said, and the four of us approached her car.

"Detective Biggs," Robyn said. "Thank you for coming. It looks like you brought the whole cavalry."

"Happy to help out, Robyn," Terry said. "Did you pick up some script revisions for Damian this morning?"

Her right hand instinctively reached over and touched a box on the front seat. The outside said *HammerMill Paper. 500 Sheets.*

"Yes," she said. "That's why I was driving so fast. Damian needs this."

"Open it for me," Terry said.

"I don't think Damian would want me to—"

"Robyn, you're in a little bit of trouble right now," Terry said. "One of us is going to open that box. If you do it, we can say you were cooperative."

"I thought Damian sent you to help me get out of a speeding ticket."

"I promise I will make your speeding ticket go away. Open the box."

The sides of the box were taped shut. "Do you have a knife?" she said.

It's not good police work to give a suspect a knife, especially when your boss is watching, so Terry politely said no. "Use your nails."

She split the tape on all four sides and lifted the lid. Blank white paper. Terry removed the top ten pages. All blank.

"Maybe it's a script for a silent film," he said.

He dug in and pulled out another hundred pages. And there, beneath the pure white paper, were plastic bags filled with pure white powder. Lots of it.

Whatever bravado Robyn had left disintegrated in an instant. "I didn't know. I swear to God I didn't know."

"I'm betting this isn't prop cocaine," Terry said.

He got a narcotics field-test kit from our car, and in less than five minutes there was no question. "Step out of the car and put your hands on the roof," Terry said.

One of the female officers patted her down.

"This is so humiliating," Robyn said. "Do I look like the kind of person who would be carrying a gun?"

"You don't look like the kind of person who'd be carrying large quantities of nose candy," Terry answered. "But you know what they say in Hollywood—looks can be deceiving."

He cuffed her, then turned and gave me his best Jack Lord imitation. "Book her, Danno."

"You have the right to remain silent," I began.

Robyn's eyes were burning with anger and wet with fear at the same time. "This is so not fair," she said. "I'm a lowly messenger making a lousy $450 a week."

Kilcullen couldn't resist jumping in. He's got six kids of his own, but he's always up for lecturing someone else's. "So you're a low-paid peon," he said. "That's the profile of a drug mule. Now before you dig yourself an even deeper hole, don't say anything until the man gets to the part about *anything you say can and will be held against you.*"

She shut up and let me finish the Miranda. "Do you understand the rights I have just read to you?"

"I graduated magna cum laude from Princeton. Of course I understand."

"My name is Detective Mike Lomax. With these rights in mind, are you willing to answer some questions?"

"No," she said. "I want my lawyer."

The L-word. I don't think any of us expected the kid to lawyer up so fast.

"Do you want the court to appoint an attorney for you?" I said.

"No, my mother is a lawyer."

"Let me guess," Terry said looking down at Robyn's license. "She handles real estate closings for the First National Bank of Upper Saddle River."

"She's an assistant prosecutor for the Bergen County Prosecutor's Office," Robyn said. "She puts scumbags in jail; she doesn't raise them."

"Officer, help the young lady into our car," I said.

"Uncooperative little shit," Kilcullen said, once Robyn was out of earshot. "What kind of a prosecutor raises her kids to talk to cops like that?"

"She's angry, she's embarrassed, and she thinks she's innocent," I said.

"Well, she thinks wrong," Terry said. "She's in possession of four or five thousand bucks worth of blow. And don't tell me she had no idea what she was delivering. She was doing what she had to do to get ahead in The Biz, and she got caught. That's jail time."

"You are really pissed at this girl," I said. "Which one of your daughters does she remind you of?"

"Up yours, Dr. Phil," Terry said.

"Looks like I hit a hot button," I said.

"Knock it off, ladies," Kilcullen said. "Barry Gerber was yanked out of his car Sunday morning. By Monday they had sucked every ounce of blood out of his body. Now we've got another abduction. You better pump this girl fast, before the people who took Damian Hedge pump him."

CHAPTER THIRTY-SEVEN

We called Anna DeRoy and told her to meet us at the station. I've worked with a lot of lawyers and Anna is the smartest I've ever had on my side.

Terry disagrees. "She graduated at the top of her class from Columbia Law School. She could be a partner in a big Wall Street firm. How smart can she be if she's a deputy DA doing drug busts for the county?"

Anna has dark hair, dark eyes and is disarmingly pretty. She doesn't look like a killer lawyer, so people who go up against her for the first time totally underestimate her.

Robyn was no exception. She checked her out, and I could see the self-satisfied smirk that said, *My mom can kick your ass around the courthouse, lady.*

"Robyn, are you sure you want to call your mother?" Anna asked once the four of us were in the interview room.

"Absolutely," Robyn said.

"What's her name?"

"Jill Higgins."

"Your last name is Tate."

"So was hers until she got a better offer. Now she's Jill Leslie Weissman Tate Higgins." Robyn paused, then added a bitchy "Esquire."

I dialed the phone and put it on speaker.

"You get to listen in on my call?" Robyn said.

Anna smiled. "Absolutely."

Somewhere in Bergen County, New Jersey, a woman was about to have her day ruined. Mom answered. "Jill Higgins."

Robyn leaned in close to the speaker. "Hello, Mom. I'm in jail. I was arrested. I'm on a speakerphone, and the cops are listening in."

Higgins didn't stop to ask any mother-daughter questions. She was all lawyer. "What are the charges?"

"I went to pick up a package for Damian and I got caught speeding. The cops looked in the package and it had some cocaine in it. I swear I didn't know. I need you to come and get me out of jail."

"Dammit, Robyn," Higgins said. "I can't. Even if I could practice in California, a sworn prosecutor can't serve as a defense attorney in a private case. Not even for her own daughter."

"They never told me that," Robyn said. The smirk was history.

"Let me talk to the arresting officer."

"Mrs. Higgins," I said. "My name is Detective Mike Lomax. I'm here with my partner, Detective Biggs, and our deputy district attorney, Anna DeRoy. Your daughter was in possession of four ounces of cocaine."

"You mean four grams, don't you, Detective?"

"No, ma'am. I mean four ounces."

We could hear Higgins breathe in sharply, then let out a long slow exhale. "First of all, since when can you search a vehicle on a speeding ticket? Second, even if the search were legal, she's obviously an unwitting drug mule."

"This is the prosecutor," Anna said. "She may or may not be unwitting, but she is definitely uncooperative. We need to ask her questions to help us in our investigation. Damian Hedge was abducted a few hours ago."

"Oh my God." It was Robyn. "How did—"

"Keep quiet," Anna said. "You'll get your turn."

"Damian Hedge was abducted?" Higgins said.

"Yes, and unwitting or not, Robyn has vital information about the people involved in this drug deal."

"This is unreal," Higgins said. "Her father and I tried to convince her to go to law school, but she, but she..." Higgins was stammering. Motherhood had trumped lawyering.

Anna took charge. "Mrs. Higgins, Damian Hedge is at great risk, and time is precious. If you can convince your daughter to cooperate I can kick the charges."

"Robyn, are you listening?" Mom said. "Do I need to *convince* you to cooperate?"

Robyn whimpered out a meek 'no.'

"She needs an attorney present," Mom said.

"Do you know someone in LA who can represent her?" Anna asked.

"No, but I will in five minutes. And dammit, Robyn, you better do whatever your lawyer tells you."

"I will."

"And do you want to know what I'm getting you after I get you a lawyer? A plane ticket. You're coming home to have a long talk with me and your father. Maybe some good can come of this, and you can get this show business bug out of your system and get on with your life."

Robyn didn't answer. She was crying.

Another starstruck kid from New Jersey gets chewed up and spit out. Hooray for Hollywood.

CHAPTER THIRTY-EIGHT

A nna, Terry, and I went upstairs for coffee and a vending
machine lunch.

"I got an old joke," Terry said. "Want to hear it?"

"I've heard them all," I said. "Spare me."

"I was talking to Anna."

"Go for it," she said.

"How come California has the most lawyers and New Jersey
has the most toxic-waste dumps?"

Anna shrugged.

"Jersey had first choice."

She laughed. "We do have a shitload of lawyers. I once dated
an agent from William Morris. His secretary had passed the bar
exam, then she spent the next two years answering phones and
making lunch reservations until they promoted her to junior
agent. All Robyn's mother has to do to find an LA lawyer in a big
hurry is pick up the yellow pages."

As it turned out, Jill Leslie Weissman Tate Higgins was not

the type to shop for a lawyer in the phone book. Within twenty minutes she had retained one of the most powerful attorneys in the state.

"I can't believe it," Anna said. "I'm squaring off against Rella."

There are a handful of people who are on a first-name basis with the public. Oprah, Angelina, and Hillary come to mind. And, if you move in legal circles in California, Rella.

Rella Shwartz started out as an LA prosecutor. She was so successful that at one point the Democrats wanted her to run for district attorney. She turned them down with two words: "Power corrupts."

Then, about thirty years ago, she went over to the dark side and became a defense attorney. It's been said that if you strangle your grandmother at high noon in Macy's window, you can probably walk if you can get Rella to defend you.

"Talk about overkill," Anna said. "It's like having Springsteen doing a supermarket opening."

Rella showed up at 1:15. She was five-feet-nothing, somewhere north of seventy-five years old, and entered the room like she had downed a couple of cans of Red Bull for lunch.

She was smartly dressed in a tailored gray suit and had a slim black leather attaché case, which was being carried by a not-so-slim black man. He too had on a gray suit, only he was wearing a skintight black silk tee underneath. Rella introduced him as "my legal assistant, De-John."

"What does he assist you with?" Terry said.

Rella smiled. "Troublemakers. He's a graduate of Muscle Beach Law School. And no, Detective, he's not carrying a weapon."

"Can't imagine he'd need one," Terry said.

Rella asked for ten minutes alone with Robyn. She only

needed five. Then she finalized the deal with Anna, and we sat down at the table. De-John waited outside the door.

"Okay, Robyn, tell us about the cocaine we found in your car," I said. "All the details. Who, what, where, how, everything."

"The whole truth and nothing but the truth," Rella said to Robyn. "And no bad language. Go ahead."

"On Monday, Damian told me to contact this guy Carlos and pick up script revisions. I called him, but he said he needed two more days."

"Can you give us his phone number?" I said.

"It's programmed into my cell, but you took that."

"We'll get it later. Keep going."

"Yesterday I arranged with Carlos to meet him at the McDonald's on Whittier Boulevard in East LA at eight o'clock this morning."

"Did you think it was strange to pick up script revisions at a fast food restaurant?" I said.

"I'm a gofer. Actually, I'm a slave. I work for Damian Hedge and whatever he asks me to do, I do it. Believe me, with Damian nothing is strange. I've gone to much weirder places and dealt with much weirder people."

"Did you suspect there were drugs in that box?"

"Don't answer that," Rella said. "Detective, this is an innocent young woman with an extremely demanding employer, in an utterly bizarre business, in a highly unconventional city. She is at the lowest rung of the food chain and cannot be expected to analyze every request that is made of her. The box she picked up could have contained Cuban cigars, stem cells, or two cheeseburgers and an order of fries. Her assignment was to pick up and deliver, not to ask questions."

"So she was only following orders," I said.

"Legitimate, forthright, seemingly innocuous orders, Detective. Her mother is an officer of the court, and I can assure you that if Damian had asked Robyn to steal a pack of Juicy Fruit from a 7-Eleven, she would have refused. But picking up a script in a restaurant from a man she believed to be an eccentric writer is perfectly normal for the totally abnormal environment she works in."

"We're not trying to incriminate your client, Counselor," Anna said. "But it might help if we knew her frame of mind."

"Her frame of mind was that of a young woman hoping to make her employer happy, so she could get ahead in a difficult business. Next question."

"Robyn, had you ever picked up packages from Carlos before?"

"I picked up script revisions from Carlos four or five times."

"How often?"

"Maybe once a month."

"And did you pay him?"

"Don't answer," Rella said. "No payment was involved. Try again, Detective."

"Did Damian ever give you anything to give Carlos in exchange for the script revisions?"

Robyn looked at Rella, who nodded. "I always gave Carlos an envelope with script notes from Damian."

"So Damian was giving Carlos script notes before you even brought back Carlos's script revisions?"

"I asked Damian that once. He said they were notes for the next project."

"Does Carlos have a last name?"

"Probably, but I never heard it." She paused. "But he does have a nickname. I've heard people call him Carjack."

"Carjack?" I said. "As in to force someone out of a car at gunpoint? So do you think that in addition to being a drug dealer this Carlos is a carjacker?"

"Stop," Rella said. "This is exactly why the Supreme Court decided that a person has the right to have an attorney present during any questioning. My client doesn't think Carlos is either a drug dealer or a carjacker. She was told he's a screenwriter, and that is all she thinks."

"Robyn, do you know why they call him Carjack?" I said.

"No."

"Did you ever hear anything about him being involved in a carjacking?"

"No. When I was little my father used to call me Robin Hood, but that didn't mean I stole from the rich and gave to the poor."

That got a smile from Rella. "Detective, I think you've pushed this carjack business far enough. Move on to something more productive."

"Can you describe Carlos to us?"

"Hispanic. About forty years old. Short, like maybe five-foot-seven. Dark hair, a mustache, and pretty decent-looking, but not great. Just kind of Spanish."

"Any distinguishing marks or tattoos?"

"One tat that I could see on his right wrist. A gun with smoke coming out of the barrel and then at the bottom there were red letters that said RIP."

"Did you get the sense that Carlos might have been mad at Damian?"

"No. He was always sort of pleasant. He asked me how I liked my job, what I wanted to do in show business, stuff like that. And very polite. He always walked me out to my car and told me to lock the doors, because it's not the best neighborhood. Then he'd watch me drive off."

"And you would always take the script revisions directly to Damian?"

"Always. He gave me specific instructions never to give them to anyone else. That's why I was upset when Detective Biggs made me open the package."

"He asked you to open it, Robyn," Anna said. "Nobody made you."

"At this point, Ms. DeRoy, it's academic," Rella said. "This young lady is walking out of here as soon as we're done, her records will be sealed, and the subject of Detective Biggs's blatantly illegal search and seizure will never have to embarrass the department in court."

"And don't think I'm not grateful for that, ma'am," Terry said. "It's a terrible habit I have, but I hear there's this twelve-step program, Blatantly Illegal Searchers and Seizers Anonymous, that might be able to help me recover."

"Did you ever pick up any packages of any kind for Barry Gerber?" I said.

"No. I never met him, but I knew Damian didn't like him."

"How did you know that?"

"Everybody knows that. It was in the papers."

The interview lasted another twenty minutes. The truth was none of us really gave a shit whether Robyn understood what she was actually doing at a McDonald's at eight in the morning. There was a thriving drug business in LA, and Damian Hedge was a frequent buyer. The fact that he got abducted at the same time one of his drug deals was going down might or might not have been relevant.

Rella stood up. "She's a little fish, Detective. Can you throw her back now so I can call her mother and turn the meter off?"

"We need her to look at some mug shots to see if she can identify Carlos for us," I said.

"Done."

"I have a question for Ms. Shwartz." It was Anna.

"Be my guest."

"Someone of your stature, with your busy schedule, doesn't usually drop everything to handle a low-level plea bargain, and I was just curious—"

"You're wondering how I got involved."

"If you don't mind my asking," Anna said.

"Robyn's mother works with an old friend of mine, Judge Miriam Span. All it took was one phone call from Judge Span."

"So you're not a friend of the family."

The tough little lady lawyer smiled broadly enough so you could catch a glint of gold from one of her back teeth. "I am now."

CHAPTER THIRTY-NINE

"It's on you boys," Kilcullen said. "You gotta telescope."

"Right. Telescope," Terry said. "That's management-speak for 'do two things at the same time.'"

"Three things," Kilcullen said. "You need to bring in this drug dealer, interview the paparazzi who shot the abduction video, find Damian Hedge before they kill him, and catch the guy who murdered Barry Gerber."

"That's four things," Terry said.

"What am I, a mathematician? See what you can get from these two shitheads who videotaped the kidnapping and then sold it to a TV station instead of calling 911. Then come back here. I put a call out to Irv Ziffer in narcotics. He was tied up in court, but he should be here by around four. If anybody knows anything about this Carlos guy, it'll be Ziff the Sniff."

"We're all over it, Loo," Terry said. "By the way, you left your car at the crime scene when you hitched a ride with us this morning. You want us to run it back for you in our spare time?"

"Kiss my fat Irish ass."

"Just trying to telescope," Terry said.

"There's one more thing I have to do," I said as Terry pulled out of the parking lot and onto Wilcox. I flipped open my cell phone. "I gotta check on that meddling limo driver who got stun-gunned."

I dialed Angel's cell.

"Mike," she said. "I'm not allowed to keep my phone on in the hospital, but I knew you would call. Did you find Damian?"

"No. How's my father?"

"He's holding court. First Dennis came, and he stayed an hour. Now three of his teamster buddies are here. One almost got kicked out for smoking a cigar in the room. Then Diana called. She's coming after she gets out of work. And Frankie got here about twenty minutes ago."

"Is Jim's heart rate back to normal rhythm?"

"Not yet. They're going to take him downstairs at four o'clock. First they had to give him blood thinners. They want to make sure there are no clots. Otherwise, they could jump-start his heart and a clot could get loose, and..." Her voice started to get teary.

"Angel, it's not gonna happen," I said. "He's been through this before. He'll be fine."

"I know, but I worry. There's a chapel downstairs in the hospital. I prayed for a while and I lit a candle."

"It's a lot smarter than lighting a cigar. Tell my father's idiot friends to behave, or I'll come over and arrest the whole lot of them."

"Don't worry. Frankie is here now. He won't let them do anything stupid."

I had to smile. It was hard to believe that my brother Frankie was in charge of *not* letting anyone do anything stupid. He'd come a long way in a short time. A year ago his gambling addiction had gotten so bad that someone had put out a contract on him. Daddy and big brother Mike to the rescue. I had the underworld connections, and Jim had the cash to bail him out. It wasn't the first time, but it was the last. Frankie spent twenty-eight days in rehab, and for the past year he's been going to Gamblers Anonymous meetings.

I could hear Big Jim and his trucker buddies yakking it up in the background. "Angel, put my father on," I said. "I want to talk to him."

It took about a minute. I could hear Jim shushing his friends. When he finally picked up the phone his voice was a feeble whisper. "Hello. Mike? Is that you?" It was pure Jim Lomax bullshit.

"You sound fantastic," I said. "So tell me, how did you come to be driving Damian's limo today?"

"Mike, my heart..." He took a deep, wheezy, theatrical breath. "My heart is still too weak for me to answer questions."

"Are you sure?"

"I'm..." He coughed a few times. "I'm sure. No questions."

"That's what I figured," I said. "That's why I told the TV crew to forget about interviewing you in your hospital room."

"You what?" His voice came booming over the phone. "The press is different. I can muster up enough strength to give them a few sound bites."

"No," I said. "I can tell you're getting agitated already. I did the right thing. Get some rest. I'll see you later."

He was in mid-yell when I snapped the phone shut.

Terry had heard enough of the conversation to figure out

what was going on. "So how's your father doing?" he said.

I was grinning. It was probably the first time I smiled all day. "He's sounding better every minute."

CHAPTER FORTY

Downtown LA was one of Joanie's favorite hangouts. We'd drive there on weekends, soaking up the little pocket neighborhoods that are built around fashion, finance, theater, art, and all varieties of commerce. She would drag me around for hours, stopping at galleries to gawk at paintings I could neither understand nor afford, bargaining with the local merchants for a copper teapot or a string of Japanese paper lanterns, and ending up in some incredible hole-in-the-wall restaurant in Chinatown, Little Tokyo, or Olvera Street.

The LA Convention and Visitors Bureau advertises downtown Los Angeles as the heart of the most vibrant city in the western hemisphere. And when Joanie was alive, it was.

The vibrancy is gone for me now, and I get a pang every time I go back. It's not on Diana's radar, so I don't go there often, but Scott and Julian Beeby, the guys who caught the abduction on video, had a loft on Mateo Street in the Warehouse District. The neighborhood is sketchy, and if you walked along Mateo late at night, you'd look over your shoulder and pick up the pace. It's a part of downtown where you'd swear even the homeless don't want to live.

Boy, would you be wrong.

Number 847 had a grimy frosted-glass front door that was reinforced with steel mesh. The panel of doorbells on the outer wall had a few readable names, but the name Beeby wasn't on any of the bells, so we rang one that said *Photog*.

The intercom was crisp and clear. "State your business."

"Detectives Lomax and Biggs from LAPD," I said. "We're looking for Scott and Julian—"

I didn't finish. We were buzzed in. "Third floor," the voice said.

The lobby, if you could call it that, was devoid of furniture. Paint was flaking off the walls and ceiling, and it smelled a little dank. We bypassed the elevator and took the stairs. There was a green metal fire-door on the third floor that had three locks, each covered with pry-proof plates. The sign on the door said, *The Brothers Beeby. Tutto è possibile.*

"My Italian's a little rusty," Terry said, "but I think it says we can get our pants pressed while we wait."

The door opened and a man in a maroon warm-up suit said, "Hi, I'm Julian Beeby. My brother and I have been expecting you."

He looked like the guy who had played Seinfeld's neurotic friend George—about forty-five-years-old, short, stocky, not fat but closing in on it. His hair was pretty much history, and he had about a week's worth of scraggle on his face.

We stepped through the door and were practically knocked on our asses. The grunge on the outside had been part of the camouflage. Inside was *fantastico*.

"Holy shit," Terry said. "It's huge." His eye caught the staircase. "And it's a duplex."

"Yeah," Julian said. "Two floors, 7,000 square feet, original bow truss ceilings, sliding glass walls, skylights, huge modern kitchen, four bedrooms, three baths, photography studio, makeup room, and tons of space for work, parties, or if you're a film company, we'll rent it out to you."

"We're not renters," Terry said. "We're cops."

"I know," Julian said. "I'm just saying."

A tall, extremely good-looking man came down the staircase and walked across the oak floor. "Hi, I'm Scott Beeby."

He was about six-two, thirty-five years old, with a smooth chiseled face that is best described in this town as soap star handsome.

"You're brothers?" I said.

"Yeah, yeah, yeah, I know," Julian said. "All the men in our family are short, fat, and bald. Scott's a freak of nature. A genetic aberration in the Beeby lineage. But my parents felt sorry for him, so we decided to keep him."

Scott smiled, all blue eyes and white teeth. "And I'm Julian's wingman. If it wasn't for me, he'd be picking up skanks."

"Yeah, yeah, yeah, and if it wasn't for me, Scott would be picking up his paycheck at the unemployment office instead of living in a veritable palace. What do you think? You like it?"

"The paparazzi business must pay pretty damn good," Terry said.

"The media buys lots of shots of celebs," Julian said. "But sometimes we make more money not selling pictures. Come here, come here, look at this."

He walked us over to a corner of the loft, where about thirty cameras were mounted to a brick wall. Broken cameras. Cases smashed, guts exposed, lenses shattered. Beneath each camera was a plaque that had a date, a famous name, and an amount of money.

"Is this what I think it is?" Terry said.

Julian clapped his hands together. "What are you thinking? What are you thinking?"

"Each one of these little brass plaques is a celebrity who got violent, busted your camera, and the amount is what you collected in the lawsuit."

"Close enough," Julian said. "Every one of these...you should pardon the expression, *stars*...got pissed off enough to get physical with us. And that cost them. Most of the time there was no lawsuit. We love settling out of court. And where you see the big amounts, like this one here for $650,000, not only was the camera broken, but my nose and two front teeth."

"For some reason they hit Julian a lot more than they hit me."

Terry studied the wall. "Sean Penn, Russell Crowe, Justin Timberlake...so you go after the hotheads."

"Oh yeah. Oh yeah. We get in their face and either get their picture, get them to throw a punch, or if we're really lucky, both. And if they're with their wives or girlfriends, and they got a little alcohol in their blood, it's practically a guaranteed twenty-, thirty-thousand-dollar night. They don't give a shit. They spend that much on blow."

"Which brings us to the subject at hand," I said. "We saw the video, but it was less than two minutes. We want to see everything you shot this morning at Damian Hedge's house."

"Be my guest," Julian said, "but we shot about four hours' worth."

"*Four* hours?"

"Well, about three hours of it is you and the other cops

working the crime scene. It won't sell for big bucks, but we'll get something. Especially with you two guys. You're pretty famous, as cops go."

I heard a whirring and turned. Scott was across the room pointing a camera at us. "Put it away," I said.

"Hey, it's my place of business," he said. "You can't stop me from taking pictures."

I walked right at him, giving him my best pissed-off copper look, which came easy. "One more shutter click and you're going to my place of business," I said. "And trust me, you'll get photographed, printed, and you'll spend the night in a room about one-thousandth the size of this loft, with a bunch of crackheads you can't sue after they get violent with you."

Scott put the camera down. "Sorry. We're here to help. We want you to find Damian and bring him back safe. He's one of our meal tickets, man."

"Forget what we saw on the video," I said. "And we're not watching four hours of crime scene crap. What did you witness before we got there?"

"Okay, okay, okay, relax. We're all on the same side," Julian said. "I got there about five. Scott and I work in shifts. He was still here sleeping."

"You got where?" I said. "Where were you shooting from?"

"Oh, there's a nice hilly area in Holmby Park across the street from Damian's house. We have a little setup behind some bushes. It's like a duck blind. I don't know what the hell we're going to do when he moves to that big house with the gates over on—"

"Mr. Beeby," I said. "Get back to the duck blind."

"Right. I didn't shoot anything till the limo pulled up. Then I started rolling camera."

"Did you see any activity before the limo got there?" I said.

"Just the local traffic. A few financial types leaving for work early. A couple of joggers."

"Any pickup trucks?"

"You mean like did they do a dry run and drive past the house before the limo got there? I don't think so. But I'm not watching the cars. I'm waiting for Damian to come out of the house, and maybe there's somebody who's coming out with him. Someone who was invited for a sleepover."

"Like who?" I said

"Like anyone. Jennifer Aniston would be ideal, but I wouldn't care if it was Phyllis Diller, Queen Latifah, or the entire string section of the LA Philharmonic. All the media whores care about is who Damian Hedge is banging these days."

"So you didn't see anything before the limo got there. Then what happened?"

"Then it's what you saw on the video. Damian comes out, driver helps him in the car, pickup drives by, they zap the driver, Damian bolts, they chloroform him—"

"How do you know it was chloroform?"

"You can't make it out on the tape, because he was struggling, but I could see it with the naked eye. The guy put a cloth over Damian's nose, and he went down. Had to be chloroform or something like it."

"How about the second person? The driver. Male or female?"

"I'm pretty sure it was a woman. It's hard to tell on the video, because I was jerking the camera from here to there. But there was something I could feel about the way she moved. Woman."

"Can you describe the truck?"

"A Chevy pickup. I don't know if the camera picked up the

logo, but I got a glimpse of it. It was dark blue, which is hard to tell on the tape because there wasn't a hell of a lot of light, but I'm pretty sure it was dark blue."

"Did you get a license?"

"No. I pointed the camera at the back of the truck, but it didn't read. I think that maybe they could have muddied it up."

"What did you do after they drove off?"

"I called Scott. I told him to come right over and keep shooting whatever went down next, while I tried to sell what we got."

"I can vouch for that," Scott said. He had relocated to a plush green armchair and lit up a cigarette.

"Thanks, wingman," I said. "If I need you to verify anything, I'll ask."

In a lame act of defiance he blew smoke in my direction. I ignored him and went back to Julian. "Did you ever think of helping the limo driver, or calling the cops?"

"Yeah, yeah, yeah, I did think about it. But I didn't want to get involved."

Nobody in Hollywood likes the piranhas with cameras who earn fortunes invading people's privacy, and these guys were easier to hate than most. "What the hell are you talking about?" I said, raising my voice. "You photograph a crime in progress, you run off to sell the film, and you didn't want to get involved? Did it ever dawn on you that maybe the limo driver needed to get to a hospital? That every minute you wasted could have cost him his life?"

Julian backed up three feet and Terry stepped in between us.

"Calm your partner down, will you," Julian said. "Let me finish, let me finish."

"I'm not here to calm anyone down," Terry said. "Finish."

"You have to understand my frame of mind," Julian said. "This is my livelihood. Getting footage like this is a once-in-a-lifetime event."

"Well that excuses everything," Terry said. "I think that's the same thing those French photographers told the police when they ran Princess Diana's car into a wall."

The wisps of hair on Julian's head were wet, the pits of his warm-up suit were dark. "Jesus, what are you comparing me to? I didn't make this thing go down. All I did was shoot it. I knew if I called the cops, they would take the video. So I decided I would give the limo driver a couple of minutes to come to. If he didn't, I was going to phone it into 911 anonymous. But he was only out about a minute or two. You can see it on the tape. Believe me, I wasn't gonna let the poor fat bastard die."

"You're one hell of a good Samaritan," Terry said. "We'll pass that on to the poor fat bastard who is now in the hospital."

"Do that, do that, do that. And tell him we'd be glad to send him copies of the video. I'll put it on DVD. Whatever he wants. No charge."

"I'm sure he'll be overwhelmed by your generosity," Terry said. "And I can't for the life of me understand why all these idiot movie stars would want to beat the shit out of you."

"I know, I know, I know," Julian said. "It's a scummy job. But look around. Look at the payoff. How else could a guy like me get to live like this?"

"And the two of you are perfectly happy to watch another human being get kidnapped and not call the cops, just so you can live in a 7,000-square-foot loft with bow truss ceilings and sliding glass walls, and rent it to movie companies?"

Julian Beeby rubbed a pudgy hand over his well-fed scraggly face. He shrugged. "Hey, man, everything's relative."

CHAPTER FORTY-ONE

Damian Hedge was not a smart man. Not that it mattered. Intellect has never been a prerequisite for movie stardom.

He was raised in Green Bay, Wisconsin, by an aunt who owned a beauty parlor. His life's values were shaped not by books, but by the loving advice of the women sitting under Aunt June's hair dryers.

A boy with your looks and charm could go far.

A spoonful of honey will catch more flies than a gallon of vinegar.

Look at this boy. He's so gorgeous. He could be a movie star.

By the time he was thirteen, Damian knew his destiny. Hollywood. At sixteen he dropped out of school and promised he'd be back someday when his picture was on the covers of all those magazines in the beauty shop.

And once Damian set his sights on something, he never gave up.

Winners never quit and quitters never win.

What he lacked in brainpower, he made up for in cunning. Damian Hedge got what he wanted because he was a master at manipulating people.

But these crazies. Nothing penetrates. Why would they kill me? What good am I to them dead? And they're lying about the money. I just haven't offered them enough.

"You look like you're thinking," Roger said.

"I'm thinking that you win," Damian said. "You don't want a million, you don't want two million, but I can offer you something that you won't be able to turn down."

"I doubt it," Roger said.

"One hundred million dollars," Damian said.

"And where would someone like you get that kind of money?"

He's interested. He didn't say no. Who could turn down a hundred million dollars? I can do this. I can get out of this.

"A man in Germany," Damian said. "A billionaire. A multi-, multi-, multi-billionaire. He offered me a hundred million dollars to marry his daughter."

"Well there's a man who doesn't think much about his daughter," Roger said. "She's lucky you turned him down."

"But I could accept it now. I could call him. He would wire you the money. A hundred million dollars."

"How do you feel right about now?" Roger said.

Just undo these straps and I'll rip your heart out from the inside. "Very weak," Damian said.

"Well, now you're lying. Aggie's got a clamp on the hose, so you ain't been bleeding the whole time, because she can turn it on and off. You ain't lost more than a pint and a half of blood, which ain't enough to make a man your size feel weak. So if you'd lie about that, you'd lie about the hundred million."

"But I swear I could get it. I swear to Christ."

"How many movies you made, boy?"

Insane. He's asking me about movies like he's interviewing me for some fan magazine. "I made fourteen so far. They grossed close to a billion dollars."

"Me and Aggie's made one. Ain't grossed a penny. That's because not too many folks have seen it, and them that did, we didn't charge nothing. I think it's time for you to see it. You game for that?"

That's it. He's a frustrated screenwriter. He wants me to help him get his movie produced. That's why he took Barry, but Barry probably told him to go fuck himself, so they killed him. "I'd like to see it," Damian said. "If I like it, I can help you get it distributed. I know the whole power structure in Hollywood. Ask anybody. If Damian Hedge likes a project, it's a green light all the way, baby."

Roger pointed a remote control at the TV set mounted in the corner of the small, low-ceilinged room. "Ain't got what you folks call production values, and Aggie edited it together on the computer, but you'll get the gist."

"I can't see the monitor very well lying flat like this," Damian said. "Can you loosen the strap a little so I can sit up?"

Roger laughed. "I look like some dumb hillbilly to you? You can see damn good enough."

Roger clicked the remote, and the picture came on. It was Roger, only he was about twenty years younger. He was holding a baby in his arms and he looked nervous but happy. He waved at the camera, then he waved the baby's hand. After about thirty seconds the picture jump-cut. Same background, only this time

Aggie was holding the baby. Her gray hair was blonde, her skin smooth, her face jubilant.

Nice body. I'd have screwed her back then. Now I'd shoot her through the head. They can't be serious about making a movie out of this.

There were more shots. Most of them featuring the baby. It was a little girl. She went from toddler to little tomboy to some Girl Scout thing, and then as Damian watched her become a young teenager, he knew.

And his bowels opened up.

"Would you look at that," Roger said. "Mister Big Time Hollywood Movie Star just shit himself."

"I think maybe he recognizes the girl in our movie," Aggie said. "Is that why you're shitting in your pants, Damian?"

"Please, please, don't kill me." Damian was crying. Not acting. Crying. Sniveling. He gasped for air between sobs. "Please, you can hate me; you can shame me; God knows you made me suffer, and maybe I deserve it, and maybe I don't, but you're not killers. You're good, God-fearing people."

"What do you know about God-fearing people?" Roger said.

Damian could feel the hate. Aggie would be softer, more compassionate. He twisted his head toward her. "I know they don't kill anyone," he said.

She looked down at Damian. "But every normal man must be tempted at times to spit on his hands, hoist the black flag, and begin to slit throats."

"Slit throats? What do you mean, slit throats?"

"It's a quote," Aggie said. "Mencken."

Damian stared up at her, his face blank.

"H. L. Mencken," she said. "The writer. You don't know him?"

"Maybe I do," Damian said. "I worked with a lot of writers. I just can't remember all their names. Give me a few of his credits."

"Go to hell," Aggie said. She removed the clamp from the hose in Damian's femoral vein and threw it across the room.

Roger pressed a button on the remote and turned the volume on the TV up high. The girl was about fifteen now. She was on a stage, dressed as Little Orphan Annie. Her voice was rich and powerful as she belted out a musical weather forecast. One that promised sun.

Tomorrow.

Damian Hedge was not nearly smart enough to appreciate the irony.

CHAPTER FORTY-TWO

It was 4:30 by the time we got back to the office. Donna, the giggly blonde, was at the front desk. "They're waiting for you two in the roll call room," she said.

"And who are *they?*" I said.

"Lt. Kilcullen and some other guy."

"What other guy?"

"I didn't ask," she said. "I figured if your boss is waiting, that ought to be enough motivation to get you up there."

"Dammit, Parisi," I said. "You're so young, and you already think like a cynical cop."

"Thanks." She giggled.

"You keep up that stupid girly giggling," I said, "and someone is going to realize you'd be damn good working undercover."

There's a large classroom upstairs with enough chairs and tables for Patrol to hold their daily roll call. The furniture is standard LAPD issue, but the walls are unique to the Hollywood station; they're plastered with movie posters.

The room was empty now except for two guys, Kilcullen and

Irv Ziffer, the best narcotics cop in LA. He's known to one and all as Ziff the Sniff because of his uncanny ability to ferret out drug deals. He's well past retirement age, but he refuses to retire, which makes both the department and his wife happy.

Ziff was wearing a garish plaid sport jacket, with crisscrossing reds, blues, browns, oranges, and greens. If there's a shirt and tie that could possibly go with it, he hasn't found them. He stood up and shook hands with me and Terry.

"Nice outfit," I said, shading my eyes. "You look like a paint salesman."

"A blind paint salesman," Terry said. "They said you were in court today. You went dressed like that?"

"All part of my strategy," Ziff said. "Defense attorney sized me up and figured I'm just some doofus cop."

"I thought your reputation preceded you," I said. "Don't lawyers quake in their briefs when you walk through the court-room door?"

"This guy was new. And arrogant. I hosed him."

"I told Ziff about the big drug bust you made today," Kilcullen said.

"Nice going," Ziff said. "The streets of LA are a lot safer now that you nabbed some twit bringing her boss his week's supply of weasel dust."

"She may be nobody," Terry said, "but she gave up this guy Carlos."

"Carlos Jacavez," Ziff said. "East LA. A bottom-feeder who works out of a Mickey D or some other fast food joint. Low-level dealer. Basically harmless."

"We should have known that you'd know him," I said.

"I got his cell number," Ziff said. "We let him swim in the

pond because he's a good CI who gives us a lot bigger fish than he is. And he doesn't sell bad junk, so nobody gets hurt."

"Do you think he had anything to do with kidnapping Damian Hedge?" I asked. "His street name is Carjack."

"Carlos Jacavez. Car Jac. Like J.Lo. It's a nickname; not his line of work."

"So then we got you to come down here in your doofus outfit, and you've got bupkis for us," I said.

"Don't give up, boys," Kilcullen said. "He's got one little tidbit I think you're going to enjoy. Irv, fill them in on the Cokettes."

"You ever hear that term before?" Ziff said.

We hadn't.

Ziff leaned back in his chair. "Okay, this business with Damian Hedge sending a PA out on a drug run...this is nothing new. It's industry-wide."

"Meaning?"

"Meaning most of the Hollywood assholes who score coke don't run right out and buy it themselves. They use assistants, like the one you busted. They're almost always young girls, so we call them the Cokettes. They're the cute little mules who bring California cornflakes back to their bosses at the studio."

"And you don't bust these kids?"

"Mike, this is harmless shit. If I'm trying to track down a shipment of heroin coming through LAX, do you think I give a rat's ass if Damian Hedge shoves another eightball up his nose? Plus, did you hear what I said about it being industry-wide? It's so rampant I'm surprised it's not an Oscar category."

"And you're saying that LAPD doesn't give a shit about rampant drug running?"

"Jesus, Mike. You're more brutal than that defense lawyer. Of course we give a shit. But…"

"There's always a 'but.'"

"Actually, I got two 'buts,'" Ziff said. "First, we don't have the manpower to stake out every burger joint, donut shop, and car wash waiting for some production assistant to pass an envelope full of cash to some low-level street pusher. And second, what's the main industry in Los Angeles? Turnip farming? It's show business. And it doesn't make sense for us to lock up our tax revenue base for indulging in recreational drugs for personal use."

"Personal use?" Terry said. "This Robyn kid was carrying enough recreational drugs to waste a village."

Ziff just shrugged. "For a guy like Hedge, that's one lost weekend with a couple of friends and a stable of hookers. It's not my policy to look the other way. It comes from higher up. But we had an incident about six months ago. Since then the brass and some heavies from the Mayor's Office have been in meetings with the big studios, trying to get them to police themselves."

"What kind of an incident?" I said.

"Last year one of these Cokettes made the buy, then got herself rolled and killed by some gangbanger. Believe me, I told the top cops we should do a lot more than sit down and give the studio heads a remedial course in drug enforcement, but they said it's one isolated incident. It pisses me off. Some little Chinese girl from East Armpit, Montana, or God-knows-where comes to Tinseltown thinking she's the next Lucy Liu. A few months later, she'd dead. All for a bag of nose candy."

"Do you know who she made the buy for?"

"This is where it gets interesting," Ziff said. "We couldn't make it stick, but we know who she was working for at the time.

Barry Gerber. Your boy who just got iced."

"That's more than interesting," I said. "And this happened last year?"

"Sometime in November," Ziff said.

I looked at Terry. "Gerber and Damian didn't have a falling-out till New Year's Eve. They were still working together in November."

"So this production assistant who got killed..." Terry said, piecing it together as he talked. "She could've done drug runs for Gerber *and* Hedge."

Ziff nodded. "I only knew about Gerber, but these girls run all kinds of errands for the heavy hitters. So she could easily have worked for both."

"What do we know about the girl who was murdered?" I said.

"Now you're getting to the part where I really do have bupkis," Ziff said. "I'm Narcotics. The case went to Robbery-Homicide over in Central."

"You said she was Chinese."

"That I remember, but I'm blanking on her name."

My adrenaline was pumping. "How about this gangbanger who killed her...did they catch him?"

"You have any idea what my caseload looks like?" Ziff said. "I got too much on my plate to work your side of the street. Talk to someone over in Central."

"I hope you boys don't have any plans for the rest of the evening," Kilcullen said.

"I have to run down to the hospital and check on my father, but I'll be back," I said. "Ziff, as usual, you're a big help. Thanks for coming down here."

"This is one hell of a place," he said pointing at the movie posters on the wall. "Where else do I get a chance to talk drug deals surrounded by De Niro, Pacino, and DiCaprio?"

"The Playboy mansion comes to mind," Terry said.

CHAPTER FORTY-THREE

Terry offered me his car, but I took a Crown Vic from our parking lot, just in case I got stuck at the hospital. The AC was busted, the springs in the driver's seat were shot, and the odometer was stuck at 81,175. I had no idea whether it was the first, second, or tenth time around.

I crept along Sunset with the rest of the rush-hour traffic and got to UCLA Medical at 6:30. My brother Frankie was in the lobby, sipping a can of Red Bull.

"How's Dad doing?" I said.

"Okay, I guess. They got his heart to stop sputtering."

"Now they just gotta work on his mouth."

"He thinks you're pissed at him," Frankie said.

"Well, he's finally got something right. How many people in his room?"

"It was like a teamsters' convention up there for a while. The guy in the second bed asked to be transferred to a quieter room. Around five o'clock they wheeled the old man into the OR, and the truckers headed home."

"I doubt if they headed straight home. Not at five o'clock. Who's with him now?"

"Angel and Diana. I just came down here for a break. Six straight hours of Big Jim is above and beyond. Did you catch the guy who stun-gunned him?"

"No. And Damian Hedge is still missing, and I don't know who killed Barry Gerber. I'm having a really rotten day, and I have to go back to work, so let's go upstairs."

"One quick phone call," he said.

He pushed a speed dial on his cell phone. After ten seconds he rolled his eyes. "Voice mail," he said to me. Then he went back to the phone. "Hey, Leah, it's Frankie. I'm with my brother now, but I'll see you real soon. Bye."

"Who's Leah?" I said as we walked toward the elevator.

"New girlfriend. She's age appropriate, doesn't drink, do drugs, or gamble. And she's not married. I figured you'd - approve."

"Not that I don't trust you, but I'd be happier if you gave me her social security number."

We headed toward the elevator. "I know you had a lousy day, but don't be too hard on Dad," he said. "I think he actually feels bad about what he did."

"He should. Dennis is an ex-cop. He would have had a better chance of saving Damian's bacon if Dad hadn't decided to help me fight crime."

We got out on the third floor and walked through a set of double doors. "Right down the hall. Room 314," Frankie said. "Oh, hey, there's Dad's doctor coming out of the room. Let's find out when we can bring him home."

The doc was totally out of shape, with a belly that strained the buttons of his white lab coat. I know the type. He tells his patients to lose weight, quit smoking, and exercise, but it's okay for him to go to seed. He was in the doorway to Jim's room, and when he saw us, he walked slowly in our direction.

"Dr. Johnson," Frankie said. "This is my brother Mike. How's our father doing?"

The doctor shook his head. "I'm sorry to tell you this, but your father has expired."

"What?" Frankie said. "What do you mean, expired?"

"His heart gave out, Mr. Lomax. He passed away just a few minutes ago."

"Oh, God, no." Frankie ran into the room. I was right behind him.

Big Jim was in the bed, a sheet pulled up over his head. Angel was sitting on the outer edge of the mattress, the upper half of her body sprawled across his chest. She was praying softly in Spanish. Diana was sitting in a chair on the other side of the bed, her face in her hands, her shoulders heaving.

"Doc, how could this happen?" Frankie said. "You said he was fine."

"Your father may have developed a clot when his heart was out of normal rhythm. There's always the risk that the defibrillator could jar it loose. We won't know till after the autopsy."

Angel lifted her head up from Jim's massive chest and looked at me. "Mike," she said. "He was hoping you'd forgive him. But you're too late."

CHAPTER FORTY-FOUR

Damian Hedge was back in the beauty salon in Green Bay. He was ten years old, and his Auntie June had just finished blow-drying his hair.

"And the Oscar for best performance by an actor," she said, using the dryer as a microphone, "goes to...Damian Hedge!"

Damian let out a loud whoop. June grabbed a Ladies' Bowling League trophy from the shelf and handed it to him.

"This is a dream come true," he said, holding his Oscar up and watching himself in the mirror. "I'd like to thank the members of the Academy, and I want to thank my aunt for making me become an actor."

"Say my name, and don't say I made you. I encouraged you."

"Take two," Damian said. "I'd like to thank the members of the Academy, and I want to thank my Auntie June for encouraging me to be an actor."

"And maybe you should plug my shop," she said.

Damian gave her a vacant stare. "What do you mean, plug?"

"If you say the name of my beauty parlor on TV, then it's like free advertising, and people will come here."

Damian shook his head. "But you won't be here."

"I won't? Where else would I be?"

"Hollywood," Damian said. "If I'm an actor, and I'm living there, then you'll be there."

She laughed. "Sweetie, by the time you're old enough to go off to Hollywood, you won't want your old Auntie June following you out there."

"Yes I will." Damian was upset. He leaned forward and put the bowling trophy on the counter. Auntie June was mixing up some stinky chemicals. She was gonna do a color job or a perm on someone. Damian tried to back away from the smell. "You can open up a bigger shop in Hollywood."

She smiled and kissed the top of his head. "June Garrison," she said, "hairdresser to the stars."

"Cool," Damian said. "Then we could—" The ammonia fumes attacked his nose and lungs and he went into a coughing jag. His body jerked forward but he was held back by the strap across his chest.

"You passed out on me, Mr. Hedge," Aggie said. "But we ain't done here." She pulled the ammonium carbonate ampule away from his nose and he gasped for air.

"That's better," Roger said. "I get insulted when people fall asleep during my movie."

"I watched it," Damian said. "Twice." His voice was a raspy whisper. The begging, the bargaining, the screaming had left his vocal cords useless.

Aggie bent down to check the level in the blood bag. Nearly four pints. Most people would be dead by now. But this boy was tough. *You hang on. The longer you hang on, the slower you die.*

Damian's eyes were closed again, but his lips, tinged with blue, were moving. Aggie put her ear close to his face.

"What's he saying?" Roger asked.

"Beats me," she said. "Some crazy talk about thanking somebody named Annie June."

CHAPTER FORTY-FIVE

I t was like a scene from a bad movie. Angel slumped on top of my father's lifeless body. Diana, sobbing, her face buried in her hands. Doctor Johnson silently looking at his shoes. Frankie standing against a wall, slowly beating it with his right hand.

I closed the door to the room. I walked toward the doctor. "This is on you, Johnson," I said. "This is all your fault."

He backed away. "Mr. Lomax, believe me, I did everything I could."

"He died from a loose blood clot?" I said. "Any first-year medical student can tell you that the patient has to be pumped with Coumadin to thin out his blood before you defibrillate and risk dislodging a clot."

"I did give him a blood thinner."

"Not enough," I said. "And you've been drinking. You reek of beer. I'd sue you for malpractice, but all that would do is cost your insurance company money. No, you drunken quack, you're gonna pay for murdering my father the old-fashioned way. Street justice."

I pulled out my gun and pointed it at his head. I could hear

Frankie call my name and Angel yell no, but Dr. Johnson drowned them all out. "Jim, Jim, your fucking kid is out of his mind. Call him off. Call him off."

My dead father sat up in bed. "Alright, game's over," he said. "Pretty good, Mike. How did you figure it out?"

"Police academy," I said, holstering my gun.

"I need a toilet," the phony doc said racing into Jim's bathroom.

Diana lifted her head up and clapped her hands together. "I am in love with one brilliant detective."

"Inspector Clouseau could have figured it out," I said. "First of all, your fake doctor is wearing a lab coat with the same fake hospital name they used in the *I.C.U.* movie."

"I didn't want to tell you," Frankie said, "but my girlfriend Leah is a stylist. She actually worked on that production. She got us the doctor outfit."

"So the lab coat gave it away?" Diana said. "We blew the whole scam because of a wardrobe malfunction?"

"That was just the tip of the iceberg," I said. "Frankie called him Dr. Johnson, but his name tag says Jensen."

"Damn," Frankie said. "Did I say Johnson?"

"Also, I can tell the difference between Diana crying and Diana laughing; the little tic in Frankie's left eye started twitching when he called from the lobby and said I'm with my brother now; and last but not least, even with Angel lying on top of him, it's not hard to figure out someone is still breathing when his belly is jiggling like a 300-pound Jell-O mold."

"Two hundred and eighty-seven," Jim said. "Don't you listen?"

Dr. Johnson-Jensen came out of the bathroom.

"This is my friend Zach Stevens," Jim said.

"I don't want to get too close," I said. "I think Zach might have crapped in his pants."

"Not funny," Zach said.

"They got diapers if you need one," Jim said.

"I don't know if he needs a diaper, but Zach definitely had his five o'clock bottle. The beer breath was a dead giveaway."

"I waited till five-fifteen," Zach said. "You were late, and I was thirsty."

I walked over to my father, who was fully clothed and sitting on the side of the bed. I leaned over and hugged him. "I'm glad you're alive," I said.

"So you can kill me, right?"

"And no jury would convict me," I said. "So now that you're back from the dead, am I supposed to be so overjoyed that I don't yell at you for that stunt you pulled this morning?"

Angel stood up, determined to stand by her man. "He only wanted to help," she said. "He knew you were talking to Damian, so he figured he would—"

"He figured he would do what he does best," I said. "Meddle."

"Hey," Jim said. "Is it a crime for a father to look out for his son?"

"I don't know." I said. "Is stupidity a crime?"

CHAPTER FORTY-SIX

A real doctor showed up and discharged Big Jim. For all I know he could have been another phony recruited by the nursing staff, who were thrilled to see the Lomax family vacate the premises.

I called Terry from the car.

"Muller's here, and we're making headway," he said. "We're just about to order dinner. What are you in the mood for?"

"Steak Florentine, roasted potatoes, a bottle of red wine, just me and Diana, somewhere in Tuscany where they haven't yet heard of Alexander Graham Bell."

"You want brown or white rice with that?"

"Surprise me. And do me a favor. Don't ask Muller who he wants to play him in a major motion picture about the Familyland case."

"Too late," Terry said. "The good news is he doesn't care. He's just happy to give some geeky-looking white boy a chance at stardom."

"I'll have the brown rice," I said. "And no MSG. See you in

twenty."

Having Muller on the case was a big plus. He didn't take much credit for solving the Familyland murders, but Terry and I knew we owed him a lot. He's only in his early thirties, but he has the insights and wisdom of a seasoned cop. He's the best computer tech in the department, and if anyone could pull some usable data out of the murky Beeby brothers' abduction video, it was Muller.

I got back to the office by 8:25, and headed for the roll call room. Halfway up the stairs I was hit with the smell of Chinese food.

"Hey, dude," Muller said. "Pull up a pair of chopsticks. It's still hot."

"And hopefully, hot is your only criteria," Terry said. "I decided to call this new takeout place." He pushed a container in my direction. "Try the General Tso's Sweatsock."

I opted for the beef with broccoli and some rice. "So, did you dissect the kidnap video?" I said to Muller.

"Most of it is you, Terry, and a bunch of other cops bumping into each other," he said, "but the first few minutes have the potential to be a top-rated clip on YouTube."

"Did you get anything on the pickup?" I asked.

"It's a late-model Chevy, registered in Texas."

"Texas? It could be a stolen license plate."

"I couldn't see the plates, but there's a couple of frames where the camera pans past the front windshield. I froze it and blew up the inspection sticker. I paid enough attention in Miss Dorling's geography class to recognize the great state of Texas. But that's all I got so far. It was shot in night vision. I'm trying to scrub the image to see if I can pick up any more details."

"Good work," I said. "Do we have anything on the Chinese

girl who got killed making a drug run for Barry Gerber?"

"I called Central, and tracked down one of the lead detectives at home," Terry said. "The girl's name is Joy Lee. She was nineteen, lived in West Covina. She worked on *I.C.U.* with Gerber and our boy Damian Hedge. She scored some coke, and before she could deliver, someone slit her throat. She bled to death."

"Did they catch the killer?"

"They're pretty sure they know who did it, but there's zero evidence. Unless you take the word of some rival gang member, which is worth less than zero."

"Well, let's bring in the guy they think did it," I said. "Even if we don't nail him for the murder of the girl, he's gonna know something."

"Good thinking Detective Lomax," Terry said. "His name is Diego Garza. He was all of fifteen."

"Was?"

"Unfortunately, Señor Garza has relocated to gangbanger heaven and is no longer available for comment."

"Shit."

"But it's interesting shit," Terry said. "Garza was murdered Friday night, about thirty-six hours before Barry disappeared. They found his body under a freeway overpass. His throat was slit. He bled out like pig in a sausage factory."

"Jesus," I said. "We got three bleeders. A Mexican kid who killed the Chinese girl, who was a drug mule for the Jewish producer. I'm on information overload."

"Well, get a bigger hard drive," Muller said, "because there's more. I just finished talking to someone at the morgue. Guess where they shipped Joy Lee's body after the autopsy?"

I waggled my chopsticks in his direction. "China?"

"Texas."

"I got a headache," I said. "Are you sure you said no MSG?"

"Oh, dude," Muller said. "We thought you said extra."

"Who did the body go to in Texas?" I said.

"It's not easy getting anything out of Records at this hour, so I don't have the details," Muller said. "But I do know that last November, Joy Lee was flown from LAX to IAH: George Bush Intercontinental Airport in Houston."

I didn't say anything for about thirty seconds. Nobody did. Finally I picked up a fortune cookie and snapped it in half. I took out the strip of paper and read it to them. "Confucius say dead Chinese girl go to Texas. Someone from Texas drive to LA in pickup truck and chop-chop gangbanger who murder girl. Then torture and kill bad producer who make Chinese girl buy drugs. Then kidnap big time Hollywood movie star. Confucius also say Muller is Caucasian geek genius."

"That's a pretty well-developed fortune cookie," Terry said. "What does it say about your lucky lottery numbers?"

"Meanwhile, we still haven't found the latest victim," I said. "I know it feels like we uncovered a lot of shit, but we could really connect the dots if we had a long talk with Damian."

The phone rang. The officer at the front desk knew we were up in the roll call room. Terry picked it up. "Detective Biggs, Homicide."

He scribbled an address down on a Post-it. "We're on our way." He hung up the phone and started cleaning up the leftover food.

I stood up. "We're on our way where?"

"The Los Angeles County Museum of Art."

"And what's on exhibit at this hour of the night?"

"The late Damian Hedge."

CHAPTER FORTY-SEVEN

We were in Terry's car with the lights flashing and the siren howling.

"The Los Angeles County Museum of Art?" I said. "Exactly where did they leave the body? The permanent collection or new acquisitions?"

"A rent-a-cop found him in a Port-O-Potty on the phase one construction site," Terry said.

LACMA is in the first stage of a massive overhaul that will probably take a decade to complete and cost at least half a billion.

"First they leave Barry Gerber in a garbage can. Then they dump Damian in the toilet," I said. "Pretty subtle."

"There's a metaphor in there somewhere," Terry said, "but I can't quite figure it out."

"Y'know, I haven't told you what happened when I visited Big Jim in the hospital. When I got to his room he was covered with a sheet, like he was dead. The idea was to get me to appreciate him more."

"Sounds like a fun family event. I'll have to try it out on my girls."

"I saw right through it, so I decided to have a little fun myself." I told him how I pulled my gun on the bogus doctor.

"And Kilcullen says you don't have a sense of humor. That's a riot. The only thing that could have made it funnier would have been if the fake doc pulled a gun, and you two guys had a shootout right there in the cardiac ward."

"Let me get to my point," I said. "When I drew my piece, I told the guy I was taking the law into my own hands because the only way I could get satisfaction was street justice. Doesn't that feel like what we've got here? A girl from Texas gets killed, and some vigilante from Texas shows up in LA and starts executing anyone connected to her death. Street justice."

"I think it's actually legal down there. Texas justice. You get on the express line in the supermarket with more than ten items, and they hang you."

The siren was driving me nuts. I flipped it off and shifted my body so I could look at Terry while he was driving. "Joy Lee was a teenager. Who's most likely to avenge the murder of a teenage girl?" I asked the man who had three teenage daughters.

"Hey, Mike, my head already went there," Terry said. "It's the first thing I thought of when I put the phrases *dead innocent girl* and *buying drugs for cokehead boss* together. If it was one of my kids, I know who would be killing the people responsible for her death. But I figured most fathers aren't as crazy as me. O.J. murdered two people. Did Nicole Simpson's father blow his brains out? Did Ronald Goldman's father slit his throat? No, they took him to court, they won a judgment he'll never pay, and now the bastard is on a golf course somewhere looking for the real killer. If someone ever hurt one of my kids, I wouldn't be looking for a lawyer. I'd beat the guy to death with my bare hands."

"So maybe Joy Lee's father is as crazy as you," I said.

"Nobody is as crazy as me, but thanks," he said. "I knew you'd come to the same obvious conclusion, but I needed you to get there on your own. So first thing tomorrow, let's see what we can do about getting a handle on Joy Lee's father."

"And mother," I said. "There were two people in that pickup and the driver might have been a woman."

Terry nodded his head and flipped the siren back on. Then he opened the window. The possibility that we were looking for two parents who were avenging the murder of their daughter was not a subject he was ready to deal with.

For now, the conversation was over.

CHAPTER FORTY-EIGHT

We didn't need directions to find the crime scene. You could see the flashing red, white, and blue cop-car lights from a mile away.

"Oh, look," Terry said. "The circus is in town. Let's join up."

The moment had passed. Terry was ready to put the fun back in crime fighting.

The museum is on Wilshire, just east of Fairfax. The area under construction was fenced in, but the fence had been cut, and the activity was centered around a cluster of five portable toilets. The door to the last one was open, and Jessica Keating stepped out.

"What's a nice girl like you doing in a shit hole like this?" Terry said.

"Holding my breath. Take a quick look before I send in my camera crew."

Damian was naked. His body had been propped up in a sitting position on the floor of the Port-O-Potty. His back was toward the door, and his head was positioned inside the open toilet.

"And you thought stuffing a guy in a garbage can was demeaning," Jessica said.

Work lights had been set up. Damian's skin was a ghostly shade of white.

"He seems to have lost his rosy red glow," Terry said.

"Same MO?" I said to Jessica.

"No blood, no sign of a wound," she said. "Let me get some pictures, then we'll move him, and I can give you a more educated guess."

We stepped aside so one of the investigators could photograph the body. "Mr. Hedge is ready for his close-up now," Terry said.

"Who found the body?" I said.

"A rent-a-cop," Jessica said. "Talk to Officer Young. She was the first responder."

If Ed Sauer was the most uncooperative cop you could have at a crime scene, Gail Young was just the opposite. She had set up a perimeter and was ready with a detailed overview of everything we needed to know.

"That guy over there with the Rottweiler is Winston Wynn, the night watchman," she said, reading from her notepad. "He doesn't work for the museum. He's with Pro-Tech Security, a private company that specializes in providing guards and 24/7 surveillance cameras for construction sites. He was making his rounds when the dog started barking at that one particular bathroom facility. He opened the door, found the body, called his dispatch, and they called 911 at twenty-forty-five hours."

"What time is that in English?" Terry said.

"Oh, sorry. A quarter to nine."

"Thanks. Go on."

"My partner and I got here at twenty...about seven minutes later, secured a perimeter, and requested backup. We now have several other teams on the scene looking for anything that might be evidence."

"That's pretty efficient, Officer Young," Terry said. He pointed at her pad. "You didn't happen to write down who killed him, and when they'll be home, so we can arrest them?"

"No, sir. I'm only on the job six months. This is my first homicide. Did I step out of line?"

"No," Terry said. "It's just that we're used to much shabbier treatment. Starting immediately, I'd like you to be first on the scene of all our homicides."

She beamed. "Thank you, Detective. That means a lot. I'll introduce you to Mr. Wynn. He's quite a character."

Winston Wynn was about fifty years old, short, and gaunt, with a tiny head and oversized ears that were set off with a diamond stud in each lobe. His Rottweiler was much easier on the eye.

"Win Wynn," he said, when Young introduced us. "My mother thought it was the kind of name that would give me a leg up in life. And look at me now. Fifty-six years old and I'm a night watchman."

If he was hoping for a reaction to his fascinating intro, he didn't get one. "Tell us how you found the body," I said.

"Marilyn found him," he said pointing to the Rotty.

"Your dog is named Marilyn?" Terry said.

"Yeah, but not after Marilyn Monroe. He's a male, so I named him after Marilyn Manson."

Terry was trying not to laugh. I could see his wheels turning, thinking about what he'd say when he got home to his Marilyn.

He shook his head and silently passed the torch to me.

"Did you hear or see anything that made you inspect this part of the site?"

"No, sir," he said. "I have to make a circuit every hour. Marilyn started barking when we got close to this clump of Port-O-Pottys. I figured maybe some wino was holed up in there. I open the door, and I recognize him on the spot. He's the actor that got kidnapped this morning. What's his name? Hodges?"

"Hedge," I said. "Damian Hedge."

"Never heard of him," Wynn said, "but I've seen his mug all day long on the TV news. No question he's dead. So I look around, and that's when I see somebody took a pair of wire cutters to the fence and dragged him in here. Beats me why they went to all that trouble. Could have left him outside the fence. Marilyn would have found him no matter what."

"And then you called 911?" I said.

"No, sir. I called my dispatch. That's Pro-Tech Edict Numero Uno. If it's not an emergency, you call the company before you call the cops."

"A dead body in the crapper is not an emergency?" Terry said.

"No, sir. He was dead. If he was still breathing, and he needed an ambulance real quick, then I would have called 911 first. Otherwise, the company wants to be in the loop ahead of LAPD. They figure us guards are either drunk or stupid, so they like to call the shots. I'm not drunk or stupid, so I always play the game by their rules."

"Did you see anybody? Hear anything?"

"Not a thing." He cleared his throat. "But I do have a professional observation, if you want to hear it."

Suddenly the strange little man with the diamond earrings

wasn't so strange. He had an intelligence and an intensity about him that I had overlooked at first. Maybe I was distracted by the Win Wynn. Or by the fact that he named his dog after a rock star who wore white makeup, black eyeliner, and lipstick and whose own name came from a cult murderer.

"We'd be glad to get your take on it," I said. "A private cop is still a cop."

"That's not the profession I'm talking about," he said. "My family owns a mortuary in Glendale. I'm a licensed funeral director and embalmer. I retired six years ago, but I've seen more dead bodies than you and ten other homicide detectives put together."

"And what did you observe about this one?" I said.

"Well, I had five or ten minutes' quality time with this Mr. Hedge before your uniforms showed up. I got to take a real long look at him. And I'm betting that boy doesn't have more than two tampons' worth of blood in his entire body. It's like he's already been to the funeral parlor, and he's all prepped and ready for his formaldehyde cocktail. I've done it myself to eight thousand, six hundred, and forty-seven people. But every one of them was dead first."

"Thank you, Mr. Wynn," I said. "Of course we can't determine the cause of death until the autopsy."

"Maybe you can't," he said. "But I can. No blood coursing through your veins. It'll kill you every time."

CHAPTER FORTY-NINE

It was 2 a.m. by the time I got back to Diana's apartment. I crawled into bed, and she grunted something romantic. I tried to respond, but I fell asleep in mid-grunt. Nineteen hours and forty-two minutes makes for an exhausting shift.

Four hours later, Diana was sitting on my side of the bed, her freshly showered body sending out notes of sweet fragrant jasmine. "You smell fantastic," I said, eyes still shut, brain still drifting.

And then I inhaled the exhilarating, intoxicating aroma of freshly brewed French roast. "Oh, God," I said. "That smells fantastic too."

"The warm blonde or the hot coffee," she said. "Pick one."

I sat up, wrapped two hands around the coffee mug, and took a long slow sip. "I don't remember ordering room service," I said. "So you must be the answer to my prayers."

"Or you're just lucky to be living with a nurse. You better not pray for this every day of the week."

"I don't know if I can take too many more days," I said. "I'm too old for this multiple homicide shit."

"Oh, please," she said. "How hard can it be to find a vampire?"

"What?" I snapped awake.

She held up the morning edition of the *L.A. Times* and read from the front page. "'Damian Hedge, who was abducted and murdered yesterday,' blah, blah, blah, but you already know that. Here's the good part. 'The man who found the body says Hedge may have been killed by some kind of vampire cultist.'"

"Oh, Christ, give me that," I said.

"Drink your coffee," she said. "I'll read it. 'Winston Wynn, a security guard at the LA County Museum of Art and a retired funeral director, told reporters that in his opinion Hedge's body had been drained of all blood, and that the murder had vampire cult overtones. Neither the police nor the coroner's office has given the official cause of Hedge's death. There is some specula-tion that Barry Gerber, whose body was found in Hollywood Hills on Monday, may have been murdered in the same ritualistic manner.'"

"Do you know what this is going to do to my investigation?" I said.

"For starters, you'll probably get phone calls from everyone who works with, lives next door to, used to date, or actually is a vampire."

"What did I say the other night, when I told you about Barry Gerber's autopsy?"

"You said the doc found a tiny incision near his groin and decided that someone had used some kind of medical device to exsanguinate him."

"And what will everyone think happened to Damian after they read the morning paper?"

"Dracula did it."

"Right. Some guy with a black cape swooped in, sank two fangs in Damian's neck, drank his blood, and flew out the window." I gulped down the rest of the coffee. It was just hot enough to hurt my throat and feel good at the same time.

I picked up the remote control and turned on the TV. I flipped between six of the major channels. Five of them were doing Damian Hedge stories; three had clips of Wynn spouting his vampire theory.

"I wonder if these TV news idiots have any idea of how much they screw up my case when they run shit like this?"

Diana leaned in and kissed me. "Are you kidding? They ran the kidnapping tape, and now they have the Vampire Hunter and a dog named after Charles Manson. This is great television. I bet they're wondering if you know how much you'll screw up their ratings if you solve this too fast."

My cell phone rang. "That's probably Terry," I said, muting the television. "At least he'll make me laugh about all this."

It wasn't Terry. It was Kilcullen. And he wasn't laughing. "I'm driving to the office," he said. "Guess what I'm listening to on the radio."

"The news," I said.

"No, I stopped listening to the news," he said. "I switched over to one of those morning zoo shows, where they don't give you the real news. They do funny little bits. They just did one about us. It said that the task force working on the Damian Hedge homicide is being issued garlic, wooden stakes, and large crucifixes. It also said that Captain Van Helsing, who is heading up the investigation, has asked the city council to authorize a budget for silver bullets. They're having a goddamn field day at our expense, Mike."

"Look, Loo—"

"I'm not finished," he said. "They've also asked listeners to call in and guess who the Hollywood Bloodsucker will strike next. Do you believe that? *The Hollywood Bloodsucker?* Hold on, I got call waiting. It's the Mayor, calling from his home number." He jumped off and came back a few seconds later. "I gotta go. Meet me in the office in an hour."

"I can be there in twenty minutes."

"Yeah, well, in twenty minutes I'll be on the carpet in the Mayor's office. Kissing his ass." He clicked off.

It was shaping up to be a really bad day. And I hadn't even gotten out of bed yet.

CHAPTER FIFTY

By eight o'clock Terry and I had a hefty Things To Do list, and Wendy Burns had drafted as many coppers as she could find to help us do them.

Kilcullen didn't get to the station until 8:20. "I hate this job," he said.

"Don't take it out on us," Terry said. "You're the one who wanted to take the lieutenant's exam."

"You're right. And I should have bailed out when I saw the first question. When you have your tongue up some politician's ass, how many times do you have to twirl it? (A) Once. (B) Twice. (C) Till he tells you to stop."

"I'm going to have to go with (D)," Terry said. "When you see how much the politician is enjoying it, and you want to be the twirlee instead of the twirler."

"What have you got for me?" Kilcullen said.

"Lots of phone tips," I said. "Apparently everyone in LA knows a vampire."

"It's going to get a lot worse," Kilcullen said. "His Honor just informed me that there's a hundred-thousand-dollar reward."

"A hundred thou?" I said. "Who put up that kind of money?"

"Pita Productions, Barry Gerber's company."

"Gerber is dead," I said. "Who authorized it?"

"Tyler Baker-Broome."

"Did anyone try to talk him out of it? It's going to open up the floodgates for every nut job in the county."

"Why don't we have a separate number just for crazies?" Terry said. "So you think you know who killed Barry and Damian? Call us at 1-800-VAMPIRE."

"Tyler didn't like either of the two victims," I said. "Why would he put up a reward?"

Terry raised his hand. "I'll take Hollywood Slimeballs for two hundred, Alex," he said. "What is, who thinks he's the next victim?"

"You think Baker-Broome is next, so he put up a reward?" Kilcullen said.

"I think Baker-Broome thinks he's next, so he put up a reward," Terry said. "Barry Gerber and Damian Hedge were superstars. They didn't get their hands dirty. So who recruited the Cokettes and set up all the drug deals?"

"Tyler," I said.

"So who does Tyler think is next on Dracula's hit list?"

"Tyler," I said.

"Then bring him in," Kilcullen said.

"On what charges?"

"Don't arrest him. Just talk to him. Tell him he'd be smarter to drop a dime on these drug dealers than to put up a hundred-thousand-dollar reward."

"No, it wouldn't," I said. "If Baker-Broome really is a target, what good is locking up dealers? Barry and Damian are not drug-type executions. Pushers don't settle their grievances by tapping a femoral vein like a beer keg. They want faster results, so they tend to use .357 magnums and make bigger holes. Whoever is behind these homicides is settling the score for a dead Cokette."

"The Chinese girl," Kilcullen said.

"You're about twelve hours behind us," I said. "I started to tell you this morning, but you had some tongue twirling to do. Her name was Joy Lee. Her body was shipped to Texas. The pickup truck that picked up Damian was from Texas."

I paused to give him a second to process it all. I didn't have to. "Go on," he said.

"Joy Lee worked for Barry, and probably for Damian. Both dead. The gangbanger who killed her also called in dead Friday night. Somebody slit his throat. Three murders, all of which could have the same motive."

"Payback," Kilcullen said.

"Terry and I were about to follow up on the lead last night when Damian Hedge's body hit the fan."

"Well, follow up on it now," he said.

"We are. We've got a team digging out everything they can on Joy Lee's mother, father, sister, brother, boyfriend, and her Girl Scout leader."

"Good work," he said. "I still think you should talk to this Tyler Baker-Broome guy. Find out who else was involved in these drug runs this little girl was making. He may be right. He might be the next victim. But he might not be the last."

Terry and I turned toward each other like a pair of magnetic dogs. "Halsey," he said.

"You're right, boss," I said. "We'll talk to Baker-Broome and find out who else might be in the line of fire."

Wendy Burns stuck her head in the door. "Quick update," she said.

Wendy is a pro. No nonsense, no drama. Terry and I have had our share of glamour cases, but Wendy likes to fly under the radar. She supervises three homicide teams, and she's the lieutenant's right-hand person. She's a born manager and Kilcullen knows it. He waved her in.

"Joy Lee's body was flown to Houston," she said, "and according to the airline, she was released to a funeral home in Katy, Texas. We contacted them to see who paid for the burial, but their computer is down."

"Computer?" Kilcullen said. "They only have one?"

"Yes, sir, and to quote the cowboy undertaker I've been talking to, 'that damn Dell's trickier than nailing jelly to a tree.' But he promised to dig through their paper files."

Kilcullen put his fingers to his temples and rubbed them.

"I don't have a Texas address for Joy Lee, because she had a California license. We've asked Texas DMV for a printout of all the people in the state with the last name of Lee who have a license. Then we'll cross-check it with anyone named Lee who has a Chevy pickup."

"How long is that gonna take?" Kilcullen said.

"Too long," she said. "They don't seem to be in a big hurry down there."

"We'd have been better off if the girl was from New York," Terry said.

"Anything else?" Kilcullen said.

"I could use a dozen more people to handle the tips that are flying in," she said. "That hundred-thousand-dollar reward hit the airwaves about thirty minutes ago, and the phones have spiked."

"Anything legitimate?" Kilcullen said.

Wendy rolled her eyes. "Lots and lots of vampire sightings. But we did get a call from a woman named Gerri Lillianchild. She doesn't buy into the vampire angle. She said Damian and Gerber were exsanguinated."

"She used that word?" I said.

"It sounded promising, so I called her back," Wendy said. "I asked how she knew they were exsanguinated, and she said her boyfriend told her."

"And how did he know?" I said.

She was grinning. "Should I let you down slowly, or can I just put you out of your misery?"

"Just shoot me right between the eyes."

"Her boyfriend knew because it was in a movie script that he read," Wendy said. "The nature of Ms. Lillianchild's frail voice led me to ask how old she was. She refused to say, but she did say that her boyfriend was ninety-two. They live in the Golden Years Senior Center in Burbank."

"A fucking nursing home?" Kilcullen said.

"That's kind of harsh," Terry said. "Some of us like to think of it as God's Waiting Room."

Kilcullen wagged a finger at Terry. "I have a good mind to send you over there, Biggs."

"Gosh, as much as I would love to meet Ms. Lillianchild and her decrepit old paramour, Mike and I are just too darn busy," Terry said. "How about you, Lieutenant? Got time for a little geriatric tongue twirling?"

Kilcullen's rosy Irish face went crimson. He had already been raked over the coals by his bosses, and now Terry was busting his balls in front of me and Wendy. It's not my job to keep Terry from crossing the line, but I try to bail him out when he does. I pushed him toward the door.

"Don't go," Kilcullen said.

We stopped in the doorway.

Kilcullen took a deep breath, and the red in his face went to a mellower shade of pink. "I appreciate the fact that you're trying to separate us, Mike," he said, "but this is my fault. I've obviously failed to motivate Detective Biggs."

"Sir, you have totally motivated us," I said. "Terry just has a defective comedy gene, and it's been spinning out of control lately."

Kilcullen nodded. "Still, it's my responsibility to motivate all my people properly. Don't go just yet."

He opened his top desk drawer and took out his book on how to motivate, captivate, and persuade. He opened it to the table of contents, and ran his finger down the page. He couldn't find what he wanted, so he turned the page and kept looking. "This will just take a minute," he said.

I don't think any of us had ever seen Brendan Kilcullen looking as humble as he did now. Terry was enjoying the moment and turned to give me a big shit-eating grin.

And that's when the book came flying across the room.

"Fuck!" Terry yelled, as it clipped him hard on the left ear.

"Hey, Biggs," Kilcullen said.

Terry was rubbing his ear. "What?"

Kilcullen blew him a kiss. "Ciao."

CHAPTER FIFTY-ONE

We tracked Tyler Baker-Broome down at home. He lived in the Hills, a short drive from our office and spitting distance from where Barry had been tossed out with the trash on El Contento.

We rang the bell, and he eyeballed us carefully through the peephole before letting us in. There were three suitcases in the front hallway.

"You going on a field trip?" I said.

"No, I signed up for the witness protection program," he said. "What the hell would you do if you were me?"

"I don't know," I said. "But I'll know better if you tell us what you know."

"I know enough to skip town. I hope I'm not a suspect, fellas, because I'm fleeing your jurisdiction."

"Who are you running from?"

"I wish I knew. Somebody is killing the people I worked with. First Barry, then Damian, and I don't want to be the next one to donate five pints of blood to the Homicidal Maniac Red Cross."

"Did you piss off your drug dealer?" I said.

"I don't have a drug dealer," he said.

"Yeah," I said. "But hypothetically, if you did have a dealer, would there be any *bad blood* between you and the sordid drug underworld that services the entertainment community?"

"No. We'd be on the best of terms," he said. "And ha ha. Bad blood. Pretty funny, Detective. But then it's not your dick on the chopping block, is it?"

"Probably because my only involvement with criminals is to catch them and put them behind bars."

"Well, why don't you catch the one who killed Barry and put him behind bars? Then I'll come back to LA and buy you a drink. Or a Mercedes. Or a little house on the prairie. Just find the bastard and lock him up."

"If you didn't have any problems with your hypothetical drug suppliers, why did they kill Joy Lee?"

"Joy Lee?" He looked at me like I had just asked about the girl who turned him down for the senior prom. "What does she have to do with it?"

I didn't answer. I just stared at him. Hard. If there's anything more intimidating than a cop who's in your face, it's a cop who's silently reading your mind. I picked it up from watching Clint Eastwood movies.

We were still standing in the hallway. Tyler headed toward the kitchen; we followed. He took a bottle of water out of the refrigerator and swigged half of it down. "What are you talking about?" he said. "What does Joy Lee have to do with any of this?"

"You tell us, T.B.," Terry said, his voice so soft it was ominous. He's a big Dirty Harry fan too. "Did I ever mention that my initials are also T.B.?"

Baker-Broome downed the rest of the water. "Joy Lee's death was a total anomaly. She was in the wrong place at the wrong time."

"Anomaly?" I said. "Nice way to put it. Especially since you're the one who paid her ten bucks an hour and sent her to the wrong place."

"I didn't tell her to argue with some crazy hophead who had an eight-inch pigsticker. She was a hick. No street smarts. That's what got her killed."

"You're right. It was all her fault," I said. "You're absolved."

"We did what we could to make it up to her. We paid her salary for the entire production schedule. Sent flowers. Had a minute of silence on the set."

"A whole minute," I said. "What a tribute. And where did you send the flowers?"

"Some funeral parlor in Texas."

"How about her paycheck? Where did you send that?"

"We sent it to her parents. Also in Texas."

"Do you have their address?"

"Probably in the studio somewhere."

"Get it for us."

He looked at his watch. "I'll call. Somebody should be in by...wait. I think I have something here in my office." He left the kitchen. We followed.

Tyler's home office reminded me of Big Jim's. Shit was piled up everywhere, and woe unto He or She who dared cross the threshold with broom or mop. He stopped in the doorway, looked around the room, then made a beeline for a pile of papers in one corner of one shelf of one bookcase. He flipped through them quickly and pulled out an envelope.

"Got it," he said. Frightening—he was a lot like Big Jim.

"They sent me one of those printed acknowledgement cards. You know, *the family of the late Joy Lee thanks you for remembering us in our time of need* bullshit. I never got around to throwing it away."

"It doesn't look like you've gotten around to throwing anything away," Terry said.

Baker-Broome handed me the envelope.

"They sent it to you here at home?" I said.

"I don't know why," he said. "The flowers came from Pita Productions, but her father called the office and said they wanted to send out personal notes to all the senior people. I guess a PA gave him our home addresses."

Terry coughed. I nodded back. Joy Lee's parents had everyone's home address. Seen and noted.

The envelope came from an address in Katy, Texas. I opened it and read the card. "Who are Agnes and Roger Dingle?" I said.

"Her parents," Tyler said. "She used to be Joy Lee Dingle, but she changed her name when she came out here. I think her drama coach in high school told her you couldn't be a movie star with a name like Dingle."

"You finish up in here, Mike," Terry said. "I've got to call the office."

He left the room, so he could tell the task force to stop sifting through everyone named Lee in the state of Texas and zero in on the Dingle family on Candlewood Park Lane in Katy.

"Where are you headed?" I said to Tyler.

"First stop, JFK in New York," he said. "After that it's none of your business."

"When are you leaving?"

"I'm having lunch with your friend Halsey Bates. We've been talking about going into business together, and this is the day we're supposed to finalize the agreement. After that I'm catching the four o'clock out of LAX."

"I can't stop you from going, but I need a way to reach you."

"You can call me on my cell when everyone who wants to kill me is locked up." He laughed. "At least the ones who are out there now. Halsey and I are going to be producing movies together, so there will always be people who want to kill me."

"One last hypothetical question," I said.

He looked at his watch again. "Sure."

"If, hypothetically, someone working on the production of *I.C.U.* was brokering drug sales in order to feed the habits of the heavy hitters, could Halsey have been involved?"

He shook his head. "Halsey hasn't had a drink or a drug since the night he killed that kid, Kirk Jacoby. He's clean and sober, and when he's not making movies, he runs this One Brick At A Time charity that he built single-handedly. He's like the white man version of Oprah. That's why I want to go into business with him. I spent the first half of my life working with assholes. Meeting Halsey is the best thing that ever happened to me. He's talked to me about you and your partner. I know you guys like him. And if you're worried that whoever killed Barry and Damian might think about whacking Halsey...don't. He hasn't done anything to piss anyone off. Me, on the other hand, I'm getting the hell out of Dodge."

"Have a safe flight," I said. I smiled. It was rather a subtle double entendre. Too bad Terry wasn't there to appreciate it.

Tyler let me out the front door. The last thing I heard were the locks snapping behind me.

CHAPTER FIFTY-TWO

Terry was waiting in the car. He took off as soon as I got in. "We're due at the morgue," he said. "Our boy Damian managed to pull off the same thing in death that he did in life. He went right to the front of the line, just like he did Sunday night at the premiere. The autopsy is scheduled for ten o'clock."

"But Craig Harvey always tells us it doesn't matter if you're a prince or a pauper, you still have to wait your turn to get cut up," I said.

"I suspect he felt that way right up until the time the Mayor called him this morning. Apparently they've found a loophole in the prince-pauper rule."

"Did anyone think to tell the Mayor that fast-tracking Damian's autopsy screws us up?" I said.

"I'm going to go out on a limb here and say even if they did, he wouldn't give a shit."

Homicide detectives don't go to autopsies because they enjoy the time away from fresh, breathable air. We go because sooner or later we're going to catch the killer and make an appearance at his trial. Since evidence that will be used in the trial is invariably uncovered at the autopsy, we'd better have been there to witness the discovery firsthand. Or as sure as God made six-hundred-dollar-an-hour retainers, some lawyer will use our absence to obfuscate, confuse, and generally create reasonable doubt in the minds of the jurors.

Eli Hand, Victor Shea, and Damian Hedge were all waiting for us when we got to the morgue.

"So, Victor," Terry said as we were suiting up, "you sell any screenplays since I saw you yesterday?"

"I might have, but how would I know?" Victor said. "My agent never returns my phone calls."

"Ah, yes, but at least you're lucky enough to have an agent," Terry said. "Do you know how many people would kill to have a real live agent ignore them? Do we have time for a quick agent joke? Show of hands."

I wasn't in the mood, but Victor raised his hand. Then with a little help from Terry, Damian's hand went up.

"And my name is Hand and I showed," Eli said, "so give us the joke."

Terry took center stage. "A screenwriter comes home one night and his front door is open. His house is trashed. He sees his wife's clothes strewn on the steps. He races upstairs and there's his wife, lying naked in bed, ravaged. He says, 'Honey, what happened?' She says, 'I was raped.' He says, 'Who did it?' She says, 'Your agent. He broke in and raped me.' The screenwriter looks at his wife dumbfounded, and he says, 'Wow...*my* agent came to *my* house?'"

Everyone laughed, except Damian.

"This one looks a lot like the last one," Eli said. "Same strap marks to restrain the victim. He's white as a sheet, and I bet we find a similar puncture to the femoral vein. Basically, it's a no-brainer. But just to be on the safe side, I'll remove the brain." Eli paused. "Alright, hearing no laughter from the audience, I think I'll get started."

"Don't blame me, Eli," Terry said. "I warmed up the crowd. You bombed on your own."

Eli did it by the numbers. Slowly, methodically, professionally. It took the better part of three hours. The bottom line was exactly what we expected. Damian Hedge had been exsanguinated.

"You were pretty quiet in there," I said to Victor as we were washing up.

"I think Hollywood is getting to me," he said. "You come here full of hopes and dreams, thinking you'll be that one guy in ten thousand that makes it big, and then you see two guys who did make it and somebody kills them."

"But Victor, these two guys were major assholes," Terry said. "Killing them may just be part of an elaborate public service effort to make Hollywood a better place to live and work."

"Thanks for trying to make me feel better," Victor said. "But I'm gonna be twenty-eight in a few months, and I'm thinking about leaving LA, moving to Pittsburgh, and taking a job in my uncle's debt collection agency."

"Victor Shea, debt collector," Terry said. "I can't picture it. At your current height and weight, you'd be lucky to repo walkers from old ladies."

"It's phone work," Victor said. "What's important is that it's a mindless nine-to-five job and I'll have plenty of time to write a novel. I have a better chance of selling a book than ever selling a movie."

"And I have a better chance of becoming Rose Bowl Queen than selling a movie, but I'm not giving up."

"Victor, do us a favor," I said. "Run upstairs to Craig Harvey's office. We asked him to pull and xerox two morgue files for us that we need to take back to the station. They should be ready by now. He said if he's out to lunch, he'll leave them on his desk."

"Craig's desk looks like Kansas during the tornado season," Victor said. "What are the names on the files?"

"Joy Lee and Diego Garza."

Victor stood and looked at me.

"Garza," I repeated. "G-A-R-Z-A. Do you need me to spell Lee?"

"No," he said. "I got it."

"Actually, you don't got it," Terry said. "Would you mind putting a rush on it? We got murders to solve."

"Sorry," Victor said and headed to the elevator.

"Damn," Terry said. "Judging by how bad that kid is as a file collector, I doubt if he's got a prayer as a debt collector."

CHAPTER FIFTY-THREE

It was 1:45, and Terry and I were starving. And when you have limited choices and even less time, it helps to be really ravenous.

We opted for McDonald's. Partly because we had been talking about it ever since we heard about Carjack offering up cocaine along with your Happy Meal. But mainly because it had the shortest line at the drive-through, so we pissed off the least amount of hungry people when we cut in at the front.

"This is the last time we ever do this," I said, after wolfing down a Number Four, which is McDonald's tasty but lethal Fat-Sodium-Carb Combo.

"I only regret that I have but one stomach lining to give to my county," Terry said. He followed it with a long, loud, near-perfect burp.

I applauded. "You have a gift," I said. "Too bad you only have daughters. A teenage boy could benefit immensely from having you as his burp guru."

"I don't want to brag," he said, "but my gas-passing expertise is not limited to my…oh, damn…how dumb can we be?"

"I didn't get a book thrown at my head this morning, so I'd say you can be exceptionally dumb."

"You said 'daughters,' and it hit me. My daughters don't look anything like me."

"Lucky for them," I said, "or they wouldn't have a shot at Rose Bowl Queen either."

"No, you twit. Sarah, Rebecca, and Emily don't look like me because they're not my biological children. They come from Marilyn's eggs and the idiot sperm donor she married before she got lucky and found me. I adopted them."

"As your partner these past hundred years, you realize I already knew that."

"My point is, I've been assuming that Joy Lee's parents are Chinese, but what if she's adopted?"

"Then Agnes and Roger might not be Asian," I said. "They could be good old-fashioned white, Texas Methodist Dingles. Of course, since we work for an equal-opportunity police department, if Ma and Pa Dingle are behind these killings, we'll lock them up regardless of race, religion, or creed. So basically this doesn't change anything."

"Well, it makes me feel better that I'm not guilty of linear thinking. Now if Wendy shows us driver's license photos of Roger and Agnes Dingle, and they're Caucasian, we won't say something stupid like, holy shit, they're not Chinese."

"I may say it anyway just so Wendy thinks you're guilty of linear thinking."

We turned onto Wilcox and were about to park in the lot, when Terry stopped the car.

"This does not bode well," he said, pointing at a large white van that was parked in front of the station. The logo on the side read *The Golden Years Senior Center, Burbank, California.*

"It looks like the old folks who called in the tip from the nursing home have arrived just in the nick of time to help us crack the case in person," I said.

"Charlie's Geriatric Angels," Terry said. "Should we go in through the back door?"

"It would be wrong," I said.

We went through the back door.

"Nice try," Wendy said when we got to our desks. "They came all the way from Burbank. Go talk to them."

"We just spent three hours locked in a room with a dead guy," Terry said. "Do we have to interview the near-dead on the same day? We should be out looking for Joy Lee's parents. I think they're in LA."

"And I think they're at home in Katy, Texas, where Roger Dingle is recovering from a double hip replacement," Wendy said.

"And who's the source on that piece of news?" I said.

"The Texas State Police. I had them track the parents down."

"The Staties?" I said.

"Just a precaution," Wendy said. "The Houston area has over a million people. But the town of Katy only has about ten thousand. If I send locals, I take the chance that the Sheriff is on the same bowling team as Roger Dingle. With the State coppers there's less chance of incest."

"Y'know, you're good," I said. "No wonder you made Detective III."

"Nice suck-up, Mike, but you still gotta go talk to Grandma and Grandpa."

"We may as well," I said. "Our prime suspects are fifteen hundred miles away. What are their names?"

"The old lady is Gerri Lillianchild. She's the one who called in the tip. His name is Myron Pecarsky. He's a little hard of hearing, so you'll have to speak up. They're waiting for you in Room One."

"Let's go, Lomax," Terry said. "Bring your defibrillator."

CHAPTER FIFTY-FOUR

If they ever have a reality TV show featuring really, really ancient people, Gerri Lillianchild and Myron Pecarsky would make the perfect couple. They were chatty, lively, and sharp as a pair of ninety-year-old tacks.

She was tiny, under five feet tall, and her weight was probably lower than her age. Her hair was bottle blonde and neatly permed, and her outfit was bright blue and—surprise, surprise—polyester.

Myron Pecarsky, who we had heard was ninety-two, could have told us he was anywhere from eighty to a hundred and ten and we'd have believed him. He was tall, about six-three, but judging by the way his body accordion folded into itself, I suspect he had been NBA height as a younger man. He had twin hearing aids, a tripod metal walking stick, and he was sporting the latest in Jewish bling around his neck: a six-pointed gold Star of David the size of a hubcap. If he ever fell into the deep end of the pool at the nursing home, he'd sink without a ripple.

When Terry and I entered the room, he stood up and banged

his cane on the floor half a dozen times, as if he needed the hammering to get our attention. "Myron Pecarsky," he bellowed. His voice was loud, raspy, and irritating. "Mrs. Lillianchild and I have been waiting. Where have you been?"

"Fighting crime, directing traffic, rescuing kittens from trees; you name it, we've had a busy day," Terry said. "What can we do for you folks?"

"I know the mastermind behind the Hollywood Bloodsucker murders," Pecarsky said.

"The Hollywood Bloodsucker is something invented by the media," Terry said.

"What?" Pecarsky said, twisting a little dial on one of his hearing aids. "You'll have to speak up. I'm getting bad reception in here."

"Are you talking about the murders of Barry Gerber and Damian Hedge?" Terry shouted.

"Of course I'm talking about Gerber and Hedge. Who else did the Hollywood Bloodsucker kill?" He repositioned his cane so he could turn his body to me. "I'm hoping you're the smart one, because your friend can't follow what I'm saying."

"I'm pretty smart," I said. I gestured toward the chair. "Have a seat, and tell us what you know."

"Thank you." He sat. "Show him the script, Gerri."

Mrs. Lillianchild pulled a large envelope from her PBS tote bag and put it on the table.

"Thank you, my dear," Pecarsky said. "What we have here, Detective, is a screenplay written by one of my clients."

"Clients?" I said.

"I'm a talent agent. Surely you've heard of Myron Pecarsky. I've handled the greats and the near-greats. Phillip Loeb, Luther

Adler, Menasha Skulnik."

"I'm impressed," I said, nice and loud, not knowing if anyone he mentioned had been a great or a near-great. "So you still have clients."

He shrugged. "Not so many. Most of them are dead. But sometimes I meet someone young and promising and I agree to take him on."

"You work out of…" I didn't want to say nursing home. "You work out of your residence?"

"What else would I do? Rent a suite on Wilshire Boulevard? All I need is a telephone and a secretary."

Mrs. Lillianchild pointed a bony finger at her chest, lest I not be a smart enough detective to figure out who Myron's secretary was.

Pecarsky went on. "And if I have to take a meeting or do a lunch, the ambulette drives me into the city and waits."

Terry's face was in pain. He wanted to be anywhere but here. I, too, was starting to wonder if Wendy Burns was as smart a manager as I thought.

"Tell us about the script you brought," I said. "And how it relates to our case."

"It's called *Bloodthirsty*," Pecarsky said. Then he winked. "You can see the connection already."

"Yes," I said. "Catchy title. Go on."

"When the movie opens, a man named Aaron gets out of jail. He's been in for seven years because he drove drunk and killed someone. A few weeks after Aaron is out of jail one of his worst enemies is murdered. Are you following me? One of his worst enemies."

"Worst enemy," I said. "Got it."

"I forget the name of the enemy," he said. "It doesn't matter."

"It was David Rosenberg," Gerri said.

"No, no," Pecarsky said, getting even louder and raspier. "You're confused. David Rosenberg is the new fellow who just moved into the home. Room 107. He was in the drapery business. The murder victim in the script was a different name."

"Are you sure?" she said. "Because with your memory—"

"Folks!" It didn't matter that he was deaf. I would have yelled anyway. "I don't need the names of fictitious characters. Just get back to the story."

"Where was I?" Pecarsky said.

Terry groaned, but Pecarsky either didn't hear him or didn't care.

"Aaron gets out of jail. One of his worst enemies is murdered," I said.

"Right," Pecarsky said. "The body is found stuffed in a garbage can. There's no sign of a wound, but when they do the autopsy, they discover that he was exsanguinated."

The pained expression on Terry's face turned into a holy-shit look.

Pecarsky knew he had said the magic word. He continued. "Two days later a second body turns up. It's another one of Aaron's worst enemies. This guy is found in a portable toilet at a construction site. Again, no wounds. But when they do the autopsy, no blood. He, too, has been exsanguinated."

Terry reached for the script sitting on the table. Mrs. Lillianchild laid her hand on top of it. "He's not finished," she said.

The two dinosaurs smiled at one another and suddenly I had a Joanie moment. This could have been us, growing old and dotty together, sharing rides in our ambulette, torturing homicide cops and thoroughly relishing every minute of it.

"Go on, sir," I said.

"You realize, of course, that what I've told you so far about my script has already happened in real life," he said.

"It certainly sounds close," I said. "When was your script written?"

"You mean, did I write it last night so I could get the reward?"

"I don't think you're that kind of an agent," I said.

"It was written at least several months ago," he said. "I know I've had it since March, maybe February."

"What's the rest of the screenplay?"

"A third person is murdered. He, too, is one of Aaron's old enemies. He, too, is exsanguinated."

"Where do they find the body?"

"A junkyard."

"Do the cops find the killer?" Terry said.

"Wouldn't you think Aaron is the killer?" Pecarsky said.

"No. Not in a movie. If three of Aaron's worst enemies are murdered, someone is setting him up to take the fall. They want the cops to arrest Aaron."

"Bingo," Pecarsky said, punctuating it with a cane thump. "So you're not so dumb after all. But my writer came up with an even better twist than that. You can read it in the script."

"Can I look at it now?" Terry said.

The old man tap-tap-tapped his cane. "Do we have a deal?"

"What do you mean?"

"The hundred-thousand-dollar reward. Once you see the writer's name on the front page, you'll know who the killer is. I can't give you a free look. Once I blow the whistle on my client, even if they make the movie, I'll never see a dime from him. You have to pay the hundred thousand."

Mrs. Lillianchild picked up the envelope and clutched it to her chest. "So, Detectives," she said. "Deal? Or no deal?"

CHAPTER FIFTY-FIVE

I don't get to use the word 'dumbfounded' every day. But I couldn't think of any other word for what I felt. Two old coots, barely fogging the mirror, seemed to know the name of the serial killer we were looking for, and they were willing to sell it to us for a hundred grand.

Ten minutes ago I was sure that a dead Chinese girl and her parents were the key to unraveling the mystery. Pecarsky hadn't mentioned any young girls—Asian or otherwise—or vengeful moms and dads, or drug dealers serving up eightballs at McDonald's and asking, "Do you want fries with that?"

All he had were the sketchy details that had been in the morning paper. But he was convincing enough to make me want to see the rest of his movie. I just wasn't going to pay the admission price. Time to negotiate.

"Mr. Pecarsky, my family has been in show business for years," I said. "Did you ever hear of Tess Delehanty?"

"No. Who was she?"

"My mother, she should rest in peace," I said, trying to put a little of Eli Hand's Jewish spin on the words. "She did hundreds of movies. With the greats and the near-greats."

"She was an actress?"

"Action films," I said. "Mostly Mama was a stuntwoman. But she had speaking parts."

He smiled and his head nodded when I said "Mama."

"And Papa still works for the studios. He drives around a lot of the bigwigs. His name is Jim Lomax."

Pecarsky may be old, but he's far from dumb. "That's the driver who was shot with a stun gun when they kidnapped Hedge," he said. "His name was in all the papers. He should sue the studio."

"Good advice, Mr. Pecarsky," I said. "I'll suggest it to Papa. You know what? I'll do even better. You're such a help already, that when he's out of the hospital, he'll drive over to your...to your..."

"It's a nursing home. You can say it. At my age I'm happy to be living anyplace above-ground."

"You have a fantastic attitude," I said. "Papa and you will get along fine. And boy, can he tell you stories about Hollywood. Especially the old days. That man can talk your ear off."

"Not a problem," Pecarsky said pointing a finger at each ear. "I got an on/off switch. If he gets boring, I turn the dial."

"Anyway, you and Mrs. Lillianchild have been so helpful, I can make you a promise. My father will drive over to see you in a limo and take you for a spin. The mall, the movies, dinner, you name it."

"We want the one that Hedge was in when they kidnapped him."

"You're a tough negotiator, but you got it," I said. "That I can guarantee you in advance. But the hundred thousand, that's not mine to give away. Your lead has to pan out."

"What am I, stupid?" he said. "I know that. But how do I know I'll get the credit if it does pan out? This business is all about credits. You want chapter and verse about how many of my clients got screwed by the studios?"

"I'm not a studio. I'm an honest cop. I come from good stock, and my girlfriend is a nice Jewish girl whose father is a rabbi."

"What's her name?"

"Diana," I said, leaving out the Trantanella. *What am I, stupid?* "Her father is Rabbi Silver. So, you give us the script, and if this helps us catch the killer, you'll get the reward."

"And I get the limo ride no matter what?" he said.

"You drive a hard bargain, but sure." I held out my hand. "Deal?"

He stared at it, still not sure, still deliberating.

"Come on, Myron," I said. "It's just you and me. A couple of *mensches*. What do we need, a *minyan*?"

That was the topper. Pecarsky broke into a big fat grin, clasped both his bony mitts around mine, and squeezed hard. "Deal."

Thank you, Dr. Hand.

Little Gerri handed me the envelope. I opened the back flap and pulled out the script.

Bloodthirsty. By Victor Shea.

CHAPTER FIFTY-SIX

I tried to flip through the pages of Victor's script, but it's hard to read in a speeding police car, so I tossed it on the floor.

"Don't tell me who the killer is," Terry said. "I don't want you to spoil the movie for me."

"I had it solved two hours ago," I said. "But now my primary suspect is recovering from hip surgery in Texas, and as for Victor, I'm totally baffled on motive. He doesn't even know any of the victims. What's the connection?"

"Frustrated writer," Terry said. "He figures if he writes a script, then acts it out for real, all the studios will fight to get their hands on it."

"That's insane. He's not the type to kill a bunch of people just to sell a screenplay."

"You'd be amazed how far people in this town will go to sell a movie," Terry said. "Plus he's familiar with medical procedures."

"We saw the kidnapping video. Victor wasn't in it."

"Writers work behind the camera. Maybe he hired people," Terry said. "And if you're applying logic here, try this on for size:

Victor knows every detail of these two crimes. As a morgue rat he's got lots more info than the general public."

"So?"

"So if he's innocent, how come he didn't say anything? Like, by the way, Detectives, these two autopsies we did here are exactly the way I described them in scenes twenty-two and thirty-seven of my new screenplay. In fact, my crimes of fiction and the recent spurt of dead celebrities are so eerily similar, that I feel it is my civic duty to step forward and report this coincidence to the authorities. But trust me, I haven't done anything illegal. It's just a serendipitous case of life imitating art."

"If he's guilty, why would he give the script to his agent before the murders are committed?" I said.

"He probably figured the old goat would never read it. Victor is always bitching that his agent can't get him a job, but at the rate Myron is going, he's gonna land Victor a lifetime contract making license plates for the state."

"And he wants a hundred Gs commission for doing it," I said. "I had to use every ounce of Jewish charm I have in my Irish body to get him to give me the script on spec."

"Now if you could only solve these nasty murders before your bar mitzvah, I'm sure your Mama, she should rest in peace, would be so proud."

"That had to be one of the weirdest interviews we've ever handled," I said. "I felt like somebody dropped us right in the middle of an episode of Geezers Gone Wild."

"Do you think Pecarsky and the old lady are getting it on?" Terry said.

"At their age?" I said. "Not every night."

"You're right. The nursing home probably posts a schedule.

Tuesdays, Bingo; Wednesdays, square dancing; Thursdays, get your freak on in the back of the ambulette on your way to the police station."

"You're just upset because some old codger is getting more sex than you."

"Mike, these days, all the old codgers are getting more sex than me."

My cell phone interrupted. It was Wendy Burns.

"Roger Dingle is in LA," she said.

"Dingle is in town," I said to Terry and put the phone on speaker.

"The trooper who went to Dingle's house got snookered," she said. "He rang the bell, got no answer, so he called the home phone. Dingle picked up, said he was bedridden and couldn't get to the door. The cop never actually saw him, but he wrote up a report that Dingle was there."

"The Texas State Police never heard of Call Forwarding?" I said.

"Sending a trooper out to see if someone is home isn't complicated police work. So they sent a greenhorn kid and he screwed up. Lucky for us, some sergeant checked his report and dispatched a second unit, who interviewed the neighbors. The Dingles packed up their pickup truck and their camper and left town two weeks ago."

"Their pickup truck *and* their camper?" I said. "So that means they're not getting blood all over the good sheets at the Beverly Wilshire Hotel. They're sucking their victims dry in the comfort and privacy of their Winnebago."

"Actually, it's a Sunline. We've got the make, model, and tags on both the truck and the trailer. I've got every cruiser in the county looking for them."

"You're positive they're here?"

"I checked with Verizon Wireless. On April 26, the Dingles forwarded their home phone to Roger's cell. They left a trail of digital breadcrumbs from cell site to cell site across the Southwest. They arrived in LA ten days ago."

I've picked up a little about cell phone technology working with Muller. I know just enough to make me dangerous. "If they've established a home base in LA," I said, "we should be able to tell which cell site is getting the heaviest usage. That would narrow it down to a five-to-ten mile radius. Then we could triangulate. It's a needle in a haystack, but we can do it."

"Dingle is smarter than that," Wendy said. "Once he got to LA he bought himself a few more mobile phones. One day he'll forward his home number to a Sprint phone. Then to a Cingular. We can't triangulate, because basically, he keeps changing haystacks."

"What is he," I said, "some kind of an engineer?"

"No, just a smart cop. He was with the Houston PD for twenty years."

"Dingle is a retired cop?" Terry said.

"Decorated," Wendy said.

"That sucks," I said. "But as much as I hate cop on cop, it's good to have him back on the suspect list. Terry and I have been trying to make sense out of this new development with Victor Shea. He's got no motive."

"Maybe Joy Lee was his girlfriend," Wendy said.

"I've got pretty good gaydar. Victor ain't the girlfriend type," I said as Terry parked the car. "We're at the morgue. We're gonna bring him in and ask him a few hundred burning questions."

We walked through the back door, sidestepping a woman on a gurney who was waiting for the welcoming committee.

There were three people sitting at their desks behind the admissions counter. Anne Jordan was the senior tech. "Anne, where's Victor Shea?" I said.

"He went home about an hour ago. Said he was feeling queasy."

"I'll bet," Terry said.

"We need his home address," I said.

She peered at me over a pair of half-glasses. It was one of those don't-mess-with-the-bureaucracy looks, like I used to get from the local librarian when I was a kid and tried to take out a book without a library card.

"We're not supposed to give out personal information about the staff," she said. "I'm guessing you don't have anything official, like a court order."

"No, just an order from the Mayor to keep your body count down."

"Sounds official enough," she said. "I'll be right back."

Two minutes later Terry and I were heading for the car. "Victor's in West Covina," I said, reading the address Anne had written on a Post-it note. "We can make it in twenty minutes."

"Let me see that," Terry said as he got behind the wheel. He eyeballed the yellow Post-it, then got out of the car and popped the trunk. He came back with one of the folders we had asked Victor to collect for us earlier.

"Joy Lee's morgue folder," he said, tossing it to me. "Check her home address."

West Covina. Same street, same house number as the one Anne Jordan had just given us for Victor Shea.

CHAPTER FIFTY-SEVEN

Victor lived in a two-story apartment building on East Amar
Avenue with faux-Spanish architecture, a smattering of
sun-scorched palm trees, and little else to recommend it.
I'd never been there, but I'd seen a thousand like it. It's the
classic starter home for the upwardly mobile underprivileged. For
six-fifty a month you can get an efficiency or a junior one-
bedroom, complete with ceiling fan, vertical blinds, and a
microwave. The neighborhood is clean, ethnically diverse, and
screams *No Charm at Affordable Prices.*

We drove slowly past his building. A block later we spotted
his car, a green Mitsubishi Eclipse with a yellow passenger-side
door and an LA County Morgue parking sticker on the windshield.

"Unless there are two pieces of shit that look like that," Terry
said, "I'm going to take a wild guess and say he's in."

Security consisted of a locked door in the center of the
building and an intercom. Victor lived in apartment 9. Terry rang
the bell.

Victor answered. "I'm not home."

"Police," Terry said. "Open up."

"I didn't do anything, Terry."

"Then you won't have any problem buzzing us in, Victor."

"Second floor, turn right," he said, hitting the buzzer.

The apartment was everything I had expected and less. To the left as we entered was somebody's old throwaway sofa, a TV, and a desk that was basically two filing cabinets and a piece of plywood. To the right was an unmade bed. Straight ahead was a kitchenette and a dining area that had two gurneys, which Victor must have liberated from the morgue, then duct-taped together to use as a dining room table. Three mismatched chairs completed the ensemble.

The walls had an illogical mix of unframed posters, some hanging on by just a few strips of tape. Everything reeked of cigarette smoke and cat piss.

"It stinks in here," Terry said. "How many cats do you have?"

"Three," Victor said. "Sometimes four."

"How many of them smoke?"

"I don't smell anything. Not after eight hours in the morgue."

"I see you've been shopping at their furniture outlet," Terry said, pointing at the gurney-dining room table hyphenate.

"Craig said I could take them," he said. "They were on their last legs. Literally. I don't steal."

"It doesn't matter. We're not the gurney police. Let's talk homicide."

"I don't kill either." There was a two-liter bottle of Wild Cherry Pepsi on the counter. Victor filled a tumbler and took a small sip. Then he took a pack of Kools from his shirt pocket, pulled one out, and lit up.

"I see you're on a health kick," Terry said.

Victor laughed. "Caffeine, sugar, nicotine, alcohol, and trans fats. Not necessarily in that order."

"Tell us about Joy Lee," Terry said, segueing from Morgue Buddy to Cop on a Mission.

Victor sipped more Pepsi and inhaled more Kool. "Joy lived next door. She wanted to be an actress."

"Were you two involved?"

"Just friends. I wrote some monologues for her."

"What does that mean?"

"Sometimes casting directors don't have anything specific to audition, but they want to meet an actor to see what he can do. So actors will bring their own material. It can be Arthur Miller, Tennessee Williams, anything. But there aren't a lot of great monologues for Asian girls, so I wrote stuff for Joy. That's how we became friends."

"So you knew she was murdered?"

"Worse than that," he said. "I was driving the van for the morgue that day. I was the one who picked up the body."

"Do you know who killed her?"

"Some gangbanger."

Terry pressed him. "The one I asked you about today? Diego Garza?"

Victor played dumb and took a drag on his cigarette.

While Terry talked, I walked around inspecting the apartment. The bedsheets were covered with cat hair. One of the cats was curled up at the head of the bed, where the pillows would be if Victor actually owned any pillows.

"That's Sebastian," Victor said. "He bites."

"Tell him I have a gun," I said. "Where are the other two or three?"

"Tony is probably on top of one of the kitchen cabinets, and Mr. G. likes to come and go through the bathroom window. He's probably out looking for the next Mrs. G. He's the reason why the cat population fluctuates around here."

Terry threw the next question at him. "Do you know who killed Barry Gerber and Damian Hedge?"

"How would I know that?"

"Because your agent came to the station and gave us a copy of a script you wrote. The first two murders in your screenplay are exact duplicates of what happened to Gerber and Hedge. Except you wrote it before they were killed."

"Wow," Victor said. "*My* agent came to *your* house?"

"Any other time and I would laugh," Terry said. "But how did you come to make up a story about people getting exsanguinated, and then a short while later two Hollywood heavies show up bloodless at your place of business?"

"Am I a suspect?"

"You're a person of interest," Terry said. "So why don't you start making this interesting for us."

Victor sipped some more Wild Cherry Pepsi. As pudgy as he was, he didn't gulp. He sipped his drink like Lady Astor at teatime. But his hand was shaking. There was a second soda bottle on the counter with a few inches of brown liquid in it. Apparently it was the ashtray. Victor dropped his cigarette in and held his glass with two hands. "I can't believe they went through with it. And now, if they get caught, it's all my fault."

"Who are *they*?" Terry said.

"Joy's parents, Roger and Aggie Dingle," Victor said. "That used to be her last name, but she changed it."

"How well do you know Roger and Aggie?"

"I only met them after Joy was killed. I called and offered to fly down to Texas with the body. I wanted to go to the funeral anyway, so it was no big deal, but they appreciated it. I think they were so devastated, they were glad not to have to fly to LA and bring her home."

"Then what?"

"After the funeral, I stayed with Roger and Aggie for a week. They needed to talk to someone about Joy's life in LA, and I was the source. I didn't mind staying down there. It was a good time for me to get away from the morgue. They mainly wanted to know about the drugs. How a nice kid like Joy gets killed on the streets over a drug deal. I told them about the Cokettes. You know what that is?"

"We do," Terry said. "Did Joy know?"

"C'mon, get real. She wasn't stupid. But she never opened a single package that she carried. That's how she rationalized it. The truth is, that maybe ninety-nine times out of a hundred, there really was a script in the envelope she was delivering."

"But none of them came from a guy named Carjack at McDonald's."

"Fuck you, Terry," Victor said. "You gonna put Joy on trial now? You want to get ahead in Hollywood, you gotta pay your dues. Would you respect her more if she were sucking some slimeball producer's cock? How about you, Terry? You're trying to get in business with Halsey Bates now. Has he asked you to bend over and grab your ankles yet?"

Terry lunged at Victor, took hold of his shirt, and yanked him hard. Wild Cherry Pepsi splashed all over both of them.

I jumped in. "Separate corners. Now," I said, pulling them apart.

Terry didn't budge. Victor sat down on the sofa and lit another cigarette. "So everything you see in the movies is true," he said. "You do rough up people to get them to talk."

"He didn't rough you up," I said. "If you want to press charges against him for spilling your soda, I'll be your witness. I could use a new partner. Next time I'm putting in for a funny one."

Victor smiled. "Sorry for that crack about Halsey," he said.

"It's okay," Terry said. "Sorry if I got Pepsi all over your good Metallica T-shirt."

"Look, Victor. We got murders to solve and maybe more to prevent," I said. "It's showtime. Tell us how you came to write that screenplay."

Victor's lungs exhaled a cloud of smoke. "It was the night after Joy's funeral," he said. "We didn't drink a lot during the wake, but the funeral ripped your heart out. A lot of her friends spoke. It was a real tribute. Anyway, Roger and Aggie and I sat in their kitchen and got totally shit-faced. Roger said he wanted to kill the people who were responsible for Joy's death."

"Did he know who they were?"

Victor nodded. "Roger and Aggie knew exactly who they were. Barry Gerber, Damian Hedge, and Tyler Baker-Broome. It was all on tape on his answering machine."

"Who left them the message?" I said.

Tears were streaming down Victor's face. "Joy."

CHAPTER FIFTY-EIGHT

We gave Victor a few minutes to pour himself a fresh glass of Pepsi and finish his cigarette. One of the cats hopped up on the sofa, walked across his lap, then curled up in a corner, ignoring him. Terry and I pulled up two chairs.

"I don't know why Garza killed her," Victor said. "I'm sure she didn't put up a fight. I think it was one of those macho gang things. Kill someone and make your bones. He just slit her throat and left her to bleed to death. She was able to call 911, and they said they're on the way, but I think she knew she wasn't gonna make it. So she made one last call."

"To her parents," I said.

"Yeah, but nobody was home. She got their machine. Roger plays the tape for hours on end. I must have heard it a hundred times. She was crying, and you could hear how scared she was. She told them she got mixed up with the wrong people. She said she knew she was doing the wrong thing, but that's what you have to do to get ahead. She said, 'Barry and Damian and Tyler all promised I was going to be a movie star, but they lied. My friend Victor told me they were just using me, but I didn't want to believe him. I trusted them.' By now the words are coming out in a wet gurgle. She says, 'Mommy, Daddy, I love you so much. I'm sorry I let you down.' Then you hear these God-awful bubbling sounds. And that was it."

"I'm sorry," Terry said. "I'm really sorry for the loss of your friend."

"Thanks." Victor exhaled and let his shoulders relax.

"Is that why you killed Barry Gerber and Damian Hedge?"

"You know I didn't kill them."

"Then answer the question you blew off before. How did you write a movie about the murders before they even happened?"

"The three of us were drunk. Roger was ranting about the system. What's the law gonna do to these guys? A fine? Suspended sentences and community service? No...Roger wanted Texas Justice. He said he's going to put a bullet in each of their brains. And that's when Aggie said, 'A bullet is too good for them. We're gonna bleed them to death. Real slow. Exsanguination.'"

"Wait a minute," I said. "It was her idea? I thought you wrote the script and they acted it out."

"No. I was already working on a screenplay about this guy Aaron who gets out of jail, and then his enemies start getting killed."

"That's the one your agent gave us," I said.

"Yeah, but in my first draft the murder weapon was a gun. I was so focused on the revenge part of the plot, I didn't care how the victims got killed. But when Aggie came up with the exsanguination idea, I knew it was perfect. So I used it."

"You mean you stole it," Terry said.

"It's not like she was gonna pitch it to a studio," Victor said. "I thought it was just crazy drunk talk. So I borrowed it."

"Some people will do anything to get ahead in Hollywood," Terry said.

"I guess I had that coming," Victor said.

My cell rang. It was Wendy.

"Tyler Baker-Broome was shot."

"Shit," I said. "Is he dead?"

"I don't know. I'll give you what I got so far."

"Hold on." I repeated what she said for Terry, then put her on speaker.

"It happened about an hour ago in Koreatown. Someone tried to nab him in a parking lot. He tried to run and got shot in the process, but he managed to dial 911. He asked for Detectives Lomax and Biggs, then the 911 operator heard a gunshot and the phone went dead. I have Detective Susan Mercier from Central Division on the other line. She's at the scene."

"Terry and I know Susan."

"That's what she said. When she found out the victim was connected to you guys, she called here. I'm going to patch her through."

Five seconds later, Detective Mercier was on the line. "Hey, guys," she said. "I've been reading about this vampire you're chasing. Is this connected?"

"Unfortunately," I said. "What's going on?"

"My partner and I just caught this and it's a little chaotic, but from what I can gather, the victim, Tyler Baker-Broome, had lunch here in a Korean restaurant, then walked to the parking lot to get his car. Somebody was laying for him, pulled a gun; the vic ran, and got shot in the process."

"Well, is he okay or not?"

"Don't know. The shooter carted him off in a pickup. The vic tried calling you guys on his cell. I thought you'd want to know."

"We appreciate it," Terry said. "Was anyone else involved?"

"Yeah, two crazy civilians," Mercier said. "Ralph and Cheryl Blanchette, tourists from Staatsburg, New York. They ate at the same restaurant and were in the parking lot getting in their car when it all went down. They decided to play superheroes, tried to follow the pickup, and got the windshield of their rent-a-car shot out. They gave up the chase in a big hurry after that."

"Did they get the plates on the pickup?" I asked.

"Yeah, and Wendy just told me it's a match for your suspect."

"Mike, I'm still on," Wendy said. "The truck belongs to Roger Dingle."

"Susan, was he with his wife?" I said.

"His wife? Now I'm confused," Susan said. "Mrs. Blanchette said there was another man in the back of the pickup. Of course she's in total shock. It could have been a woman."

"Damn! It's not a woman." Terry started yelling into the phone. "Susan, this is Terry. How noisy is it where you are?"

"It's a crime scene, Terry. There's a bit of a buzz."

"Tell everyone to shut up for thirty seconds," he said.

He took out his cell and started dialing. In the background I could hear Susan Mercier yelling at everyone to keep quiet. Then she came back on. "It's as quiet as it's gonna get," she said. "Oh, shit, now someone's cell phone is ringing."

"Answer it," Terry said.

"Whosoever cell is ringing, answer it," she yelled.

"The phone doesn't belong to anybody at the scene," Terry yelled back. "Find it and answer it."

I could hear a commotion in the background, and then someone called out, "Under the car." And then the phone stopped ringing, and I heard Susan yell, "Hello!"

Terry was standing right next to me, talking into his cell phone. "Hey, Susan," he said. "It's Terry."

"Son of a bitch," she said. "There was a second cell phone that wound up under a car. You just called, so you must know who it belongs to."

"A friend of mine," Terry said. "The other guy in the back of Dingle's pickup truck. His name is Halsey Bates."

CHAPTER FIFTY-NINE

"This is your case," Susan Mercier said. "Do you want to come down here and take over?"

Terry and I said no in unison.

"We're in West Covina," I said. "We don't have time to drive to Koreatown and walk a crime scene. We have to find Halsey and Tyler fast."

Wendy Burns was still conferenced into the call. "And how do we do that?" she said.

"We're with Victor Shea, the guy who wrote the script," Terry said. "He's been semi-cooperative, and if anyone can help us figure out what Roger and Aggie Dingle are going to do next, Victor can. We'll see what we can get out of him. Wendy, the best you can do is help us find that camper."

"I have an APB out," Wendy said. "The problem is, the camper isn't rolling. It's hidden. In a garage, in a warehouse, in an airplane hangar. Even if it's out in the open, do you know how many RVs, campers, and trailers there are in this town?"

"She's right," I said. "Big Jim has a dozen of them parked in his truck barn. If they're hunkered down, they'll be harder to find than weapons of mass destruction."

"Do what you can," Terry said. "Susan, thanks. We owe you."

We hung up. Everything had been on speaker. We didn't have to fill Victor in on the details. He backed away from us and held his hands up.

"This is not my fault," Victor said.

"Sure it is," I said. "Why didn't you tell us what you knew? It's only by luck that Myron Pecarsky showed us the script. You could have stopped this from going down, but you didn't."

"I tried," he said. "I swear I tried. I called Tyler, and I warned him."

"*You* warned him? When?"

"Late last night after the news broke about Damian."

"What did he say?"

"I didn't actually talk to him," Victor said. "His home number is unlisted. So I called his office at Pita and left a message on his voice mail, but I have no idea if he ever got it."

"What was the message?"

"I said this is the Hollywood Bloodsucker, and you're next. I tried to do it in a Dracula voice, but I think I sounded more like Arnold Schwarzenegger."

"And did you call Halsey and warn him too?" Terry said.

"No." It came out whiny. Then he said it again. "No!" He sounded indignant this time. "Halsey isn't on Roger and Aggie's hit list. Joy never mentioned his name. I thought he was safe from them. I'm the only one who wants him...Oh, God. I think I know what's happening." He shook his head to escape the thought, then turned away from us.

Terry grabbed him and spun him around. "What? What's happening?" His right fist was raised. We have our own little version of the good cop, bad cop act, but Terry wasn't acting. This was genuine rage. I wondered if he'd be just as angry if Halsey Bates, the key to his retirement plans, hadn't been a victim.

"Easy, partner," I said. I turned to Victor. "What were you saying about Halsey? You're the only one who wants him *what?*"

Victor's eyes were moist again. He dropped his voice to a whisper. "Dead. I'm the only one who wants Halsey dead."

"Why?" I said. "I didn't even know you knew him."

"I don't."

"Then why?"

"Halsey Bates killed the man I loved. Kirk Jacoby."

"The actor," I said. "The one who was killed in the drunk driving accident."

"Kirk and I were lovers," Victor said. "Halsey killed him, and all he did was four and a half years. Fifty-four lousy months for snuffing out a beautiful young man's entire life. And he spent all that time building his help-the-homeless charity, and when he got out, Barry Gerber gave him a big directing job and he just picked up his life. Everyone in the world forgave him. Everyone but me. I wanted him to pay."

"So you asked Roger and Aggie to kill him," I said.

Victor laughed. "Yeah, one night down in Texas, I said, hey, Roger, do me a favor. If you ever actually come to LA and murder those other assholes, would you mind killing this Halsey Bates guy for me?"

"Okay," I said, "if that's not what happened, what did?"

"I'm not the type to kill anyone just because I want them dead," Victor said. "So I wrote about it. It's in the script Myron gave you."

"Aaron is Halsey Bates," Terry said. "He's been in jail for a drunk driving homicide, and he gets out after a couple of years."

"Seven," Victor said. "Which still isn't enough."

"But then his enemies start getting killed," Terry said. "So how does that hurt Aaron? He's obviously being set up."

"Right. He knows it and the audience knows it. But you have to read the ending and see how Aaron gets it in the end," Victor said with a self-satisfied smile.

"Victor, we're knee-deep in dead bodies, with two more on the butcher's table as we speak," I said. "Just tell us the ending."

He looked hurt. "It reads better than me just telling it," he said, "but if that's what you want…"

"That's what we want," I said. "And we want it now."

"Aaron is being set up by a character whose name is Victor Ashe."

"I'm just guessing here," Terry said, "but Victor Ashe sounds like he could be Victor Shea."

"I wasn't trying to be subtle," Victor said. "I'm making a statement. Anyway, after the third murder the Victor character confesses to Aaron that he framed him. So Aaron kills him."

"With a catheter?" Terry said.

"No, with a gun."

"So Aaron kills the real killer," Terry said. "I think the cops in this movie have it way too easy."

"That's the big twist. Actually, Victor had alerted the cops, and they show up just as Aaron pulls the trigger. So the cops witness Aaron in the act of murdering Victor."

"Just like in real life," Terry said. "What's the ending?"

"Aaron winds up back in jail. In the last scene a lawyer brings him a letter. It's from Victor saying, 'You killed someone I love, but you only got seven years. Now you're in jail for the rest of your life. Justice has been done.'"

Victor lit up another Kool. "So, what do you think?"

"It's pure gold, baby," Terry said. "I'm ready to green-light it myself. I only have one little problem. I still don't understand why Halsey Bates is out cold in the back of Roger Dingle's pickup truck."

Victor shrugged. "I guess that's my fault. When I was in Texas I told Roger and Aggie how much I hated Halsey, and that the only way I could ever kill him off was in a movie script. And Roger said, don't bother writing it. I'll kill him for you."

"So you stole his bloodsucking technique for your script, and he borrowed your victim to murder in real life," Terry said.

"I didn't think he'd kill anybody. Especially Halsey. He didn't have to do that for me. Believe me, I didn't ask him. I think he's just doing it as a friend."

"Well, that is one hell of a real good friend," Terry said. "Like me and Mike. We do all kinds of stuff for each other all the time. Never thought about asking him to suck the life's blood out of someone, but heck, with three ex-wives, I may just want to rethink the meaning of the word friendship."

"Where are Roger and Aggie now?" I said.

"I don't know," Victor said. "I swear. You heard that lady cop on the phone. They could be hiding that camper anywhere."

"I also heard her say something else," I said. "She said, the problem is, that camper isn't rolling." I looked at Terry, and he was immediately on the same page.

"Right," he said. "So maybe instead of trying to figure out where they're parked, we should start thinking about how to get them rolling."

CHAPTER SIXTY

Roger hadn't planned to take two of them out at the same time. But there they were in the Korean restaurant. Tyler Baker-Broome and Halsey Bates. Together. A God-given opportunity.

"I can handle them both," Roger told Aggie.

He did. But it was messy.

He had to shoot Baker-Broome. Some nosy parkers heard the shot and tried to chase them down, so Roger put a few bullets into their windshield. That changed their tune real quick.

When the pickup was safely on the freeway and the two men secured under a tarp in the bed of the truck, Roger slid open the rear window of the cab and leaned in. "We almost had us a parade there," he said.

"That's what happens when you go shooting off your gun," Aggie said. "Tends to attract a crowd."

That was Aggie. No credit for what he accomplished. Just finding fault with what he did wrong. "One shot," he said. "It got the job done."

"Maybe, but it's a whole lot noisier than chloroform."

"I got the first one with the chloroform. Did you think the second one was gonna stand around waiting for me to put a rag to his face? He was dialing the cops while he was running. I had to think on my feet."

"It's over now," she said. "Just make sure both of them are out good and cold when we get to the campground."

Getting the two men inside the camper without being noticed was easy enough. The problem was where to put them.

They only had one embalming table. Since Baker-Broome was bleeding out just fine on his own, they decided to strap Halsey to the table.

"Where do you reckon we oughta put the one you shot?" Aggie asked.

"Well, he ain't gonna fit in the microwave," Roger said. "Only available spot is our bed."

Aggie's mouth twisted into a frown. "I'll be darned if I'm gonna let him bleed to death all over my good linens," she said. She stripped the mattress and covered it with plastic garbage bags. Then she cut off Baker-Broome's shirt and wrapped his bleeding shoulder with rags and an old blanket they used when they stopped along the road to picnic. It didn't stop the flow of blood. It just soaked it up.

"Mr. Baker-Broome's circulatory system is on automatic pilot," Aggie said. "We might as well start bleeding the other one."

Halsey was still unconscious. Roger gave him another noseful of chloroform to keep him that way. He was strapped to the same cold metal table where Barry Gerber and Damian Hedge had died before him. Aggie opened the sterile packaging that sealed the TruFlow catheter tray, picked out a 16-gauge needle, and attached it to a syringe. She punctured Halsey's femoral vein, drew out some blood, and disconnected the syringe from the needle.

She then carefully inserted a guide wire through the needle. Once it was in place, she backed the needle off, leaving only the guide wire in the vein.

"You're getting pretty good at this," Roger said.

"It ain't that hard, really," she said. "Just needs a little concentration and a steady hand. Like quilting. Give me the vessel dilator, please."

Roger placed the dilator in her hand and she slid it over the guide wire, working it into the vein, expanding the original needle hole. "This should be plenty wide," she said, backing off the vessel dilator and sliding the catheter over the guide wire and into the vein. Finally, she removed the guide wire and secured the catheter to Halsey's leg.

"He's ready to bleed," she said. "Should I wake him before I start?"

A moan came from their bed. "Please…"

"No, keep him under for a while," Roger said. "Just start him bleeding. Let me deal with this other one." He turned his attention back to Tyler.

"Who are you?" Tyler said.

Roger stood over him. "I'm Roger Dingle. That's my wife Aggie. You knew our daughter."

"Joy…Joy Lee," Tyler said, whispering her name.

"So you remember her."

"Yes, we all loved—"

"Do you remember sending her to her death?"

"I didn't. It was all Barry. I swear—"

"Save your breath," Roger said. "You don't got too many more of them left."

One of Roger's cell phones rang.

"We're busy here," Aggie said. "Don't answer it. Just let it go to the voice mail."

Roger ignored her and flipped open his cell. "Hello."

"Roger, it's Victor Shea."

"Victor, it's been a while. How are things in Los Angeles?"

"The police are after me."

"The police are after you," Roger repeated, gesturing for Aggie to get close to the phone and listen in. "Now what did you go and do?"

"I didn't do anything, but LAPD made a connection between Barry Gerber, Damian Hedge, and Joy. They know she worked for them, and they know she was doing the drug run for Barry and Damian when she got killed."

"So why are the cops after you?"

"They know I was friends with Joy and that I spent time with you after she died. Two detectives came looking for me at the morgue, but I snuck out before they could find me. They want to grill me."

"So don't say nothing. You have the right to remain silent and all that horseshit."

"Roger, I know you're in LA," Victor said.

Aggie's cheek was pressed against Roger's. She shook her head vigorously.

"That's crazy talk," Roger said. "We're sitting here on the porch in Katy, Texas."

"Roger, I'm not stupid," Victor said. "The people you wanted dead are either murdered or kidnapped. And it's all happening the way Aggie and you planned it that night."

Aggie pulled the phone closer to her face. "Victor, what have you told the cops so far?" she said.

"Hey, Aggie," Victor said. "I didn't tell them anything. But I can't avoid them much longer. And if they find me and I lie to them, I'm an accessory to murder. You did what you had to do, but I don't want to be dragged into it. I don't want to go to jail."

"So why did you call?" Aggie said. "Just to whine? Or to tell us that you're gonna rat us out?"

"To warn you," Victor said. "I'm trying to give you time to get away. You're only about 125 miles from Tijuana. If I can stall the cops for three hours, you can get over the border to Mexico."

"Three hours is the best you can do?" Roger said. "We could use a little more time."

"Roger, you know how much I loved your daughter, but I can't buy you more time just so you can exsanguinate Tyler Baker-Broome and Halsey Bates. Just let them go and make a run for it."

"Baker-Broome is pretty much drained dry on his own," Aggie said. "Mr. Bates has a little ways to go."

"You're killing him on my account, aren't you?" Victor said.

"What the hell are you talking about?" Roger said

"You know I have a grudge against Halsey," Victor said. "I thought you were doing it for me."

"You think I'm getting back at that homo for getting drunk and killing your boyfriend?" Roger said.

"I thought—"

"You thought wrong, boy. This is my retribution. Mine and Aggie's. Halsey Bates killed our daughter. The vengeance is all ours."

"But he didn't kill her," Victor said. "He wasn't involved in the drug—"

"He was the boss. The director. I'm not stupid. I know who's in charge of making a movie. The day he got out of prison, who was the first person to show up and give him a job? That fat Jew Barry Gerber. Bates knew what Gerber was making Joy do, but he decided to look the other way. He's as guilty as the rest of them."

"Roger, where are you?" Victor said. "Maybe we should get together and talk this over."

"No. You said you don't want to be involved, and you're right. Aggie and I are pulling up stakes."

"How fast can you get out of LA?"

"You give us them three hours you promised, and we'll be out of the country."

"I can do it," Victor said. "Just hurry."

"Thank you," Roger said. "Thanks for helping."

"Victor..." It was Aggie.

"Yes, ma'am?"

"What was your friend's name? The one Halsey Bates killed?"

"Kirk. Kirk Jacoby."

"We can only send Halsey Bates to hell once," she said, "but I'll make sure he knows that his ticket was paid for by Joy and your friend Kirk."

"Don't," Victor said. "Please don't. I appreciate the gesture, but..."

"It's okay, Victor," Aggie said. "Don't thank us. All you've done for our family, it's the least we could do for you."

CHAPTER SIXTY-ONE

V ictor hung up the phone. "Wow, I thought I knew about cop shit, but this is way cool. You actually warn the bad guys that you're coming after them."

"We're not warning them," I said. "We're flushing them out. They're about to murder two people. There's no time for a standard search and rescue. We need to get them out in the open fast."

I flipped open my cell phone and called Julie Burton at KLAJ.

"Mike," she said. "I knew you'd call. Is this about the latest kidnappings? Please tell me you're giving me that exclusive you promised."

"I'd rather give it to that tough boss of yours, Angela Martin. Put her on."

"Gosh...bad timing," Julie said. "Angela's not in the office today."

"From what I heard, Angela hasn't been in the office for months. You really conned me, Jules."

"So I'm a media bitch," she said. "It's not a crime."

"Actually, it is. I think they call it obstruction of justice."

"I apologize. Did you call to arrest me?"

"I just wanted you to know I'm not as dumb a detective as you thought," I said. "And now that we're back on the same team, I do have an exclusive."

"You're kidding me. Did you arrest the Hollywood Blood-sucker?"

"No, but we might be able to if you help."

"Tell me. I'll do whatever it takes."

"There's a dark blue Chevy pickup with Texas plates that I'm hoping is headed south out of LA. He may or may not be towing a twenty-eight-foot Sunline trailer. I want you to get their description out to the public. Put it on your TV station, your local radio, even your website."

"Oh man, this is huge," she said.

I gave her the license plates and an LAPD hotline number. "Anyone who sees them should call the cops, but under no circumstances should they attempt to stop the vehicle."

"Like an Amber alert," she said. "Is the Hollywood Blood-sucker in the truck? Are Tyler Baker-Broome and Halsey Bates in the trailer?"

"No comment, Julie."

"Mike, this is fantastic," she said. "What else can you tell me?"

"I can tell you that you have the exclusive, but not for long. How fast can you be on the air?"

"Minutes. I promise. Thanks, I owe you."

I hung up. "Now we just have to hope that these nutjobs hit the road before they do their vampire thing on Tyler and Halsey."

"Roger and Aggie are making a big mistake," Victor said.

"I'd say they've made several already," Terry said.

"Halsey didn't do anything to hurt Joy. They're going to kill him for all the wrong reasons."

"Not to go all LAPD on you," Terry said, "but where we come from, there are no right reasons."

"Hey, if we catch them," Victor said, "do I get the hundred-thousand-dollar reward?"

"Your agent already has a claim on that," I said.

"Myron?" Victor said. "That old coot sold me out. He gave you my script because he thought I was the killer. I'm not. How does he get the money?"

"Technically, he led us to you."

"But you already knew me."

"Victor, we don't make the call on who gets the reward," I said. "But he's your agent. This is Hollywood. Just shut up and split it with him."

"Split it? You mean like fifty-fifty? No way. He gets fifteen percent tops. That would leave me with eighty-five thousand. I could live with that."

Victor lit up another cigarette while he entertained the thought. "Wow," he said, getting the word and a lungful of smoke out in the same breath. "Do you guys know what I could do with eighty-five thousand bucks?"

Terry turned his head from left to right, slowly scanning the room. "Hopefully," he said, "you'd buy some disinfectant."

CHAPTER SIXTY-TWO

We turned on Victor's radio and TV. The radio hit first. "This just in," the announcer said. "A KLAJ exclusive on the Hollywood Bloodsucker." He laid out the details, making it sound like the station and the police had been working together around the clock on a citywide vampire hunt.

KLAJ TV was slower to get the word out. They were in the middle of a pod of uninterruptible commercials, and the station manager must have decided that peddling Pine-Sol, Metamucil, and I Can't Believe It's Not Butter was more important than tracking down serial killers.

Victor was loving every minute of it. "This is too cool," he said. "I may write it into my next movie."

"Let's see if it works first," Terry said. "Of course if it back fires, we can always sell it as the sequel to *Dumb and Dumber*."

"You guys have a lot at stake," Victor said. "If you screw this up, you're gonna make LAPD look really bad. And if Roger and Aggie kill Halsey, your whole movie career is in the toilet."

"It won't do a hell of a lot for Halsey's career either," Terry said.

After the fifth commercial a card came on that said 'Bulletin,' and an announcer wasted more time by explaining that they were interrupting their regularly scheduled programming for a bulletin.

Finally, they cut to a newsroom. The guy behind the desk had removed his jacket. Nothing says Urgent News like an anchorman in shirtsleeves. As he described the pickup, the trailer, and the Texas plates, a card came on-screen spelling it all out for the viewers.

"Oh good," Terry said. "Now we can also count on the civic-minded hearing impaired."

"How long do you think it will take for someone to spot them?" Victor said.

"Five bucks says we get the first phone call in three and half minutes," Terry said. "Lomax, you want the over or the under?"

"Under," I said, looking at my watch.

"You guys are betting on when the tip is going to come in?" Victor said.

"We're not betting," Terry said. "Betting is against the law."

"Freaking cool, man," Victor said. "This is so gonna be in my next movie."

"Don't wet your pants," Terry said. "And if you write it into a movie, make it fifty bucks. Five sounds too lame, but it's all I can afford."

My cell phone rang two minutes and forty seconds into the bet. "Pay up," I said to Terry and took the call.

It was Big Jim.

"Hey Mike, I just caught that bulletin on TV," he said.

"Dad, I'm working here. Don't tie up my phone."

"I didn't call the hotline," he said. "I'm just calling you. Can't a guy with a bad heart call his son?"

"Not when I'm in the middle of a crime wave. Call your other son." I hung up.

"Three minutes and counting," Terry said. Thirty seconds later, he grinned. "Now you pay up."

I barely had the fiver out of my wallet when my phone rang. This time it was Wendy Burns.

"I think we got them," she said. "I got a call from a woman at the KOA in Pomona."

"Damn," I said. "It's an RV campground. Why didn't I think of that?"

"I didn't realize LA was a hot spot for campers," Wendy said. "You know the place?"

"It's across from the Fairplex," I said. "I used to go to the LA County Fair as a kid. I just haven't thought about it in years. Are they holed up there?"

"Not anymore," Wendy said. "Hang on. I'm going to patch the tipster through. Her name is Shirley Klinghoffer. Go ahead ma'am, you're on with Detective Lomax."

I hit the speaker button and a woman's voice came on. "My husband and I heard the bulletin about the Chevy pickup and the Sunline with the Texas plates. The people you're looking for were parked in space number 179. We're in 182."

"And you saw them leave?" I said.

"Hard to miss," she said. "They had a canopy carport next to their trailer. They went tear-assing out of here so fast, they side-swiped it on the way out."

"How long ago was that, Mrs. Klinghoffer?"

"A few minutes before we saw the bulletin on the TV."

"Did you see which way they went?"

"We're at the far end of the campground. We can't see the

front gate from back here, but we can see the road. A few minutes after they left, you could see them heading south on White Avenue."

"This is very helpful, ma'am. Is there anything else you can think of?"

"No. Except, I'd be willing to haul out their garbage if I could keep that canopy carport. Ours is getting kind of ratty."

I got that gnawing feeling in my gut. I asked the question I really didn't want to hear the answer to. "What garbage, ma'am?"

"Before they left, they dumped a load of trash and covered it with a tarp. Did they think nobody would notice? There's a strict no-dumping policy here."

"Ma'am, don't go near that trash pile," I said. "We're sending some police officers out to investigate. Detective Burns is going to put you on hold for a minute. Don't hang up."

Two clicks later and Wendy said, "She's off. Let me get some units out to Pomona."

"And a bloodmobile," I said. "I'm betting whoever's in that trash pile is going to need a transfusion. And get us a chopper."

"Where?"

"If the Dingles are making for the border, they'll have to go west on the 10 and south on 57. Start the chopper up there, then have him follow 57 toward the Santa Ana Freeway. Terry and I are in West Covina, maybe five miles from the KOA. We should be able to head east and cut them off."

I hung up.

"We can take Amar to Grand Avenue," Victor said. "It cuts southeast toward Diamond Bar. It runs right into 57. They're pulling a trailer. We can catch them easy."

"We?" I said.

"The three of us," Victor said. "I should go. I know them. I can talk sense to them."

"Are you crazy?" Terry said. "Do you want to wind up back in the morgue? It's not as much fun when you're horizontal."

I don't know how many civilians dream about riding in the back of a speeding police car, chasing down a pair of mass murderers, but I'm sure Victor is one of them.

"But—" he said.

"Butt out," Terry said. "Now sit down and drink your Pepsi or I'll handcuff you to the chair."

Victor's head dropped and his expression went from wild anticipation to a pitiful pout. "Fine," he said and sat down.

Terry and I raced out the door.

In hindsight, we definitely should have handcuffed Victor to that chair.

CHAPTER SIXTY-THREE

"Put your prom dress on, honey," Terry yelled as we ran for the car.

He popped the trunk. "Would you like the chiffon, the taffeta, or we have a lovely crepe de chine," he said as I peeled off my jacket and grabbed a vest. "Ah, I see you're going with the Kevlar. Excellent choice."

"Are you *ever* serious?" I said, putting an LAPD windbreaker on over the body armor.

"I figure Roger Dingle will be serious. One of us should keep it light."

We headed east loud and fast. I checked my weapon. Then I checked Terry, who was staring straight ahead, both hands on the wheel. His usual look-Mom-I'm-in-a-high-speed-chase demonic grin wasn't there. He looked humorless. Never a good sign.

Neither of us said a word till we crossed Lemon on our way to Grand. Finally, Terry spoke. "Shoulda, woulda, coulda."

"Don't go there," I said.

"Shoulda gave Tyler protection. Woulda kept him from getting snatched. Coulda saved his life."

"I thought you're the designated Keep It Light Guy," I said.

"Hey, if Marilyn can have mood swings every five minutes, so can I."

"We don't even know that Tyler is dead."

"One of them is under that tarp at the campground. Maybe both. I guarantee you the Dingles weren't dumping their recyclables."

"Just because somebody kills two Hollywood assholes, it's not our job to offer a safe haven to all the rest of them," I said. "The last thing Tyler said to me was 'I'm getting the hell out of Dodge.' He could have asked for police protection, but he didn't. His choice, not ours."

Terry twisted up the corner of his mouth. "Whatever," he said.

Translation: technically I was right, but that didn't make it any easier for him to deal with. If Terry has one flaw as a homicide detective, it's that sometimes he thinks he could have prevented some of the murders we have to solve. I think it has something to do with having two aunts who were nuns.

We were headed south on Grand when my cell rang. It was Wendy. She gave me the bad news. I repeated it for Terry. "Cops on the scene at the KOA found a body under the tarp," I said. "It's Tyler."

He nodded. "What about Halsey?"

"No sign of him."

"So it's just the one dead guy," he said. "Kind of a slow day at the old campground."

I gave Wendy our location and asked about the chopper.

"Twelve minutes out," she said. "We got another sighting from a motorist. You called it. They're headed south on 57. Male behind the wheel of the pickup matches Roger Dingle's description. The female suspect wasn't in the cab of the truck. She's probably in the trailer with the other hostage."

We had to make a hard left across four lanes of northbound traffic on Grand to pick up the Orange freeway on-ramp. Fortunately, Terry had the lights, the siren, and the balls.

"And you thought Damian Hedge was good at car chase scenes," he said. "Hey, there's the Diamond Bar golf course. Kilcullen plays there."

There were cars on the freeway, but for LA it was light. Traffic was moving at a good clip. We cleared the left lane and about five minutes later we could see a trailer about a mile ahead.

"I think I see them," I said to Wendy, and gave her the mile marker. "I know this road. There's a Boy Scout reservation to the west of us. I used to go camping there as a kid. There's about a five-mile stretch of undeveloped county land just south of Diamond Bar. Dingle is armed, and I'd rather take them out where there aren't any civilians. You have any units up ahead of us?"

"I've got backup headed north," she said. "I can put them in the southbound lane in front of the camper, and we'll box him in. Just hang back till all units are in place."

Terry pulled into the right lane and slowed down, keeping about a quarter of a mile behind the camper. We were close enough now to confirm. It was them. I let Wendy know.

"Intercept units are about two miles ahead of you," she said.

All signs of civilization disappeared, and I looked around at the familiar LA topography. Brown-gray hills and brown-green vegetation. Henry David Thoreau himself would be hard-pressed to find inspiration. I'm a native, but as far as I'm concerned, without its ocean, Southern California is downright ugly.

"What the hell?" Terry said.

A car whizzed by us on the left. It was a green Mitsubishi Eclipse with a yellow door on the passenger side.

"It's Victor," I said.

"What the hell does he think he's doing?"

Whatever he was doing, he was doing it fast. He sped past us and was barreling down on the trailer. Terry sped up, but somehow the little piece-of-crap Mitsubishi was outrunning us.

As the road ahead angled downhill, the trailer picked up momentum. The Eclipse picked up even more.

"He's passing him," Terry said.

Roger was in the right lane. Victor passed him and kept on going in the left lane. He was now about twenty feet in front of the trailer. The gap widened to fifty feet.

"What is that crazy bastard doing?" Terry said.

It didn't take long to get an answer. Victor was about a hundred feet in front of the trailer when he pulled sharply into the right lane. And then his taillights went cherry red.

Roger slammed on his brakes, but the laws of physics weren't on his side. The heavy load was moving downhill too fast, and the little Eclipse was stopping too soon.

I felt like I was watching it in slow motion, and all I could think of was *the irresistible force is about to meet the immovable object.*

I took a logic course in college. On the first day our professor, Dr. Herbert Sontz, asked the class what happens when an irresistible force meets an immovable object? Lots of theories popped up, the most popular of which was the title of that song by Frank Sinatra. Something's Gotta Give.

But Dr. Sontz shot them all down. He then spent the rest of

the hour explaining that it is logically impossible to have these two entities in the same universe. "You can't have a force that cannot be resisted," he said, "and an object that cannot be moved by any force."

I had always agreed with Professor Sontz's logic. I assumed that some whimsical, totally illogical poet came up with the concept, but in the real world there's no such thing as an irresistible force meeting an immovable object.

But as I watched the Chevy pickup with its twenty-eight-foot Sunline plow into Victor's little Japanese tin can on wheels, I had one thought. This car wreck comes pretty damn close.

CHAPTER SIXTY-FOUR

If you're going to force a vehicle twenty times your size to ram you at ninety miles an hour, it helps if you're a good driver.

Victor Shea was the Richard Petty of morgue attendants.

Just as he was rear-ended, Victor hit the gas pedal. The net effect was that he managed to pull away just enough so that the back half of his Eclipse got accordioned but he managed to avoid being completely flattened.

Roger's rig wound up getting the worst of it. Like a drunk at the top of a staircase wearing oversized clown shoes, he went camper over teakettle, careening across the highway in several directions.

The trailer sparked along on its side in the left lane, while the pickup gouged a trench in the right shoulder before it finally came to rest. The peppy little Eclipse rolled once, then hung tough till it skittered to a stop against a guardrail.

It was a spectacular crash, worthy of a NASCAR highlight reel. And miraculously, as the TV sportscasters love to say, nobody was hurt.

Well, not badly. The real hurting came after the crash.

Victor staggered out of the Eclipse. His head was bleeding, which could only mean that his brain was even more scrambled than when he decided to play Junior Crimestopper.

His walk was loopy as he made his way toward the pickup. At the same time Roger leaped from the cab with a forty-five in his hand.

"Roger," Victor called out, "we need to talk."

Terry and I were out of our car, screaming at Victor to hit the dirt.

Victor kept walking, only slowing down long enough to yell out his faulty logic in our direction. "I can help. Let me talk to Roger."

But apparently Roger was not in a talking mood. He was more in a shooting mood. He fired once. And thanks to the quality firearm training he had received from the United States Marine Corps and the Houston Police Department, one shot was all it took.

Victor went down.

We were next on Roger's hit list.

Luckily, we had a big ass car to hide behind. And guns.

We crouched behind the car and fired.

Roger fired back, zigging, zagging, rolling to the ground, and finally diving over the side of an embankment and into the thick brush.

We ran to the edge of the tree line. A bullet splintered a branch barely an inch from my ear. We dove to the ground.

In the movies when a bullet just misses a cop's head, he rolls, gets up, and keeps firing. Not me. Not Terry. Our bodies were pressed hard against the earth.

"Jesus, that was close," Terry said. "Are you okay?"

"No," I said. "I mean, there are no bullet holes in me, but I'm probably gonna have nightmares for a few weeks. If my ears were as big as yours, he'd have shot one of them off."

"We are definitely not going in after him," Terry said.

"No sense of adventure?" I said. "Or are you just too lazy to break in a new partner?"

"I saw *Rambo*," Terry said. "This guy is in the same league. Only an idiot would follow him into those woods. And since Victor's already been shot, we don't have any idiots left."

He was right. Besides, we had plenty of cleanup work to do. Victor was lying in the road bleeding, Halsey was hopefully in the camper with some blood still coursing through his veins, and Aggie Dingle was a wild card.

The last thing I had said to Wendy before the bullets started flying was "there's been a collision. Suspect vehicle hit a civilian car. Send paramedics and a couple of wreckers."

I called her back. "Still need paramedics, and if you're keeping score, the civilian in that car wreck is now a gunshot victim. Male suspect escaped on foot through the woods. He's armed. Female suspect still in the camper. We're going in. That chopper is now the designated MedEvac unit. Tell him to fly faster."

Terry and I closed in on the camper. The windows were broken, so if Aggie were conscious, she'd hear me.

"Police," I yelled. "Come out with your hands in the air."

It's the traditional greeting all bad guys and gals are entitled to. I think it may be part of the Bill of Rights, or the Marquis of Queensbury's rules, and while I personally think it's kind of dumb to lose the element of surprise by warning the people you're coming after that you're coming after them, it's also kind of un-American not to.

I waited for the response. A hail of bullets. A Jimmy Cagney-esque, "Come and get me, copper." Or a highly unoriginal, but totally communicative, "Fuck you." I've had them all. I'm happy with anything but the bullets.

Much to my amazement, Aggie hollered back, "Don't shoot. I'm coming out."

I was reminded that there's another reason why I'm honor-bound to yell those warnings. Sometimes, like today, the con-frontation ends with a whimper and not with a bang, bang, bang. There's a lot to be said for low drama.

Aggie climbed nimbly out of the window. She walked toward us with her hands held high. She looked like a throwback to another era. A farm wife. The left side of *American Gothic*. Her gray hair was in a bun—or at least what was left of a bun after a hard day abducting, exsanguinating, and skidding across the freeway in her home away from home. If I actually knew what gingham was, I'd have guessed that the plaid cotton dress she had on was just that. The light blue flowery apron tied around her waist was splotched with dark brown stains that I knew weren't gravy.

"Cuff her," I said to Terry. "I'm going in for Halsey."

The trailer was lying on its side. I climbed up and lowered myself through a broken window. Déjà vu. Hadn't I just hauled my ass into a downed Winnebago not too long ago? It was last year in a parking lot in Familyland, and the guy I was trying to rescue was my partner. It worked out well then. I was hoping I could go two for two. I called out Halsey's name. I got back a faint groan.

There was a metal table lying on its side. I crawled toward it and felt the warm sticky liquid under my hands and knees. Blood. Lots of it.

Halsey was strapped to the table. Naked. A catheter was dangling from his groin. Blood was trickling out. Too risky to try to remove it. I pinched the tube and the blood stopped.

"You're going to be okay," I said, not knowing if what I was promising was even remotely close to medical reality. "Help is coming."

I undid the straps and lowered Halsey to the floor, which was actually the wall of the camper.

"Thanks," he said in a whisper.

"Don't talk," I said.

Like most directors, Halsey doesn't take direction well. He kept talking.

"Thanks," he said. "This will make a brilliant scene in the movie."

CHAPTER SIXTY-FIVE

We were at the Pomona Valley Medical Center. Victor was listed as stable, which is not exactly the word I would have used for him. The good news was the crazy bastard was expected to live.

Halsey was another story. His tank was on E when he got to the hospital. Even though the docs had managed to get the needle back up to F, their official medical prognosis was "still not out of the woods."

"Roger Dingle is the guy who's still not out of the woods," Terry said, "but if you topped Halsey off with premium, how come he's not up and humming?"

"Organ failure." The doc's nametag said Karan Mahajan. I didn't try to pronounce it.

"Which organ?" I said.

"What gives me the most concern is his kidneys. His heart is a little erratic as well. The human body is not like a sponge, Detective. If it goes dry, you can't just plump it up and expect it to be good to go. Blood carries oxygen, and Mr. Bates was oxygen deprived long enough for his organs to start shutting down. His whole system has been shocked."

"Will he live?" I said.

"He's in his mid-forties, reasonably good health," the doc said. "The odds are in his favor."

"When can we talk to him?" I said.

"Not tonight. But assuming he bounces back, he'll bounce back fast. Why don't you call the nurses' station tomorrow after 9 a.m."

"And Victor Shea?" I said.

"Not my patient," Mahajan said. "But they both came into ER together. Young man, gunshot wound to the thigh, no complications from what I heard. Check with the head nurse, but my guess is he can answer questions now."

"Let's start with why he's such an idiot," Terry said.

"And we thought the cigarettes were going to kill him," I said.

We thanked the doc and walked down the hall to Victor's room. He was sitting up in bed watching TV. He hit the mute button.

"They interrupted *Wheel of Fortune* with a bulletin that Tyler was dead, and one of the two Hollywood Bloodsuckers was caught," he said. "Of course, they don't say squat about me, but the night is young. How's Halsey?"

"Alive, no thanks to you," I said.

"No thanks to me? I stopped the trailer. I thought you guys were chasing him, but then you slowed down."

"We needed time to get our backup in place," Terry said. "It's called police work."

"Well, if you waited any longer, he'd have bled to death. As far as I'm concerned I saved his life, which is total dramatic irony," Victor said. "Halsey kills my boyfriend in a car crash, and I go ahead and save his life in a car crash. It sounds like a Lifetime movie."

"How are you feeling?" Terry said.

"Pretty good."

"Good enough to be arrested?"

"For what?"

"Take your pick," Terry said. "You broke at least half a dozen laws out there this afternoon. We might be able to overlook going ninety-five in a fifty-five-mile-an-hour zone, or obstruction of justice, or helping a mass murderer escape, but your little high-speed fender-bender constitutes assault with a deadly weapon. You have the right to remain silent—"

"Are you serious?" Victor said. "You're really going to arrest me?"

"I think our boss will be a little ticked off if we don't," Terry said. He finished giving Victor the Miranda warning.

"This is fantastic," Victor said. "Thank you."

"I've had trouble tracking your logic all day," Terry said. "You can get five years for an ADW. Why are you so grateful?"

"My movie script. It's all playing out," Victor said. "Sure, I'll have to do a rewrite, but now the whole thing is practically autobiographical. And my character is the star. He works at the morgue, so he sees the victims, he has a relationship with the killers—and now you're hauling me off to jail."

"Actually, you're going to spend the night here. There's a cop outside your door with orders to shoot you if you so much as try to sneak outside for a cigarette."

Victor beamed. "This is cool. Way cool."

Three people were dead, one was hanging on, and by now

the man behind it all was probably in Tijuana chomping on enchiladas and washing them down with cerveza fría. And any minute now, Kilcullen, his boss, and all his boss's bosses would be screaming, "Bring me the heads of Mike Lomax and Terry Biggs."

Cool. Way cool.

CHAPTER SIXTY-SIX

It was almost 9 p.m. when I got to Diana's apartment. Before I could even shut the door, she ran across the room and flung herself into my arms.

"What did I do to deserve this?" I said.

"You came home alive," she said, kissing me and pressing her face to my neck.

"I come home alive lots of nights," I said. "I don't usually get this kind of reception."

"You don't usually get shot at."

"Who told you I got shot at?"

"Marilyn."

"And did she tell you I had on a bulletproof vest?"

"What good would that do?" Diana said. "The bullet missed your brain by a few inches."

"And how does Marilyn know that?"

"Terry told her. They have an agreement," Diana said. "She can ask anything. He has to tell her the whole truth and nothing but the truth."

"He has to tell her the whole truth about me?"

"If she asks."

"And then she has to call up and tell you? Is that part of the agreement?"

She squeezed me hard and kissed me again. "I can't believe you almost got killed."

"I've been shot at before. The bullet whizzed by. It's no big deal."

She pulled back, and I could see the tears streaming down her face. "What if it didn't whiz by? What if it whizzed into that big fat stupid brain of yours that keeps trying to convince me that it's no big deal?"

"I'm sorry," I said. "I know this is major to you, but this is why most cops don't tell their wives or girlfriends all the details. *How was your day, honey* is a loaded question. It's a dangerous job. I know it. You know it. But the last place I want to talk about it is here. With you."

She gave me a nod that hinted at acceptance. At least for now. I wiped a tear from her cheek. "So then, I take it you're happy to see me," I said.

"You want dinner?" she said.

"I'm starved. Let's drive down to the In-N-Out Burger."

"No, I mean dinner here."

"Is 'dinner' a euphemism for sex?"

She shook her head. "No, that would be 'dessert.' I mean I'll make you dinner."

"Can I start with dessert?"

"Come into the kitchen. I'll make you an omelet."

"I'd rather go for a cheeseburger. Or pizza."

"You have to have eggs," she said. "They're a symbol for new life, a new beginning."

"Who's having a new beginning?"

"You are," she said. "You're the one who almost got shot."

"Are you going to have some of my eggs?" I said. "Then the two of us could have a new beginning together."

"You had a near-death experience," she said. "You're in shock. Please don't ask me to marry you."

"I wasn't going to ask you to marry me."

"Then what does 'the two of us could have a new beginning together' mean?"

"I don't know," I said. "I just don't want to eat my omelet by myself. Maybe we should live together."

She looked around the room. Then she turned back to me. "Mike, we do live together."

"We room together," I said. "Sometimes my rented place. Most times your rented place. What if we bought a house? What if we had an *our place*?"

"A house," she said. "Just a house? No wedding dress, no bridesmaids, no throwing bouquets? You're not asking me to marry you?"

"I'm just asking you to break your lease."

The tears started rolling again. "Okay," she said. "We'll buy a house."

"Wow," I said. "That was easy."

"No, it wasn't."

I put my arms around her and held her. "I love you," I said.

"I love you too." She pulled back. "Now let's go crack some eggs."

"You're positive that pizza doesn't qualify for new beginnings?" I said.

She took my hand and pulled me toward the kitchen. She made me a mushroom, chive, and feta cheese omelet. It was fantastic.

An hour later I had dessert. It was even more fantastic.

But I was really exhausted, so I only had one helping.

CHAPTER SIXTY-SEVEN

"Thanks for outing me," I said to Terry when he picked me up the next morning.

"Meaning what?"

"Meaning you told Marilyn that I almost took a bullet, and she told Diana, who had a major meltdown."

"I have a deal with Marilyn. I tell her everything. She repeats nothing," Terry said. "Apparently she's not holding up her end of the deal. Sorry if she caused you any domestic distress. When I get home tonight she's going to get a good spanking."

"It worked out for the best. Diana suddenly decided that I was worth keeping around long term. We're going to buy a house together. So actually, you can give Marilyn a big thank-you."

"I'll do better than that," Terry said. "When I get home tonight she's going to get a good spanking."

It was only 6:45 when we got in, but Wendy was already at her desk. "Roger Dingle was caught on surveillance at the Brea Mall an hour after he took off. He helped himself to a 1994 Chevy Camaro."

"Which he probably drove across the border to Mexico," I said.

"And sold for twice the book value," Terry said.

"Not quite," Wendy said. "The car turned up on the U.S. side in San Ysidro. Odds are he walked across the border."

"And his poor wife is here with us," Terry said. "Don't they know that separate vacations weaken the matrimonial bond?"

We cranked out paperwork until Aggie's court-appointed attorney showed up at 8:30. Ed Kaufman was a solid lawyer, easier to work with than most, and well past retirement age. So were most of his jokes. When we sat down in the interview room, he led off with one of his old standbys.

"Do you believe this case the judge assigned me? As Mary Jo Buttafuco said, 'I need this like I need another hole in the head.'"

Aggie Dingle just stared at him.

"Your client doesn't think you're that funny," Terry said.

"It doesn't matter," Kaufman said. "This is my one and only appearance. Mrs. Dingle has asked the judge for a different attorney."

"They're charging me with killing men," Aggie said, "so I think I'll do better with a woman. And not Jewish. Gerber was Jewish."

"That's her strategy for success," Kaufman said. "A non-Jewish female lawyer. I suggested Sandra Day O'Connor."

"Since we have evidence up the yin-yang that your client murdered Diego Garza, Barry Gerber, Damian Hedge, and Tyler Baker-Broome," I said, "can we get to something of consequence? Like, where's her husband?"

"I ain't admitting I killed them," Aggie said, "but even if I did, I would be guilty because of insanity. Either of you got kids? Somebody murdered one of them, what would you do?"

"Mrs. Dingle," I said, "we're sorry for the loss of your daughter, but we're not the judge and jury. We're cops, and since you're married to a cop, you know why we're here. Where's your husband now?"

"Who knows?" she said.

"You do," I said. "This was all carefully orchestrated. You had to have contingency plans. Was there a specific time and place you were supposed to meet if you got split up?"

"Not a specific time," she said. "Just the place."

"Where is that?"

"The pearly gates," she said.

"Heaven?" I said. "You murder four people and you actually think you and your husband are going to meet up in heaven?"

She stared at me, a sly smile on her face. "I thought you just told me you wasn't the judge and jury."

"Detective Lomax," Kaufman said, "where my client winds up after she dies is of no value to this interview. Do you have any real questions?"

"Your husband is in Mexico," I said. "Is he coming back?"

"Quién sabe?" she said.

"Who's next on his hit list?"

No answer.

"Counselor," I said, "please tell your client that the DA is willing to cut a deal if she cooperates, but if she stonewalls us she and her husband are going to wind up celebrating their final wedding anniversary on death row."

"You think you can scare me, Detective?" Aggie said. "A year ago, Roger and me had all kinds of retirement plans. But then our little girl got murdered. The lies those men told Joy, the things they made her do, that all led up to her death. The state of California don't have no justice for that. Only choice we had was Mom-and-Pop justice."

Her eyes grew watery and began to spill over. Tears rolled down her cheeks.

"I got no regrets," she said. "None whatsoever. It ain't the golden years that we planned for, but without my daughter, them golden years is all tarnished anyways. Roger's not coming back, Detective. Me and him, we said our good-byes. We gave up everything to do what we had to do. And I don't think no jury is gonna put me on death row for doing it."

I looked at Terry. He shook his head slowly. He had no questions. Aggie Dingle might be a murderer, but she was the most sympathetic murderer we'd ever run across.

"Thank you, Mrs. Dingle," I said. "Counselor, the interview is over."

Ed Kaufman's chin was resting on his hands, and he was staring at the woman who was about to become his former client. "Mrs. Dingle," he said. "I apologize for the jokes, and I'm truly sorry for the loss of your daughter. If you ever change your mind about a female attorney, I'd be honored to defend you."

I was willing to bet that a lot of defense lawyers would be equally honored. Not just because it was a high-profile case, but because even with the evidence stacked up in our favor, the DA would have a tough time convincing a jury that this teary-eyed symbol of American motherhood should spend the rest of her life rotting in jail.

CHAPTER SIXTY-EIGHT

"**I** called the hospital," Terry said. "Halsey is sitting up, taking nourishment, and ready for visitors."

"Does that mean his adoring fans?" I said. "Or can he be debriefed by LAPD Homicide?"

"That's the beauty of us," Terry said. "We're both."

We got to the Pomona Valley Medical Center at noon. Halsey was getting the full celebrity treatment. To keep the gawkers at bay, they had put him on the top floor in a private suite. It wasn't private enough. There, sitting in a leather armchair, drinking out of a Starbuck's cup, was my father.

"What the hell are you doing here?" I said.

"This man and I were both rendered powerless by deadly assassins," Jim said. "We both faced the specter of death, wrestled the Grim Reaper to the ground, and emerged triumphant. Now I am here to give comfort and support to my stun gun soul mate. What the hell are you doing here?"

"We're the metaphor police," I said. "You're under arrest."

"It's good to see you two haven't changed," Halsey said. "Let

— *343* —

me repeat what I attempted to say in my semi-conscious state yesterday. Thank you for saving my life."

"We had a lot of help," I said.

"You mean Victor Shea?" Halsey said.

"The jury is out on whether he actually helped," Terry said.

"He was in here this morning," Halsey said. "He took a bullet for me."

"Noble, but dumb," Terry said. "He also almost got you killed in a car wreck, and he helped the man who was trying to kill you get away."

"That's not the way Victor tells it," Halsey said.

"He's a screenwriter," Terry said. "He gets paid to make shit up."

"Halsey was just telling me what those bastards put him through," Jim said. "They were laying for him in the parking lot of that Korean restaurant. After he and Tyler had lunch—"

"Stop," I said. "As long as I have both ends of the horse in the room, why don't we hear it straight from the horse's mouth."

"Y'know, Michael," Jim said, "I feel like putting you back in my will, just so I can take you out again. Go ahead, Halsey."

"It's like Jim said. They were waiting in the parking lot. I found out later that they had originally come for Tyler, but I was the bonus. Stun one, get one free. Tyler and I had just made a handshake agreement on our new partnership over lunch. He had been warned that he might be next and he was in a hurry to get out of town. We were going to have the lawyers draw everything up, and we would both sign it when it was safe for him to come back to Los Angeles."

"Did you ever think that you were in danger?" I said.

"At first, yeah. I thought maybe they were killing people connected to *I.C.U.* But then over lunch Tyler told me about the Joy Lee connection. I knew her, but I didn't know about the drug-running. I left the drugging part of my past behind. Ever since I was in prison I've been working to help get people back on the right track. Next week we're opening another rescue mission."

"So getting back to you and Tyler in the parking lot," I said. "You didn't think you were a target."

"Neither did I," Jim said, "and that's when we both got stun-gunned."

"Dammit, Dad," I said.

Halsey laughed. "I think he's just doing that to piss you off, Mike. Anyway, Tyler and I were walking to our cars, and like typical Hollywood assholes, we both already had our cell phones in our hands, ready to check for messages. We were saying good-bye when I got zapped. Never felt anything like it in my life. I pieced together later that Tyler started running. Roger went after him with a real gun and shot him. They lifted me into the back of the pickup and chloroformed me. Next thing I know, I'm naked on a table in a trailer and they're trying to bleed me dry."

"Did you know who they were?" I said.

"They didn't hide it. Tyler knew right away. They told me because they wanted me to know. They showed us home movies of Joy growing up, so we could understand what they had lost."

"And justify why it was okay to kill you," Terry said.

"I tried to tell them that I had nothing to do with her death," Halsey said. "But they blamed me. They told me I was the boss. I should have protected her. They don't know a hell of a lot about moviemaking. There was only one boss, and that was Barry."

"They had no problem telling you who they were, because they were confident that you'd be too dead to tell anyone," I said.

"Did they tell you where they were going to go after they killed you?"

"Roger's still out there, isn't he?" Halsey said.

"He's on the loose for now," I said, "but we'll get him."

"I think their original plan was to kill the four of us, drive home to Texas, and go back to living their lives," he said. "But once they found out that you knew who they were, they knew they could never go back. At one point Roger said to me, 'Tomorrow this time me and Aggie will be sitting on a beach in Mexico and having a pitcher of sangria, while some coroner is yanking out your black heart and tossing it on a scale.' It was pretty graphic. You don't forget something like that."

"He didn't say which beach in Mexico, did he?" I asked.

Halsey smiled. "No. And I had a lot on my mind, so I didn't ask."

"Is there anything else you can tell us that will help us track down Roger Dingle?" I said.

"I watched his home movies," Halsey said. "It's pretty clear who he was. A good husband, a loving father, just an all-around nice guy. But the day his daughter was murdered that man died with her. Now he's obsessed with her memory and the need to punish the people responsible for her death."

"He could come back," Big Jim said. "Mike, I think you should give him police protection."

"And I think you should mind your own business," I said. I turned to Halsey. "My father is not authorized to make the offer, but if you want, I can get you police protection."

"There's a strapping young cop standing outside of Victor's room," Halsey said. "I wouldn't mind having him tuck me in every night."

"Sorry," I said. "We're the police department, not a dating service."

"In that case, I'll pass, but thanks for the offer. So, tell me... what's going to happen to Joy Lee's mother?"

"It's up to a jury," I said. "For now, she's in jail."

"Can I visit her?" Halsey said.

"Visit her?" Big Jim said. Apparently he decided he had minded his own business long enough. "The woman tried to kill you. Why in God's name would you want to visit her?"

I knew why. Terry knew why too, and I could see by the look on his face that he wasn't happy about it.

"Halsey's a director," Terry said to Jim. "And in case you hadn't noticed, there's a movie in all of this."

CHAPTER SIXTY-NINE

We were back in the office by 3, and on Kilcullen's carpet at 3:01.

"There's a press conference in an hour," he said. "The Mayor would like you to be there."

"Fuck the Mayor," I said.

"Jesus, Lomax, I would expect something like that from your partner," Kilcullen said.

"He beat me to it," Terry said. "But for the record, fuck the Mayor from me too."

"The press is going to have questions," Kilcullen said. "Who better to handle them than you guys?"

"I'll bet they'll have questions," I said. "Like where's Roger Dingle? How did you manage to let him get away? Who's this civilian Victor Shea who you recruited to help you flush out the killers, and then you let botch up the arrest and apprehension? Now Detective, can we take your picture please? Just hop up on this cross, and keep your legs together, because we only have three nails."

"You think the press is going to come after you?" Kilcullen said.

"We only caught one out of two bad guys," I said. "And you don't get kudos for batting five hundred when you let a mass murderer get away."

"But the one you caught was the Hollywood Bloodsucker."

"What are you talking about?" I said.

"The wife. Mrs. Dingle. She was the one who did the actual bleeding. Mel Berger in the Mayor's Office thinks we should paint her as the real killer, the actual bloodsucker. That makes the husband who got away seem more like an accomplice. Less of a threat that he's out there."

"Mel Berger in the Mayor's Office came up with that?" I said.

"Yeah."

"In that case, I would like to amend my previous response and say fuck Mel Berger."

Kilcullen turned to Terry for help. "Biggs, do you want to tell me what got into your partner?"

"I think it's what almost got into him," Terry said. "He came this close to taking a .45 slug to the frontal lobe. It could be a little post-traumatic stress."

"Well that would explain a lot."

"I'm not finished," Terry said. "Or it could just be that he's fed up with your nonstop political bullshit, and you finally pushed him over the edge."

"I'm going with the PTSD," Kilcullen said. "Mike, why don't you set something up with one of the department shrinks? Take some time off if you need it."

"I don't need time off," I said. "Strike that. I do. It's Friday afternoon, and I plan on driving to Santa Barbara with Diana for the weekend. No cell phone. No pager. No contact till Monday morning. But I'm not suffering from PTSD."

"Then what's your problem?"

I hadn't realized I had a problem until I exploded at my boss. But once the powder keg blew, I was pretty sure I knew what set it off. "I think it might be a touch of Stockholm syndrome," I said.

"Meaning?"

"I feel more compassion for the killers than I do for the victims. Aggie and Roger Dingle couldn't have children of their own. Talk about identifying. Joanie and I had the same problem. But they were lucky. They got to adopt a little Chinese girl. And they invested everything they had in her. Terry and I saw the video they played for their victims. They loved that kid. And then she got mixed up with a bunch of Hollywood scumbags who put her in harm's way, and she got her throat slit. The last thing those two people heard from their daughter was a message she left on their answering machine. She ran out of blood and air trying to tell them how much she loved them and how sorry she was for letting them down."

I realized I was shouting and I stopped. I took a long, slow breath and dropped my voice back down to a civilized level. "So don't expect me to stand up at a press conference and demonize Aggie and Roger Dingle for avenging Joy Lee's death. Because if it was one of your daughters, Brendan, or one of Terry's daughters, you both know what you'd be doing. You'd kill the bastards who killed your little girl, and you wouldn't think twice about it."

Kilcullen got up from his desk and walked to the door. "Stay here," he said and left. Terry and I sat there, not talking. A few minutes later, Kilcullen came back with three cups of black coffee.

"It must really suck for you guys to have a boss who's a recovering alcoholic," he said. "There was a time when I would have been able to open my desk drawer and pull out a bottle of Irish whiskey. But I'm afraid the best I can do at this stage of my life is a cup of this highly suspect warm brown beverage that we brew."

He handed us each a cup.

"I'd like to propose a toast to two of the smartest, most dedicated cops I've ever had the honor of working with." He looked squarely at Terry. "And one of the least funny. Job well done, boys. Job well done."

CHAPTER SEVENTY

Kilcullen went to the press conference on his own. He got back to the office just as I was getting ready to leave for the weekend.

"Santa Barbara is a good choice," he said. "There are some beautiful bed-and-breakfasts right on the beach. After what you've been through this week, the sun, the sea, and the sand will do you a world of good. They have a way of recharging your battery and restoring your soul. You got a place all picked out?"

I nodded.

"Sally and I have a favorite place down there," he said. "I wouldn't be surprised if it's the same one."

He was fishing. But I wasn't biting. It was none of his business where I was going for the weekend.

"It's called Country Inn By The Sea," he said.

"It sounds perfect," I said. Then I winked.

He winked back, completely convinced that his keen detective mind had psyched out the exact spot where I was going to find my serenity and spirituality.

Five hours later Diana and I checked into the Bellagio Hotel in Vegas.

The sand, the surf, and breakfast at sunrise might work for Brendan and Sally Kilcullen, but Diana and I needed noise, music, craps, blackjack, glitz, booze, 24-hour room service, and sex. Not necessarily in that order.

We left our cell phones in LA and never looked at a newspaper or turned on the television. And no place helps you keep the outside world out like Vegas. By the end of the weekend my battery was recharged, my soul was restored, and my bank account was shy three thousand bucks. Worth every penny of it.

Monday morning Kilcullen hit Terry and me with the bad news.

"We got a call from the Mexicans," he said. "Roger Dingle is dead. He checked into a fleabag hotel Thursday night. Ate his gun on Sunday."

"I guess this story was never going to have a happy ending," Terry said.

"The Mayor would disagree with you on that," Kilcullen said.

"A cop blowing his brains out is never a happy ending," I said. "Even a cop that's gone sour."

"I never understood why cops have only one way of committing suicide," Terry said. "It's such a cliché. The department should come up with a few interesting alternatives and start teaching them in police academy."

"Somebody's got to go and tell Dingle's widow that her husband won't be joining her," Kilcullen said.

"We'll tell her," I said.

"It doesn't have to be you."

"Yes it does," I said.

"It's all yours. Then get back here and start on something new," Kilcullen said. "You look rested. You must have had a good weekend."

I nodded. "A great weekend."

"What did I tell you?" he said patting me on the back. "Mother Nature works wonders."

So does 48 hours of sleaze.

CHAPTER SEVENTY-ONE

Once he ditched the car in San Ysidro, Roger Dingle could have walked across the border to Tijuana in a few minutes. But then he'd be in Mexico on foot. He needed wheels.

The traffic was moving slow enough to catch a ride, but Roger didn't want just anyone who would drive him over and drop him off. He needed a traveling companion. It took forty minutes before the good ole boy in the Dodge Ram 350 showed up.

There's my ticket, Roger thought, sticking out his thumb.

"Arvin," the guy said as Roger hopped in the cab. "Arvin Skett."

"Wyatt," Roger said.

"Like Wyatt Earp," Skett said. "But I'm betting you ain't no frontier marshal."

"Try unemployed construction worker," Roger said.

"You're traveling light," Arvin said. "I guess you're not staying long enough to need a change of underwear."

"I'm lucky I got pants on," Roger said. "I had a fight with my old lady and stormed out of the house. Took the Greyhound down from LA to San Ysidro. I got some cash and a credit card, so I figure I can buy whatever I need down here."

"If you don't mind me asking, what did you and the little woman fight about?"

"Same old shit. Me not working, her not spreading her legs."

"I feel your pain, bro," Arvin said. "But you're in luck. You came to the leg-spreading capital of the world, and ole Arvin Skett will be your tour guide."

"You know your way around?"

"Wyatt, you know how some people go to church? This is my church. Once a month on a Thursday night, I drive down here from SD for tacos, tequila, and sweet Mexican pussy. You like 'em young?"

Roger laughed. "I'm fifty-three years old. These days they're all young."

"No, I mean like fifteen, fourteen, even twelve. You ever fuck a twelve-year-old?"

Roger put his hand to his jacket pocket and pressed it hard against the gun. He mustered up a smile. "I don't believe I ever fucked a twelve-year-old. Even when I was twelve."

"That's a good one," Arvin said. "Me, I wouldn't spend a dime to hump one of those fat old Mexican whores. They got pussies that hang down off 'em like saddlebags. If you want, we can team up."

The invitation had come faster than Roger had hoped for. He took it slow, careful not to pounce on it. "Team up?" Roger said. "Like how?"

"Like we get a couple of el cheapo rooms at the Roach Motel, grab some food, some tequila, and then I'll take you to Bonita's. She specializes in young Mexican poonanny. Sweet, tight, and for a few extra pesos, shaved. How about it, Wyatt? You game?"

Sitting behind the wheel, Arvin looked to be about Roger's height. He was a little thinner, a little younger, but he had the same salt-and-pepper hair. His face didn't look a lot like Roger's, but that was no problem. Arvin wasn't going to have much of a face left to identify.

"I don't know," Roger said. "It's damn white of you to ask, but I don't want to cramp your style."

"Are you kidding me?" Arvin said. "I drive a Budget Rent-a-Car van at the San Diego airport. I deal with hundreds of total strangers every day. I sized you up when you were standing on the road with your thumb out, and I said to myself, there is one straight shooter. Otherwise, I would never have picked you up. Nothing's more fun than Thursday night in TJ with Arvin Skett. Except for Friday and Saturday. Come Sunday, I'll drive you back to the bus terminal in San Ysidro, or you can hop a ride with me to SD. What do you say?"

"Arvin, this is my lucky day," Roger said. "I couldn't have gotten a better ride if I prayed for it."

CHAPTER SEVENTY-TWO

A
rvin was in a drunken stupor when Roger blew his head off with the .45. He debated whether or not to leave a suicide note. If he were actually killing himself he wouldn't have bothered. But he figured a note would give the scene that much more authenticity and make it easy on the Mexican cops to determine cause of death.

He kept it short. *I'm sorry. Please ship my body back to Katy, TX. Gracias.*

Of course, they wouldn't ship it anywhere. The police would take his wallet and run the name Roger Dingle through their computer. Then they'd contact LAPD to let them know that they had the remains of the guy you're looking for, and LA would ask for positive ID.

No problemo. Someone at the Tijuana police would contact someone at the local morgue and ask for fingerprints on the gringo suicide victim. Eventually, they'd realize that they had Roger Dingle's wallet and somebody else's faceless corpse. But that would take time. Mexican time. By then Roger would have returned to LA and finished what he had started.

Roger took one last look at Arvin Skett's body and felt a pang of regret. Arvin was lying on the bed, the .45 in his right hand, his blood and brains spattered from the pillow to the far wall. Damn shame, Roger thought. I hate having to leave that gun behind. I've had it a good twenty years.

A half hour later he was driving across the border in the Dodge pickup. The guard waved him on through. "Welcome back to the U.S., Mr. Skett."

Sunday night he checked into the Best Western on Century Boulevard close to LAX. He used Arvin's credit card. He'd have rather paid cash, but the card wouldn't be reported stolen until Arvin was identified, and his cop sense told him that since 9/11 anyone who checked into an airport hotel using cash would raise red flags.

Monday he shopped for the things he needed to do the job. That night he made the six o'clock news. *Roger Dingle, the mass murderer known as the Hollywood Bloodsucker, has taken his own life in a motel in Tijuana.*

Then they cut to Halsey Bates, the only survivor of the vicious killing spree. Bates prattled on about the tragedy of Joy Lee and her parents. But that was the past, and he wanted to talk about the future. He was dedicating another rescue mission on Wednesday at noon. They expected at least five hundred home-less people for the inaugural celebratory lunch.

"Five hundred and one," Roger said to the television set.

Tuesday was painfully long. Roger spent most of the day in his hotel room flipping from news channel to news channel. The good news was he was still dead.

On Wednesday at 4 a.m. he checked out of the hotel and

drove downtown. The new rescue mission was on East Fifth Street, the heart of Skid Row. Roger parked ten blocks away. The windshield would fill up with tickets until they finally impounded the truck. He didn't care. He wasn't coming back.

It was still dark out. He hopped out of the cab and made sure there was no one in sight. Then he got the wheelchair out of the back. He had bought it used, then beat it up some more. Finally, to give it a little character, he plastered a dozen bumper stickers to the metal sides and the vinyl seat. His favorite was *Jesus Loves You. Everyone Else Thinks You're An Asshole.*

He hadn't shaved in nearly a week, and his clothes were torn and well stained. This wasn't Roger's first outing as a homeless man. Two years ago, a new sport had caught on in Houston. Bum hunting. Packs of teenage boys would attack homeless men with paintball guns and baseball bats. Roger was still with the Houston PD then, and he had gone undercover. He dressed in rags, staggering around in alleys and side streets for five nights until a gang of teenage boys pounced on him.

They were all white and rich, and their lawyers blamed their senseless acts on the Bumfight videos, which were corrupting the nation's youth. They all got jail time, and Roger got a commendation from the department. Joy and Aggie had been at the awards ceremony. It seemed like a lifetime ago. It was. Joy's lifetime.

He wheeled himself toward East Fifth. Halfway there he saw a large black man urinating against a wall. "Hey bro," Roger yelled.

"What do you want, crip," the man said.

"If you can lift that monster you got in your hand, you can probably push an old man down to the Nickel."

The guy laughed and zipped up. "You got the monster part right, but what is it about me that makes you think I'd want to push an old white cripple around the Row? What's in it for me?"

"I'm a real good tipper," Roger said. "Especially if you like Jack."

"Jack who?"

"Daniels."

"Yeah, right. You ain't got Jack shit, whitey."

Roger had a backpack strapped to his chest. He reached in and produced a pint of Jack Daniels. "Have a taste," he said.

The man broke the seal and unscrewed the cap. He took a swallow, then a second. "This is top-shelf," he said. "Where'd you get this?"

"I hit the lottery. Now, you interested in pushing me downtown? I have a lunch date. I'm going to the grand opening of that new rescue mission, and I want to be at the front of the line."

The black man took another swig. "I got your booze, and I got two good legs," he said. "Why do I have to push you anywhere?"

Roger tapped the backpack and got the distinct sound of glass hitting glass. "You only got one bottle, Brother. I told you I hit the lottery."

"Buckle up, dude," the guy said. "You don't mind me drinking and driving, do you?"

"What do I look like?" Roger said. "A cop?"

CHAPTER SEVENTY-THREE

They stopped off for breakfast. Roger had bacon, eggs, toast, and coffee. The black man had four doughnuts and a Coke.

"My name is Carl," he said. "My friends call me Chain Gang."

"That sounds like a story I might want to hear," Roger said.

"Not on the first date," Carl said, pouring the rest of the first pint of Jack into his Coke. "You got a name?"

"Heywood," Roger said. "Last name is Yafuckoff."

"Heywood Yafuckoff. What kind of a—" Carl let out a loud cackling laugh. "Hey would you fuck off. That's a good one. There's more to you than meets the eye, Cracker. You can afford booze and breakfast, but you show up six hours early for a free lunch."

"What can I tell you? I love grand openings," Roger said. "They're so festive."

They killed five hours and three pints. When the doors to the mission opened, they were at the head of the line. Carl wheeled Roger to the front row. He pulled his baseball cap low, slouched in his wheelchair, and took inventory.

Roger was here on a mission. He didn't expect to escape, but as he looked around the room, he began to get his hopes up. There were no cops. Just two security guards, one white, one black, both old. I can take them, he thought. And the nuns, the priests, and the other do-gooders who were opening their new home to crazy people in rags were no threat either.

The only thing between me and that front door are five hundred of the least motivated life forms on the planet, Roger thought. I should have hired Carl to run interference for me.

And then Halsey entered. The nuns started applauding and the rest of the room joined in. He was wearing khaki pants and a pink sweater. Pink, Roger thought, and his mind flashed to the photos he'd seen of Jackie Kennedy dressed in pink that day in Dallas.

Blood shows up real good on pink, Roger thought.

Halsey stood at a podium just six feet in front of Roger and began to speak. Roger slipped his hand under his thigh and wrapped his fingers around the grip of his Ka-bar. It was the same knife he had used on the pigs and the Mexican kid. It's just as well I don't have my gun, he thought. I'll get a lot more blood with a blade.

Halsey knew his audience, so he kept the speech short. Roger couldn't focus on what Halsey was preaching. Every now and then he'd pick up a few phrases. *New beginnings...always hope...I know hardship too...my goal is to help...*and more bullshit, bullshit, bullshit.

In two minutes it was over. Polite applause. Halsey stepped away from the podium.

"Halsey, we love you," Roger yelled. "Come shake hands."

Halsey smiled, stepped up to the wheelchair, and bent over, his arm extended. Roger's hand whipped out from under his leg and thrust the Ka-bar directly toward Halsey's heart.

There was a scream, and Halsey fell to the ground, his pink sweater drenched in blood.

CHAPTER SEVENTY-FOUR

R oger Dingle completely blindsided us. We had been watching for him, but we never saw him walk in.

There were half a dozen undercover cops in the room, but most of us were either in the back or on the sides, covering every possible escape route. What we didn't count on was the suicide bomber mentality. Roger didn't care if he got caught. All he wanted was to kill Halsey Bates.

I had scanned the crowd while Halsey was speaking. Then I watched him as he approached the guy in the wheelchair. Even as I was thinking, this is a bad idea, I saw the knife come up and the center of Halsey's sweater go red. Then he hit the floor. Hard.

All hell broke loose. The crowd began to push their way out, pushing me with them. I plastered myself to a wall and radioed for backup and paramedics. Then I started fighting my way toward the man in the wheelchair.

Terry got there before me. He grabbed Roger's right arm and pulled him to the ground. I didn't know if Roger still had the knife, but I could see blood all over Terry's face and his priest's collar. Then a large black man fell on top of Roger and helped roll him over so Terry could get the cuffs on.

Halsey was flat on his back in a puddle of blood. Someone yelled, "He could have AIDS," and people backed off quickly— all except a few for whom catching the virus was no longer an issue.

I put my hand behind Halsey's head and tipped him forward. "Hang on," I said. "We'll get you to the hospital."

"No, I'm fine, really. It just hurts a little." He reached behind his head and rubbed it. "How bad is it back there?" he said.

I pulled my hand away from his head. It was wet and sticky with blood. And then I realized. Halsey was bleeding from the back of his head. I lifted his sweater. The blood on it wasn't coming from Halsey. The vest had done its job.

"It looks like the knife hit him square in the metal shock plate," Terry said. "But it didn't penetrate. The blood all over his sweater is Roger's. The vest stopped the knife, but his hand had so much momentum, it kept going right along the blade. He practically sliced it off. He's bleeding bad."

I turned back to Halsey. "And you?"

"I'm okay. I just hit my head on the way down. We have a nurse here. She can patch me up. I really want to stay and feed these people."

"And how about you?" I said to the big black man who had helped Terry get Roger cuffed.

"I'm fine," he said. He stood up. "And assuming you don't arrest good Samaritans for helping, I'm gonna just take my stuff and go."

He picked up his backpack, and I heard the clinking of glass.

"Empties," he said. "I get a nickel for each one I return."

"Do you have an ID?" I said.

He laughed. "Nobody here has an ID. And even if they did, I wouldn't believe it. I didn't do nothing wrong," he said. "Am I free to go?"

"Sure," I said. "And thanks for your help. Do you have a name?"

"Only if it's required by law."

"How about just a first name," I said.

He flashed a big smile. "Heywood."

CHAPTER SEVENTY-FIVE

There were five of us in Terry and Marilyn's dining room. Jett, their black Lab, was under the table. Terry, Marilyn, and Diana had consumed the better part of three bottles of Kendall Jackson chardonnay, and were well on their way to joining the dog. I was the designated driver, so I let the three of them do the heavy drinking.

We were having our Case Closed dinner. Marilyn made jambalaya. Diana and I brought pecan pie and ice cream. Terry had just rehashed the details of Roger Dingle's capture at the rescue mission for the third time.

"I would have loved to see you in your priest's outfit," Diana said.

"I'm going to wear part of it later on tonight," Terry said. "But I have to wait for you and Mike to leave. Only Marilyn gets to see me."

"Which part are you wearing?" Marilyn said.

"The collar and the black socks."

"Wouldn't you have wanted to see Mike in his homeless

outfit?" Marilyn said. "I wish we had pictures."

"I've seen Mike dressed like a homeless man," Diana said. "On Sundays during football season. How did you guys figure out that Roger Dingle didn't commit suicide?"

"His wife told us," I said. "Not on purpose. She didn't give him up. But on Monday when Terry and I broke the news to her that her husband was dead, she thanked us, and that was it. It just didn't feel like the right reaction."

"But different women react differently," Diana said. "How do you know what the right reaction is?"

"You just do," Terry said. "Like if they told Marilyn I was dead, she'd call the insurance man and start remodeling the kitchen. Aggie Dingle reacted like...like she didn't believe us. I think she knew Roger would try to kill Halsey before he'd ever kill himself."

"Now what happens to them?" Marilyn said.

"It's up to the system," I said. "Aggie may get out one day when she's eighty years old. Avenging her daughter may resonate if she gets the right judge and jury. But Roger murdered this guy Arvin Skett in Mexico just to get his truck and his ID. Best guess, he'll die in prison."

"It's all very sad," Diana said. "They were leading a perfectly normal happy life, and their daughter gets killed and look where it ended up."

"What would you do, honey?" Marilyn said to Terry.

"What would I do about what?"

"What would you do if, God forbid, somebody ever murdered one of the girls?"

"No question," Terry said. "I'd buy an AK-47 and get revenge."

"What if they murdered me?" Marilyn said.

"No question on that one either," he said. "Internet dating."

Marilyn punched him in the shoulder. Then she kissed him.

"I'd like to propose a toast," Diana slurred. "To our two favorite crime fighters. Congratulations on another case closed."

"I'd like to propose a toast too," Terry said, lifting his glass. "To the victor."

"You're a little sloshed," Marilyn said. "There's two of you. To the victors."

"No, no, no," Terry said. "I'm toasting the one and only Victor, the kid who works in the morgue. As of this afternoon, he's a free man."

"What?" Marilyn said. "He interferes with a high-speed police chase, almost gets you and Mike killed, and they let him go?"

"They dropped the felony charges and slapped him on the wrist with some community service," Terry said.

"Community service?" Marilyn said, the chardonnay causing her to mangle both of the words. "How could they—"

"He's got no priors," I said, "and according to Halsey, that dumbass stunt of Victor's saved his life. He is forever indebted to Victor Shea, and more than a little attracted to him. In fact, it was Halsey who pulled the political strings that got Victor off the hook."

"But that's not all, folks," Terry said. "The boy is not only free, he is now rich. Halsey is also going to produce and direct Victor's movie."

"What movie?" Marilyn said.

"This case we just wrapped up," Terry said. "Halsey thinks it can be a blockbuster."

Marilyn was getting angry. "But it's your case."

"I know," Terry said. "But Halsey wants to come at it from

Victor's point of view. Victor knew Aggie and Roger. He was close to Joy Lee, whose murder was their underlying motive. He works in the morgue. He even got in the middle of a high-speed chase that resulted in one arrest and one escape."

"And one bullet," I said. "Which was taken by guess who."

"Hell, if I had $250,000, I'd have optioned Victor's story myself," Terry said.

Marilyn stood up. "He got $250,000?"

"It'll be in tomorrow morning's newspapers," Terry said. "When we released Victor late this afternoon, Halsey showed up with a contract and a bunch of reporters. He gave Victor a pen, leaned over, and the kid signed right there on Halsey's back. It was a great stunt. A true tribute to the late, great, exsanguinated Barry Gerber."

Marilyn took a fourth bottle of wine from the counter and grabbed the corkscrew. "He should have gotten five years in jail. Instead he gets $250,000?"

Terry nodded. "Two-fifty is what we heard. But you know Hollywood. It might only be $150,000."

"That's way more than you and Mike got," Marilyn said.

"I told Mike we'd get more money if he'd sleep with Halsey," Terry said. "But you know how resistant he is to change."

"So Halsey is doing Victor's Bloodsucker story and our Family-land movie," Marilyn said. "Which one is he making first?"

"Victor's," I said.

"What about ours?"

"It's in something called turnaround," Terry said.

"What does that mean?"

"I asked Big Jim to explain it to me," I said. "From what I understand, it means they *say* they're gonna make your movie, but they don't."

Marilyn began refilling their three glasses with wine. "So they just lie to you?"

"They don't exactly lie," Terry said. "They just promise they're gonna make your movie someday, but that day never comes."

"Do we get to keep the $25,000 Halsey already paid us?" Marilyn said.

"Absolutely," I said. "And God knows it was easy money. We just did our jobs, and somebody paid us to option it for a feature. I'd be glad to do that any day of the week."

"So then that's what you guys should do," Diana said. "Just go out there and solve another big case and sell that one too."

"You make it sound so simple," I said.

"It may be the wine," Diana said, "but I think you guys are the smartest, bravest cops in the whole city."

"You left out funniest," Terry said.

Diana raised her glass. "To Mike and Terry."

Marilyn raised her glass. "To Mike and Diana."

I raised my glass. "To Terry and Marilyn."

Terry raised his glass. "To show business."

THANK YOU

If you want to write a crime novel, call a cop. I called some of the best. I am indebted to Detectives Wendy Berndt, Elizabeth Estupinan, and Leonard DeLeon of the Los Angeles Police Department, and to Undersheriff Frank P. Faluotico of the Ulster County Sheriff's Office, all of whom took time from their demanding jobs to help me pursue my life of crime.

I'd also like to thank Craig R. Harvey, Chief Coroner Investigator and Chief of Operations at the County of Los Angeles Department of Coroner. I needed to experience the L.A. County Morgue up close and personal, and Craig gave me an education I'll never forget.

Thanks to Dr. Paul Pagnozzi, who taught me how to exsanguinate; Mike Jackman, my film production guru; Rick Cook, my Texas connection; Tony Melone, V.P. at Verizon Wireless; Ron Frank, my weights and measures expert; Jonathan Berg, Mencken scholar; Wendy Karp, who taught me never to leave profredding to amatures; and to my Los Angeles location scout, Matthew Diamond, who knows all the best places to dump a dead body.

A big thank-you-I-love-you-guys to everyone at MacAdam

Cage—Scott Allen, Melanie Mitchell, Dorothy Carico Smith, Julie Burton, Melissa Little, Karan Mahajan, Dave Adams, and especially to David Poindexter, who had the faith to publish my first novel and who continues to be the biggest champion of the Lomax and Biggs series.

I am particularly grateful to all the booksellers, librarians, fan magazines, bloggers, and readers, who have gone out of their way to be supportive. And to my editor, Jason Wood, who flew 3,000 miles to help me shuffle index cards, iron out story points, and deliver on deadline—thanks, kiddo; you rock.

And despite the fact that I can hear the band trying to drown me out and get me off the stage, I want to thank the love of my life, my wife Emily, who somehow manages to be both the wind beneath my wings and the person who keeps me grounded.